MW01491863

6 GUYS, 1 GIRL
1 NIGHT

ALSO BY JILL KELLY

Fiction

When Your Mother Doesn't

The Color of Longing

Fog of Dead Souls

Broken Boys

Nonfiction

Sober Truths: The Making of an Honest Woman

Sober Play: Using Creativity for a More Joyful Recovery

Candy Girl: How I Gave up Sugar
and Created a Sweeter Life between Meals

6 GUYS, 1 GIRL
1 NIGHT

by

Jill Kelly

Copyright © 2018 by Jill Kelly

This book is a work of fiction. References to real people, events, establishments, organizations, or locales are intended only to provide a sense of accuracy and authenticity. All other characters, and all incidents and dialog, are from the author's imagination and are used fictitiously.

All rights reserved. No part of this book may be used or reproduced by any means, graphic, electronic, mechanical, or digital, including photocopying, recording, taping, or by any information storage retrieval system without the express written permission of the author except in the case of brief quotations embodied in critical articles and reviews.

Cover and book design by
Amy Livingstone, Sacred Art Studio
sacredartstudio.net

Cover photo by
Jill Kelly

ISBN-13:978-1726329590
(3 Cats Publishing)
ISBN-10:1726329593

For all of us who've made bad choices.

1

On the Tuesday in August that changed everything, Derek Walsh woke up with a dry mouth and a headache. He tried to remember how much scotch they'd had after dinner, whether they'd smoked one joint or two as they listened to his vinyl, but it was more of a blur than he wanted to admit. Whatever it had been, it had been too much. He moved his leg over onto Karina's side of the bed but it was cold. He glanced over at the clock. 8:45. He hadn't heard his wife get up, hadn't heard her leave. He was getting too old for this.

He sat up and swung his legs to the floor with a groan. He felt terrible. He wasn't hung over often, but his capacity for drink and drugs was fading as fast as his morning erections. He thought about Julie. How she told him she'd been drunk or hung over most of the decade they were together. He hadn't realized she had a problem until she told him she was going to treatment. How had he not seen all that? How had she kept it all hidden if she felt like he did now?

He knew he needed to get moving. A run would make him feel better and the heat of high summer would hit full force in another hour. He pulled on his shorts and tank top and want downstairs.

The kitchen was a mess, dishes piled in the sink, unwiped counter tops. He groaned again. Since Karina was teaching summer classes and he wasn't, the mess was his to deal with. He'd do it later. He found a clean glass, filled it from the tap, and drank it down.

He started off strong as he always did, a surge of energy and adrenalin up the hill towards the hospital, but he slowed after a few blocks and ten minutes later, he turned around. Between the hangover and the poor sleep of middle age, there was no way he was going to go five miles.

As he turned onto his street, he saw the taillights of the mail carrier rounding the corner. He pulled the mail out of the box and went into the kitchen where he poured a tall glass of orange juice and drank it down. Then he took the mail into the dining room and sorted it on the table. A couple of bills, ads from the market up on Rivermont, a letter from the university about the fall faculty workshop, and then a slim envelope in a familiar handwriting. Something from Pete Chandling.

He frowned when he saw the Priority Mail sticker. He and Pete still wrote to each other, both preferring letters to email, but nothing was ever a rush. He opened the envelope. Instead of a letter from Pete, there was a typed letter signed by a name he didn't recognize and a sticky note: "Did you get this too?"

Derek frowned again, then sat down at the table and read.

Dear Peter Chandling,

My name is Jason Kirchner and I am searching for my birth father. My birth mother, Rhonda Ordway, got pregnant while she was a student at Western Willamette College in Salem, Oregon, in 1972, and gave me up for adoption. In tracking her down, I discovered that you and five of your fraternity brothers got my mother drunk and had sex with her in somebody's apartment. One of you is my father.

I have six names. You're the only one who is local so I'm starting with you. I hope you are man enough to meet with me.

Jason Kirchner

Derek put the letter down slowly. Then he got up, walked into the kitchen, and vomited into the sink.

2

"This is Pete. Leave a message."

"It's Derek. I got the letter. Call me."

It had taken Derek nearly 10 minutes to stop retching into the sink. He was glad for the spasms, the choking, the sour taste in his mouth as the orange juice came back up and burned his throat. It helped him not have to think. But eventually he was as empty as he could be and he straightened up, rinsed his mouth, and went back to the table.

He remembered. Of course, he remembered. Not her name. Even seeing it on the page conjured nothing. He couldn't visualize her either. Not whether she was blonde or dark, short or tall. Not even what her breasts were like. But the event of it, the doing of it, that he remembered.

He remembered Fred Landon leaning in the passenger window of Pete's old Volvo. Pete was driving and he was riding shotgun. He always rode shotgun. In the back were Jim and Lonnie. And Fred leaning in the window with the invitation.

"We're all set." Fred's eyes had glowed with excitement, and he winked and smirked in that annoying way that the frat brothers made great fun of. "I'm going first, of course, then Murcheson, since it's his apartment, and then you guys figure out who's next. I'd say wait out here 10 minutes and then come on in. It's around the back and up the stairs." He pointed down the street to a small set of concrete stairs. "We'll leave the door unlocked." He slapped the window sill and stuck his hand out for Derek to shake. Then he hustled over to his car and helped the girl out and they disappeared around the building. She was small and slim. He could see that in his mind.

Someone had asked, "She wants to do this, right?" Jim? No, not Jim. Not Pete either. Must have been Lonnie. But he didn't remember anyone responding.

What he remembered next was rummaging through Pete's glove compartment for paper. Pete had a little notebook he used for mileage and gas records. Already the accountant. Derek saw himself ripping out a clean sheet from the back and tearing the sheet into four pieces of different lengths. Then he mixed them up, placed them in his hand so no one could see the length of the paper, and offered them around. "Shortest goes last," he said.

Jim had said something smart like "We don't need to draw for that" or "You go last, Pete. That's a given." Everyone had laughed.

Derek could feel the energy that had hung in the car all these years later—excitement, trepidation. He could see the white paper in his hand. He'd drawn the second to shortest. Pete would go third after Murcheson, then Jim, then him. Lonnie would be last.

He got up from the dining table. He felt queasy and his head pounded. The run, the vomited orange juice, the hangover that he'd done nothing to medicate. He looked at the clock. 10:17. He got a beer out of the fridge and drank it down. The cold carbonation was soothing. He rummaged through the fridge. Found tuna, lettuce, and bread. Made a sandwich. He took it out to the patio with another beer. He thought about calling Pete again but he didn't want to seem freaked out.

He sat down and looked out into the gulch of old trees that separated his property from the houses on the next street over. He watched the leaves shimmer in the small breeze. He saw the flash of red as a cardinal flew from branch to branch, heard the chittering of a smaller bird.

He remembered that the four of them had stood on the sidewalk outside the building for a while. There had been beer in the trunk, and he and Pete shared one. It was warm out. Fall maybe? Late spring? Maybe Jim had passed a joint. He always had one on him.

It was a surprisingly big place, that apartment. Big open rooms compared to the frat house. But it was still full of the crap furniture they all had in those days. Murcheson was watching TV. Johnny Carson talking to Rob Reiner. Funny how that detail was so clear. They'd all stood there watching. They must have been really stoned. Finally, the other guys sat down on the sofa, but he remembered not wanting to crowd in with them so he'd pulled a straight chair from the dining table and sat next to Murcheson and a little behind him. It had felt awkward to sit there. He didn't like not being part of the inner circle. That part of the memory was also clear.

Were there muffled noises from the bedroom? He couldn't be sure. Maybe Fred's voice, the girl's voice. Mostly it was the audience laughing at Carson and Reiner although he didn't remember any of them laughing. Or talking for that matter. At some point, Fred must have come out of the bedroom, for in his mind's eye, Derek could see Murcheson heave himself up out of the chair and go into the bedroom and close the door. And then more memories came back. Fred going out the front door, Murcheson coming out of the bedroom, lighting a cigarette. He went into the kitchen, got a beer and a slice of cold pizza, and took his chair again in front of the TV.

It was Pete's turn then but he hadn't stood right up and gone in. That Derek remembered too. Instead Pete had glanced his way with a strange look. Derek couldn't see the look in his memory, only felt his own curiosity about whether Pete had been clowning around or was stoned silly. Now he wondered if Pete had been afraid.

Jim had spoken then. "Pete" was all he said, and Pete went to the bedroom door. He'd hesitated again and looked back at Derek for just a second and then he'd gone in and shut the door.

When Pete came out, the Carson show was over and an old Glenn Ford western was on. Pete hadn't looked at them, just turned and went down the hall to the bathroom. Jim didn't hesitate. He stood up from the couch, grinned at the three of them, and went into the bedroom. Derek went to the bathroom when Pete came out. He found some mouthwash in the cabinet over the sink and took a swig. What a funny small thing to think of.

Pete took Jim's place on the sofa. He didn't look at Derek.

When Jim came out, he grinned at them again. "You're up, Walsh," he'd said, clasping Derek's shoulder with his hand in passing. Derek could still feel that hand on his shoulder. Then his memory went blank until he stepped into the bedroom.

He heard the screen door slide open. It was Karina. "Hey, weren't you going to lunch with Todd?"

"Shit," he said. "What time is it?"

"Ten to one."

"Shit, shit, shit." He handed his wife the phone. "Will you call him and tell I'm on my way? Fifteen minutes at the latest."

She laughed, shook her head. "What have you been doing all morning?"

"You wouldn't believe me if I told you," he said over his shoulder.

It was dark in the house after the bright sun of the terrace. He started up the stairs and then remembered the letter, went back down and carried it up with him, placing it way in the back of a drawer of his desk. Then he changed his clothes and left.

3

Peter Chandling sat sweating in his green Miata just outside the entrance to Crema, a coffeehouse in SE Portland. He'd been there 15 minutes watching people go in. Young men to be exact. He assumed that Jason Kirchner would look familiar. But he hadn't seen anyone he recognized.

He wished he had a drink. The nervousness was miserable. He checked his pager. No response from Harv. His AA sponsor worked as a shop supervisor for a manufacturing plant and was seldom available during the day. He only worked with men who'd been sober a good while, men who could manage their own lives. And that hadn't been a problem for Pete until now. For the last eight years, he'd stayed out of drama and chaos. But this—he couldn't have foreseen this. He knew he should have gone to the Monday night men's group and talked to someone afterwards, but he just couldn't talk about it with anyone but Harv. Harv already knew about that night in the apartment. Pete had told him during his 5th Step confession.

He looked at his watch. It was 4:35 and he needed to go in. He needed to face this and make whatever amends he could.

The big room in the coffee shop was mostly empty. He took off his sunglasses and looked around. Two women in the corner. Three slackers at different tables on their computers. An older couple with two little kids, one in a stroller. He went up to the counter and ordered a chamomile tea. Maybe it would settle his stomach. As he handed the counter clerk his debit card, he heard his name.

He turned and looked at the young man behind him. Jason Kirchner was tall. His light brown hair was long and just this side of shaggy, his brown eyes deep set. He had pleasant features but they bordered on the nondescript. A forgettable face that Pete would remember forever.

"Jason," Pete said.

"Yes."

Pete turned back to the clerk, signed the receipt, and picked up his tea.

"I'm over here," said the kid, and he led the way to a back corner table for two. He waited for Pete to take the booth seat against the wall and then sat down across from him. An untouched iced coffee sat in the middle of the table.

"I wasn't sure if you'd show up." The kid's face was closed, not quite blank but hard to read.

"It was the least I could do. How can I be of help?"

"A DNA sample would be a good start."

"I'm happy to give you one," Pete said, "but I'm not your father."

The kid tensed his jaw and shook his head. "How do you know? Because you're too short?"

Pete could feel himself blush. The kid was at least 6 feet and he wasn't. "Well, there's that," he said, "but mostly because I didn't have sex with your mother that night."

Jason sat back. He looked out the window and then looked back at Pete. "Are you bull-shitting me?"

"No."

"You were there, right?"

Pete screwed up his courage and looked Jason in the eye. "Yes, I'm very sorry to say that I was."

"And you went into the bedroom while the others watched TV, right?"

Pete hesitated and then nodded. He wanted to ask how Kirchner knew all this but he didn't have control of the conversation.

Jason leaned forward on his elbows. Not exactly menacing but Pete felt pinned into the corner. "Why did you go in the bedroom if you weren't going to have sex with her?"

The shame choked Pete's throat and he took a sip of the tea.

"Well?"

"I…I did plan to have sex with her. But once I got in there, I…I couldn't do it."

"You mean you changed your mind?"

"No, I couldn't…you know…get it up." He kept his eyes on the tea cup.

"That's not what my mother said."

Pete looked up at him. "Your mother told you about that night?"

"No." Something else passed across the young man's face. Anger? Sorrow? Then it closed and he said, "She told her husband and he told me."

"Well, I don't know what she said—or he said—but I didn't have sex with her. I…" He put up his hands as if to ward off something. "I got on the bed with her and we fooled around some but I couldn't… nothing happened. So I lay there with her for a while and then I got dressed and left. That's it." He looked out the window and then very slowly looked at the young man across from him. He saw the kid's jaw tighten again and his lips purse. A small shiver of fear ran through Pete. "I'm so sorry. I know an apology is not enough. I don't know what else to say."

"Did my mother want to have sex with you? Did she know you? Did she like you?"

"I don't…I didn't really know her. I met her that evening or maybe I'd met her before that. I don't remember. We all hung out at this tavern, and she was there that night."

"Was it your idea? Gang-banging my mother?"

Pete winced at the ugly words. "No," he said as quickly as he could. "No, it wasn't my idea."

"Whose idea was it?"

"I don't know. We were all out there at the tavern, we were drinking and playing pool, and somebody suggested we go back to this guy's apartment and party there."

Kirchner hesitated and then said slowly, "So if it was a party..."

Pete could see him trying to figure this all out.

"If it was a party, why was my mom the only girl there?"

With every passing moment, Pete felt more guilt, more shame. "Okay," he said. "It wasn't a party exactly. It was, I don't know, just an idea, an impulse. Somebody said let's go to the apartment and take her with us and see what happens."

Jason sat back in his chair. He shook his head again. Then he said, "Did you drive my mom there?"

"No, I didn't."

"You didn't have a car?"

"No, I had a car but I drove the other guys."

"Who drove my mother?"

Pete didn't know what to do. He didn't want to implicate Fred. It wasn't his place to do that. "I can't tell you that."

"Why? Some fraternity oath bullshit?"

"No," Pete said, although that was true. They'd taken strong oaths of loyalty in the fraternity. Not about this specifically. He'd never talked to any of them afterwards about this. It was as if it hadn't happened. But they'd made sacred vows to protect each other. Even the members they didn't like much, like Fred. "No," he said again. "To tell you the truth, I don't know how she got home."

Kirchner didn't say anything and then he looked at Pete and said, "You're scum. You know that, right?"

Pete looked at the kid and then looked away. The shame boiled up in him and he felt light-headed, almost dizzy.

Kirchner pulled a backpack off the bench next to Pete and opened a zip compartment, took out a DNA swab tube, and handed it to Pete. "Just run it around in your mouth."

"You don't believe me," said Pete.

"I don't know," he said. "I don't see why I should."

Pete took the tube, opened the little kit, and did as the kid asked. He handed the two parts to Kirchner, who closed it up and put it in his backpack. "How long does it take?" he said.

"What do you care? You said it can't be you."

"It can't."

"Well, then." Kirchner stood up. "I'll be in touch."

"About what?" said Pete. He was struggling to figure out what else could happen.

"About all this. It's not over. Not by a long shot." He turned his back on Pete and moved to the door and went through it. A minute or so later, Kirchner walked down the street past the window where Pete sat. Pete looked up as he passed and the kid shot him a look of hatred and pain so intense that Pete had to close his eyes against it.

He'd told himself all these years that he hadn't had sex with the girl and therefore he'd done nothing wrong, but he knew he was guilty just the same. And he saw that he'd known it all along.

4

Derek left two more messages that afternoon for Pete. He and Todd had a long lunch and he drank a lot. He could feel Todd's disapproval when he ordered the second pitcher of beer, but he didn't care. He wasn't driving—well, not all that far. A couple of miles to home and he knew the way like the back of his hand.

He didn't tell Todd about the letter. He'd never told Todd about that night. He could have. He'd known Todd then. In fact, he'd known him since 4th grade, but in those college years, they didn't see each other much. In '72, Todd had just come back from Vietnam. He was married, had a baby daughter, and was living in DC. He'd re-enlisted but instead of a second tour in country, he'd gone to work for the Pentagon. They wrote to each other once in a while, made the occasional phone call. But Todd wasn't a part of his college life and they'd never talked about it much. He might have mentioned the night in the apartment to him at some point, but he didn't think so, so he wasn't bringing it up now.

Todd just wasn't the right person to talk to about any of this. They had very different ideas about women. Derek had jumped head first into the sexual revolution. He had grown up on *Playboy*, its photos, its centerfolds, and its philosophy. Hugh Hefner's ideas about women and the female body spoke to something in him, and he wanted to experience as many relationships as he could. It wasn't all about the sex for him. He worked hard to be a sensitive and considerate lover. It was about being in love. That drug was his addiction. In his 20s, he often had two or three primary relationships going at once.

Todd was, well, the only word for it was *old-fashioned*. He'd been married twice, had a daughter from each. His first marriage had ended bitterly, but his second marriage now to a smart, funny woman was strong. And as his daughters grew older, he made it clear to Derek that he didn't approve of the younger and younger women in Derek's bed. "If you had daughters, you'd know how I feel," he'd said once. So Derek found himself with nowhere to go with his panic over the letter. He was counting on Pete to be the voice of reason.

5

Pete didn't leave the coffee shop right away. He couldn't find the strength to get up and go home to his wife. So he just sat there, feeling, remembering, hating himself for what he'd been involved in. He hadn't been all that drunk that night. His really heavy drinking was still a couple of years into the future and most of that would be done alone. But in those early years, he always went along with the guys on the trips to Ozwalt's tavern and he drank his share unless he was driving. A DUI or drunk-and-disorderly would have broken the hearts of his teetotaling Methodist parents, who were footing the bill for his studies.

That night though, he had been the reason for going to Ozwalt's. He'd gotten a D on a philosophy paper. The first D of his academic career. He and the professor didn't get along, and their world view was miles apart. He knew the grade was unfair but he had no one to complain to about it. Most of his frat brothers could have cared less about his grades since they didn't care about their own. They weren't going to listen to him. Even Derek and Jim told him to forget about it. And they urged him to go out drinking instead of rewriting the paper as the professor had suggested. Derek and Jim were his best buddies and so of course he went. They drank a couple of pitchers, played some pool, let Pete win a game or two. He'd felt a lot better.

Then as they were getting ready to leave, Fred had come over, bringing the girl with him. "Guys, this is Rhonda. Say hi, Rhonda."

"Did you say 'Rhonda'?" Jim looked at Derek and Pete and they broke out into a chorus of "Help me, Rhonda, help, help me, Rhonda."

The girl had laughed and blushed. She was cute. Small with long blond hair and a nice body. He remembered tight jeans and a white blouse with colored embroidery around the low neckline. It was both sexy and sweet. Pete had been attracted to her right away.

"Yes," she'd said. "Rhonda, that's me. How can I help?"

They'd all cracked up at that. Derek had said, "Oh, baby, baby!" And Jim had said, "Let me count the ways." Then she put out her hand to Derek, who shook it and told her his name. "Hi Derek," she said. And then she shook hands around and repeated their names.

Pete found this really charming and he thought this might be a girl he could date. If Fred wasn't interested, that is. Fred was a senior, and of course he would have first say in that. But Fred had a girlfriend already and he seemed pretty serious about her. So Pete might have a chance.

They sat back down in their booth and Pete moved in next to the wall so Rhonda could sit next to him with Fred next to her and the other three across the table. There was still some beer, though by then it was warm and flat, but Fred handed her a glass and encouraged her to drink it down. Then Jim started clowning around, probably also to impress the girl, and there was a lot of laughing and fun.

Fred ordered another pitcher and the guys all groaned. They'd had enough but the moment was too good to let go of. Derek started talking to Rhonda and anybody who would listen about the Beach Boys and how he and Jim and Pete were taking a road trip to see them play in Vancouver, BC, and maybe Rhonda would want to go along.

He hadn't thought about that part of the evening for a very long time. How it had started out as such fun and then had become something else.

"Sir?"

He looked up at the scruffy young man in front of him.

"Sir, we're closing now."

Pete nodded and got up and went out to his car. Someone had keyed the full-length of the driver's side of the Miata. He was pretty sure he knew who.

<u>6</u>

Derek finally reached Pete that evening. He waited until Karina was well asleep before getting out of bed and heading downstairs. As an extra precaution, he took the portable phone outside, leaving the door open for increased reception. He pushed 3 on the speed dial and heard it ring 3,000 miles away.

"Peter Chandling," said the familiar voice.

"It's Derek."

"Hey, hold on. Nance, it's Derek. I'm going out to the deck to talk with him."

Derek heard the second familiar voice. "Okay. Tell him hi for me."

"Nancy says hi."

"Tell her the same from me." Derek liked Nancy. She had been Jim's girlfriend for a decade and the three of them, no, the four of them with Pete, had spent a lot of time together. When Nancy and Jim had broken up—Jim said it was his choice but Derek suspected it was Nancy's idea—Derek thought about making a move on her, but he'd met his second wife Mindy by then and they were talking marriage. A couple of years later, Nancy had married Pete. Derek was surprised. They seemed an odd couple from the look of it. She was a head taller than Pete, who'd always favored petite girls.

But in other ways, it made sense. She was a good woman, smart, a nurse. She was a union advocate at her hospital and Pete was equally liberal and an occasional activist. Nancy was also an ardent feminist, and Derek had long wondered if she despised him for his many relationships. He wondered now if Pete had told her about the letter and what her response had been.

He heard Pete settle into the creaky porch swing in the yard. He and Pete had had many a conversation out on that swing.

Then Pete said, "I met with him today."

"Kirchner?"

"Of course Kirchner. Isn't that what you called about?" There was anger in Pete's voice and something else Derek couldn't identify.

"Yeah, sure. Calm down. Let's start over. How are you?"

"I don't know. Not good. Terrified even."

Derek felt suddenly much calmer. Pete was a worry wart, a doomsday kind of guy, and maybe he could carry this for all of them. Obviously, Kirchner had singled him out already as the dad. "Hmmm. Where to start?" he said. "Which one of us does he look like?"

"Nobody really. I mean I couldn't tell. He's tall, he's got light brown hair, he's got, I don't know, regular looks. I wasn't struck with any resemblance to any of us."

"That's a relief."

"Why? That doesn't mean you aren't the father."

"You mean that you or I aren't the father, don't you?

"Well, like I told him, I can't be."

"How does that work? Do you have some sterility issue you've never mentioned?"

"No, it means I didn't have sex with her."

"Yes, you did. I saw you go in there."

"Yeah, I went in there but I couldn't do it."

"You mean…"

"Geez, Walsh, do I have to spell it out?"

"But you never said anything."

"What was I going to say? Something that would humiliate me in front of all of you? And in front of Murcheson? It was just easier to let you guys think that I, well, participated."

"I can't believe you never told me this. I'm your best friend."

Pete was quiet for a little bit. "Well, I might have told you, but we never talked about it, about that night. I wasn't about to bring it up."

"I don't know what to say."

"There isn't anything to say. He still asked me for a DNA swab and I gave it to him."

"What? That wasn't a wise thing to do."

"Why not? I'm not the father."

"Yes, but giving him the swab means you admitted being there."

"Of course I admitted being there. You think I should have lied about this?"

"You could have said you had no memory of being there."

"That would have been its own lie, Derek. I do remember. I wish I didn't but I do."

There was silence then. Derek could hear the crickets in the gulch, the rustling of leaves and grasses as the night creatures went about their lives. It was a relief to focus on them, not on Pete, not on all of this. Finally, he came back to it. "Did you talk about any of the rest of us?"

"No," Pete said quickly. "Of course not. When he asked me who had driven his ... her to the apartment, I said I couldn't tell him that. Truth is, I don't know."

"But you didn't tell him it was all Fred's idea."

"No, I didn't mention any of you by name. I'm sure of it. But, Derek, it doesn't matter that it was Fred's idea. We all were part of it."

"Except you."

"The fact that I didn't sleep with her isn't going to matter to a jury. I was there. I didn't stop it. You didn't stop it."

"Did you think about stopping it? I sure didn't."

Pete hesitated just a beat and then said, "No. I didn't either." He sighed. "What are we going to do, Derek?"

"I don't know. What did Kirchner say he was going to do?"

"He didn't. Just that it wasn't over."

"He didn't talk about suing us then."

"No."

"Then why did you bring up a jury?"

"I don't know. Worst-case scenario, I guess."

"Are you going to tell Nancy about this?"

Pete was silent again for a long moment. "I don't know. I don't know that we would survive this. You know how she is about women's rights and men's wrongs. Will you tell Karina?"

"Not now, maybe not ever." Derek heard a door slide open on Pete's end and Nancy's voice. "One last question," he said. "How did he find out who you were?" But the connection was broken. There was just the dial tone.

7

Derek sat out on the patio for a long time after the phone call. He thought about Pete going into that bedroom. He'd stayed in there at least 20 minutes. Jim had commented on it. "Pete's really taking his time."

He hadn't responded but Murcheson had. "Good for him" or "Atta boy" or something similar. Now he knew it had all been for show. To impress them. To fit in. Pete had been a transfer pledge from some rural college in Tennessee where he'd belonged to another chapter of the same fraternity. All the guys liked him right away, but they'd never let him forget he was a latecomer to the party. He must have felt he had something to prove.

Is that why he himself had done it? Had something to prove? That wasn't what he remembered. He'd seen it as an experience, something new to add to his list, his future memoir. He'd been willing to try anything: booze, dope, acid, mescaline. And especially anything that involved women. The spring before that night at the apartment, he and Jim and Fred had driven all night to Reno and gone to the Mustang Ranch. The fact that the brothel was now legal had taken some of the excitement away from it, but it was still the real thing and he and Jim were underage and that helped make it even more of an adventure. Only Fred had been allowed into the bar, but the owner was happy to take their money for time with the girls, especially when Derek said he was writing an article on the ranch for *Playboy*. Fortunately, the guy didn't ask him for any press credentials or call him on it.

The place wasn't what he'd expected. There wasn't a ranch house, just interconnected trailers. There weren't any cows or horses, and they saw only one cowboy type, a guy in jeans and a Stetson. That was disappointing.

Derek had picked a black girl to sleep with. Salem, hell Oregon, didn't have many blacks and he didn't know when he'd get another chance. She wasn't his type: short, stocky, pendulous tits. But she was black. In the end, he was disappointed that she wasn't more exotic. She had experience and was willing to do whatever he asked if he paid for it, but he'd thought somehow she'd be different. A different feel to her skin, a different smell to her body, but she was just a woman. However, he had impressed her. All his years of prolonging ejaculation so that he could satisfy a woman had paid off, and she had told him so. He'd walked away proud of himself.

Afterwards they'd driven into Reno and gotten some breakfast. Fred had bragged about doing it four times, how he'd spent all his money on the woman, how Derek and Jim would have to pay for breakfast and the gas home.

The reality of it hadn't been all that great, but he and Jim and Fred talked it up when they got back to the frat house. Cutting classes, making the road trip, sleeping with "hookers" in a famous brothel. They were the envy of all the brothers.

So maybe there had been some of that in his being there that night at Murcheson's apartment. Impressing the other guys. Although none of them had ever talked about it at the frat, not even Fred. So how impressive was that?

A night breeze came up out of the gulch and rippled across his skin. It was cool but he was sweating. A deep uneasiness was settling into his gut. He went inside, poured three fingers of scotch into a tumbler, and drank it down before he headed back upstairs to Karina.

8

Pete too sat outside after the phone call. He was deeply disappointed in Derek's response. He had expected solidarity and mutual concern, not castigation for telling the truth. He needed somebody to sympathize with him, with his fear, with his guilt and disgust with himself. That night had been a shared experience. They were all guilty of doing something despicable but Derek didn't seem to feel guilty or ashamed. How was that? He'd always thought of Derek as a stand-up guy, a loyal friend, someone he could turn to if he was in trouble. Now he wasn't so sure.

"Okay to join you?" Nancy stood in the doorway.

"Sure. Come on out."

She moved to the edge of the deck and he heard the lighter and her quick inhale. The one cigarette of the day she allowed herself. She'd been a smoker when he met her, and he'd told her right away that that was a deal-breaker for him. She'd quit soon after and had stuck to the single indulgence for the last eight years.

"What did Derek want?"

The guilt rose up in him then, hot misery. He thought about pushing it down but he knew not speaking of it would be worse. He'd already committed to the path ahead when he'd agreed to meet with Kirchner. He would have to follow it through, no matter what happened.

"Sit down, Nance. I need to tell you something."

Pete hadn't watched his wife's face as he told her of the letter and the meeting with Kirchner. But now that he was finished, now that he was in tears, he looked over at her. Her jaw was set, her usually soft mouth tight and grim. That was the only word for it. And he felt as grim as she looked.

She got up and went to the edge of the deck again. After a long moment, he heard the lighter, saw her face light up in the deepening dusk. He said nothing. She also said nothing until she had finished and crushed out the butt and put it in her pocket. Then she came back and sat down next to him. "Tell me what happened in the room," she said. "All of it."

He told her what he could remember. That the room was mostly dark although there was no curtain on the window and some light came from a street lamp in the distance. That the girl was lying on the bed.

"You mean Rhonda?"

"Yes."

"We have to call her that, Pete. She wasn't anonymous. She wasn't a stranger. "

"Yeah, I see that. Rhonda was lying on the bed. She was...naked, she wasn't covered up in any way."

"Was she awake?"

"Yes, of course." Pete could hear his defensiveness, his vehemence.

"Was she drunk?"

"I don't know. I don't know how much she'd had to drink before we met her at the tavern but she didn't seem drunk there at all. I don't know if Fred gave her more to drink in the car or when she got to the apartment."

"Fred. Do I know Fred?"

"No, I haven't seen him since college. He wasn't a friend of mine, just a brother."

"Just a brother," his wife said.

"Oh Nance, I know how lame and awful this all sounds. I...don't what to say."

She sighed. "What was Fred's part in this?"

He told her. She sighed again. "Finish telling me about what happened in the room."

Shame burned through him. "I took off my clothes and lay down next to her."

"So you intended to have sex with her."

Pete finally looked his wife in the eye. He nodded.

"But you didn't."

"No, I…I kissed her, I held her, but I couldn't get an erection." Pete felt himself blush. He shook his head.

"You know why you couldn't get an erection, don't you?"

He frowned.

"Because you're a decent guy."

He could see some sympathy finally in her eyes. He felt a small shift, a bit of relief. She smiled at him although it was a sad smile.

"Then what?" she said.

"I just held her until…"

"Until what?"

He hesitated.

"Until what, Pete?"

"Until I thought enough time had gone by and I wouldn't embarrass myself in front of my friends."

Her look changed then and he knew he'd said too much, even if it was the truth.

"I thought Fred wasn't your friend."

"He wasn't. It was Derek and Jim I was…" He paused.

"…afraid of." She said it for him. "You and the Musketeers. Always the damn Musketeers. The three swordsmen." She shook her head. "I always thought it was a joke, the penis as sword. Now I see it was no joke at all." She got up and he could see the burden he'd laid on her.

"Did you try to stop any of it, Pete?"

"It wouldn't have done any good."

"That wasn't my question."

"No, I didn't."

She turned away then and went into the house. He called after her, "I told her my name, Nancy. Doesn't that count for something? I told Rhonda my name in the bedroom."

But she either didn't hear or didn't care.

9

Bruce Houghton was the husband of one of Derek's colleagues. He was also a lawyer. Wednesday morning, Derek called for an appointment, and Bruce invited him to the house for coffee—it was just up the street. But Derek declined, preferring an office visit. It was now 1:30 and the two men sat in comfortable leather chairs in the offices Houghton used in an old bank building downtown.

Derek had also declined the coffee, tea, and pale ale Houghton offered. They'd been through the how-you-been pleasantries and the requisite discussion of major league baseball. And then the pause had come in the conversation, and Houghton sat waiting for Derek to say what he needed.

"I can only guess at how this works," Derek said, "but I need our conversation to be confidential and so I assume I pay you something, like they do in the movies."

"Okay," said Houghton. "How about a hundred bucks?"

Derek thought that was a little steep, but he pulled out his checkbook and wrote the check on the little coffee table between them. Then he handed it to the lawyer, who put it back on the little table.

"Tell me what's up."

All the neutrality, all the bravado Derek had mustered to get him there began to falter. It was one thing to think about talking to somebody about this, another to actually do it. So he pulled out the copy of the letter Pete had sent and handed it to Houghton, who read it and handed it back.

"Pete is?"

"A good friend, a fraternity brother."

The lawyer looked over at him. "Are you on Kirchner's list?"

"I assume so."

"Are you his father?"

"I don't know."

"Could you be?"

Derek nodded.

"So are you here about paternity concerns? What your legal responsibilities are?"

"No, actually that didn't cross my mind." He hesitated just a moment. Then he said, "I need to know if I can be charged with rape."

If Houghton was surprised, he didn't show it. He got up and left the office. Derek could hear him talking to the woman who'd shown him in. Derek looked out the window at the old magnolia that shaded the office. The blooms were huge, creamy white with brown edges from the heat. He listened to the murmur of the voices. Then Houghton came back and sat down again.

"Here's what I can tell you with a quick search. Oregon has a 6-year statute of limitation on filing rape charges and that of course is long past."

Relief washed over Derek.

"However, if there is DNA evidence, there is no statute of limitation on filing."

"Kirchner has the DNA from one of us."

"Yes, but that's only proof of paternity. The DNA for the rape has to come from the scene. From on or in the woman's body, the sheets, towels, and so on. Basically from a rape kit or other items at the scene." Houghton paused. "Did she report this?"

"No, I don't think so. We were never questioned. In fact, we never spoke of it again, any of us."

"Did you ever see her again?"

"Not that I know of."

"Then if there was no investigation of the scene, there will be no DNA that pertains to the crime. So under Oregon law, you can't be prosecuted."

"That's a relief." He looked at Houghton, whose face showed nothing. He wondered what the other man thought of him. Wondered if he'd tell his wife despite the professional confidentiality. Wondered if he and Houghton could see each other at cocktail parties and not talk about this.

"Any other questions, Derek?"

"Yes, one. What if one of us confesses?"

"As your lawyer, I wouldn't advise it."

"No, I'm not planning to. But what if one of the others confesses and implicates me or the rest of us. What then?"

"It would be your word against his. He can't confess for all of you."

"So I would have to lie about my involvement. Would I have to do that under oath?"

Houghton smiled but there was no mirth in it. "As your lawyer, I cannot advise you to lie under oath. That's perjury and it has a heavy penalty. But I don't see this going to court with no DNA evidence. Is the woman still alive?"

"I don't know."

"You might try to find out. If she's not, it will most likely go nowhere."

"Okay, thanks. This has been really helpful." Derek stood up, suddenly anxious to get away from the lawyer and his knowledge of his guilt. He put out his hand and Houghton shook it. Then he moved to the door.

"One thing, Derek. While it's true that Kirchner can't sue you or the others, he can ruin your life in other ways."

Derek stopped and turned.

Houghton went on. "Public accusations, letters to the press, a shit storm. I don't know that he will. But legal isn't his only recourse to hurt you." He looked Derek in the eye. "Come back if you need me. And Derek? Don't admit anything to anybody."

10

Derek arrived in Seattle early Friday morning. He got his duffel from baggage claim and went outside to wait for Jim. He took big gulps of the cool air, such a relief from the wet-cotton heat of central Virginia. He'd had a couple of Bloody Mary's at the airport in Charlotte and then slept all the way west, but the cooler temperatures began to clear his head right away. The trip out was ostensibly a reunion of the three old friends or so he told Karina. He didn't have to be on campus for another two weeks, she was still busy with her summer program, he had the time. She was used to his abrupt decisions, his need to get away, and so he'd bought a ticket and called Jim.

Derek assumed that Pete had sent Jim the letter too, but that wasn't the case. Jim said he hadn't heard from Pete in several months. Derek was pleased somehow. It meant that he and Pete were tighter than Pete and Jim. Not that it was a contest but he was pleased nonetheless. Derek didn't mention the letter on the phone, just asked if Jim could take a few days off from his work at the talent agency for a road trip to Portland. Now they were going to head down I-5 and meet Pete when he got off work.

He watched the cars come and go, picking up passengers. People looked different here. Mostly white and Asian faces. Much more casual clothing except for the ubiquitous power suits. There was something about the whole energy of the Northwest that he missed even though it had been 20 years since he'd lived here.

He began to grow impatient. Jim was always late. He was dependable that way. Derek needed coffee and some breakfast and he realized he should have told Jim an hour later than his actual arrival time so he could have done that in the airport. Now he'd have to get Jim to stop on the way out of town and that wouldn't be easy. When Jim was behind the wheel, there was no stopping unless Jim needed something.

Derek thought about going inside, finding a restaurant but he didn't move. And soon enough, there was Jim rolling down the passenger window of another rapper SUV, this one black with tinted windows. Jim was still a personality on the Seattle music scene although with the death of Kurt Cobain, the grunge scene, where Jim had made his money, had dwindled to very little that was innovative or even clever. He and Derek often went 'round and 'round about this in the late-night phone calls they shared, calls that were fueled by weed or scotch.

Derek put his bag in the back seat and got in the front. No hug, no handshake. That wasn't their style.

"How do you like her?" Jim said.

"The car? Looks a lot like the last one."

"No, this one is way cooler."

Derek laughed. "Tell me about it."

And Jim proceeded to do just that, spending the next 20 minutes extolling the virtues of his latest toy. It was only when he got to the outrageously expensive sound system that the two of them had something to talk about. Derek still preferred the "real" sound of vinyl and had maintained his pristine collection all these years, while Jim liked the "clean" sound of digital. But they could agree on the tunes coming out of the speakers as Jim played some of their old favorites from Super Tramp and Roxy Music and of course *Pet Sounds*. They were coming into Olympia when Jim finally wound down about the car.

With a certain amount of pleading, Derek got him to stop at a café where he could get some bacon and eggs and coffee. It wasn't a leisurely meal as Jim was antsy as always to be back on the road. Derek put off mentioning the letter until they were back on I-5. Finally he said, "I got a copy of a letter from Pete, a letter he received. That's really why I came out. I'm surprised you didn't get a copy too."

Jim looked at him. "Why would I? What's it about?"

"I'll read it to you." He pulled the letter out of his back pack and read it aloud.

"Whoa! Does Pete think he's the dad?"

"No, he says he can't be. Says he didn't have sex with her."

"How come?"

"Well, you can ask him that."

Jim shook his head. "That's pretty out there for Pete. I would never have thought he'd have the balls for something like that. Did Pete say who the other guys were?"

Derek looked at him. "Come on, Jim. You know who they were. You were there."

"Me? No way. Although it sounds intriguing. But nope."

"Come on. We went out to Ozwalt's. Fred Landon picked up some girl and we all went back to that apartment. You, me, Pete, and Lonnie somebody. What was his last name? A soft, blond guy. Tillstrom. That's it. Lonnie Tillstrom. And Fred and Tom Murcheson, Fred's cousin. You remember him. He was a Sig Delt a couple of years ahead of us. He'd already graduated and was going to law school in Salem. We were the six guys."

"Yeah, I remember the guys of course but I don't know what you're talking about. Sorry, buddy."

Derek looked at Jim and Jim looked back. He could see that Jim believed what he was saying. There was no guile, nothing hidden behind his eyes. He was serious. Derek searched his own memories but kept coming up with Jim in the back seat of Pete's car, Jim's hand on his shoulder, Jim's voice saying "You're up, Walsh."

"I don't know, Jim," he said, "I remember you as being there."

"Well, that probably makes sense since we used to do most things together, but I didn't do this one with you. I'm sure of it. Look, you talked to Pete about this, right? Did he mention me in that conversation?"

Derek thought back. "No. No, he didn't."

"Who did he mention?"

"Fred. And Murcheson."

"See? He doesn't remember me there either. I think your memory's playing tricks on you, Walsh."

"Maybe," Derek said. "Maybe."

They were silent then through Centralia and Chehalis, Derek trying to figure out how Jim could have forgotten that night, for he was sure as anything that Jim had been with them. Maybe it hadn't meant anything to him or maybe he'd done worse things since then and that night wasn't worth remembering. He didn't know about Murcheson or Lonnie, but he would guess that Fred wouldn't remember it either. Anybody who could plan something like that wouldn't be bothered enough to take note.

Finally Jim spoke. "Didn't the letter say there was a list? Did Pete send you that too?"

"No, he didn't. We didn't even talk about it."

"Well, if he's got it, that will clear things up about my being there."

"You're right," Derek said, "it will." *Or not.*

"Is Pete going to meet with this guy? Is that why you came out, to coach him through it?"

"He's already met with him. What's worse, he gave the guy his DNA."

"You're shitting me." Jim hit the steering wheel with the palm of his hand. "What a stupid thing to do."

"You know Chandling. He's not going to lie about anything… ever. He just won't."

"Even if it means going to prison?"

"No one's going to prison over this," and Derek told Jim what the lawyer had told him.

"Well, that's a relief," said Jim. "No one meant her any harm. And clearly she agreed to go along."

"Yeah."

"But why did Pete give his DNA if he can't be the father?"

"The guy asked him. I think Pete was intimidated. And I think he felt guilty."

"Why? He didn't do anything."

"He thinks he should have stopped us."

"As if Pete could have stopped Fred from doing anything. Or Murcheson, from what I remember of him." Jim handed Derek the CD case and told him to pick something. Then he said, "Have you heard from any of those other guys? Has the kid—what's his name again?"

"Kirchner."

"Has Kirchner contacted any of the others?"

"I don't know. I think just Pete."

"Because he was local."

"Yeah, like the letter says."

"Sounds like a mess."

"That it is," said Derek.

There was silence then for a mile or so, and then *Smiley Smile* came on and Derek sat back and sang along. He was relieved that Jim hadn't asked him about his own involvement in the whole thing.

11

By the time Jim and Derek got to Pete's house in southeast Portland, it was well after 6. They had stopped for a couple of beers and played some pool to give Pete time to get home from work. There was no answer to Derek's knock although Pete's Miata was in the driveway so he tried the door and found it unlocked. He called out for Pete but got no answer so the two men went back towards the kitchen and saw Pete out on the deck, scrubbing down the Weber. Jim went straight to the fridge for beers while Derek opened the slider and went out to Pete.

"Good-looking steaks there, Pete," said Derek, nodding at the plate next to the grill.

Pete turned and grinned. "Only the best for my friends. You know that!"

The men hugged briefly. Derek was always glad to see Pete. There was something safe and steady about him, something reassuring and soothing. Maybe it was the fact that Pete's folks had been missionaries in South America and he had that solid church background, something Derek's family hadn't given him. Maybe it was the fact that he was two years older, the older brother that Derek hadn't had. Whatever it was, Derek felt steady around Pete.

Jim came out then, two beers in hand. "Thanks for keeping the beer stocked, Chandling." He gave one to Derek.

Pete grinned. "As I told Walsh, I want the best for my friends." Then he went inside and came out with a tray of chips and salsa and a bottle of sparkling water and a glass for himself, and the men sat down around a table not far from the grill.

For a while, they kept the talk small and safe. How much better the weather in Portland was than in Virginia. What chance the Yankees and the Giants had in the pennant races. Derek's recent promotion to head of the sociology department. The miserable decline in the quality of the tunes and lyrics in popular music. There was a lot of laughter and it felt like old times. Somewhere in there, Pete put the steaks on and convinced Derek to make a salad. Jim made a run for more beer and for ice cream for dessert.

Derek waited until the sound of Jim's engine had faded and then he went to the slider and called to Pete to come inside for a minute. He stood at the chopping board, dicing red peppers and cucumber, and when Pete came in, he said, "Was there a reason you didn't send Jim a copy of Kirchner's letter?"

Pete sighed. "I knew you'd take it seriously. I wasn't so sure about him."

"Good call because he says he wasn't there."

"You're joking."

"No, when I read the letter to him, he looked blank. Said he had no idea what that was all about."

Pete frowned. "But he was there. I know he was there."

"I do too, but he says no."

Pete shook his head. "How can that be? I can see him there. In the car. In the apartment. Sitting on the couch next to Lonnie watching TV."

"Carson, right?"

"What?"

"Carson was on TV that night."

"You're right. What a memory! And I can see him coming out of the bedroom. He asked me to take him back to the frat house, to come back for you guys later. Do you remember that?"

"I don't remember that but I do remember that there were three of us on the way back to the house instead of four. You, me, and Lonnie in the back seat."

"Yeah. I drove Jim back to the house and came right back and you guys were waiting for me down on the sidewalk."

"That's right. We waited downstairs."

"I remember thinking you guys had been pretty quick because it only took me about 20 minutes to get to the house and back."

"That's because Lonnie didn't go into the bedroom that night."

"He didn't? He never said."

"Of course not. Just like you didn't."

Pete shot him a look and then they were both quiet. Pete moved over to the refrigerator and pulled out two bottles of salad dressing and put them on the island. Derek put all the chopped vegetables into the big salad bowl and dumped in mixed greens and tossed it all with his hands.

"Then only four of you can be the father," Pete said. He leaned against the counter and looked Derek in the eye.

"I guess so," Derek said.

"Are you going to meet with Kirchner while you're here? Are you going to give him a sample?"

Derek looked at Pete and then looked back at the salad. "My lawyer says not to give him anything, not to admit anything." He told Pete about the conversation with Houghton.

Pete said nothing for a few seconds. Then he spoke up. "That's not right, Derek. What if he's your son?" He paused and looked at him. "What if he's your son?" he said again and shook his head and went out to check on the steaks.

Derek didn't like disappointing Pete. He felt chastised and he didn't like that either. But he shook it off and found plates and silverware and carried them out to the table. He went back in for the salad and the dressings, then made a third trip for paper towels and steak sauce. Pete had put the steaks on the table on a platter. He covered them with one of the dinner plates, then poured himself some more sparkling water and sat down at the table.

Derek sat down too. "Where's Nancy?" he said. "Is she travelling?"

Pete looked at him. "She's gone to stay with her mother for a while."

"Is everything okay?"

"With her mother? Yes. With Nancy and me? No."

"You told her then."

"I had to, Derek. I couldn't *not* tell her."

Derek nodded. After a minute, he said, "Are you guys going to be all right?"

Pete shrugged. "I don't know. It's a big thing for someone with her beliefs to forgive. You know, the part she's angriest about is not that I was going to have sex with the girl but that I did it to impress all of you, not because I was horny or drunk or even curious. The 'power of the good ol' boys,' she called it."

"Ouch!"

"Yeah, but no matter what happens, I'm glad I told her. I couldn't live with the guilt." He looked at Derek. "I take it you haven't told Karina."

"No. I'm not sure there's any good to be had from doing that, for her or for me."

"Unless this goes public."

"Let's hope that doesn't happen."

"I'm not sure we have any say in that." Pete looked at his watch. "Where's Leeder? He's been gone a long time."

"How far is the store?"

"About six blocks."

"He's probably chatting up some cashier."

"Not at that store. They're all older than we are," Pete said.

"That wouldn't stop Leeder," they said in unison and burst out laughing.

They waited some more. Talked about the new mobile phone that Jim was having installed in his car, and they spun off into talk of technology and the latest gadgets. Just as they were getting ready to start eating without him, they heard Jim in the kitchen. They went in to see what had taken so long.

"You won't believe this but some asshole sideswiped my car and then just drove off. There was a witness so we called the police and I had to fill out a report."

"Are you okay?" Derek said.

"Yeah, I'm fine. That car's built like a tank." He pulled a fifth of Jack Daniels out of one of the paper bags he'd placed on the island. "You want one, Walsh?"

Derek nodded, then said, "Did you get a license number?"

"Only a partial. What a jerk! Let's eat. I'm starved."

They went out to the deck and during dinner, Jim described what had happened. His uneventful trip to the store for ice cream and beer. His stop at the liquor store. His exit from the parking lot and the accident as he turned into the lane. "The guy was not paying attention. He was way over the center lane and he just ran into me and then sped off. Probably didn't care about his little pickup enough to stop."

"I don't want to sound paranoid but it might have been Kirchner," Pete said and he told them about the keying of his car the afternoon he met Kirchner.

Derek scoffed. "You can't think the two events are related. How would he know what Jim looks like or what he's driving? That doesn't make any sense."

"And I wasn't even there that night," said Jim. "He has no reason to harm me. This is crazy."

"Come on, Leeder," Pete said. "Derek and I both know you were there that night. We remember it clearly." He recited his memories again.

"Sorry to disappoint you, Pete, but I wasn't there. I don't remember any of this."

"That's just not possible," Pete said.

"What can I tell you, man? It was nearly thirty years ago and our memories aren't what they used to be. Isn't that right, Derek?"

"Yeah, but I too remember you being there, Jim."

"A collective delusion is the only explanation. Anyway, am I on the list? Kirchner's list?"

"I don't know," Pete said. "I haven't seen the list."

"So Walsh might not be on it either."

"I suppose that's possible," Pete said slowly.

"Maybe she did this more than once," Jim said. "Maybe she mixed you up with other guys. Anyway, her memory isn't going to be all that perfect after all these years either."

"Maybe so," Derek said, although he felt uneasy saying it. He wanted Jim to be right, that the girl hadn't named him or Jim in the event. Obviously she'd listed Pete and he would have to deal with whatever came his way in that regard, but maybe he and Jim wouldn't be implicated at all. He felt a twinge of hope.

Pete said nothing more and they let the subject drop. They did next what they always did. Smoked some dope with Pete abstaining, played music on Pete's fabulous sound system, reminisced about concerts and road trips. Derek brought up the excursion to the Mustang Ranch but Jim didn't remember that either and Derek began to seriously doubt his own memory.

12

It was almost 11 the next morning before Derek surfaced from the guest room. Pete was at the kitchen table, drinking tea and reading the *New York Times*. "Tomorrow's paper?"

"No," said Pete. "Last week's. I never get to it until Saturday. You still reading it every day?"

"Yes and no. Karina keeps giving me a subscription but they pile up during the semester. I read some of the international stuff, let all the New York stuff go."

"Still wishing you lived there?"

"Sure. Or at least spent the summers there, but Karina's teaching now in the summers and she won't let me go alone."

"She's smart, that girl."

"Yes, I always seem to get into trouble when I travel on my own." Derek moved into the kitchen and explored the contents of the fridge.

"There's a pot of tea on the counter, bagels, cereal, if you want it. Thought maybe we'd go out for some lunch in a bit."

"Is it too early for a beer?"

"Don't ask me," Pete said.

"Jim still sleeping?"

"Hell no. He left about 9, said he was going to visit his sister. Said to look for him about 4."

Derek laughed. "Yeah, right."

Jim did have a sister and she lived in Portland, but he hadn't seen her in a decade or more. Jim's many connections in the music business up and down the West Coast had resulted in women friends of all ages who were usually glad to see him, especially if he showed up with flowers and chocolate.

Derek brought a beer and some cheese and bread over to the table. He offered the food to Pete, who shook his head. Pete didn't speak again until Derek had eaten and gotten through the baseball scores. Then he said, "I was thinking I would call Kirchner and we would meet with him this afternoon. Get him to show us the list."

Derek looked over at him, then out the window into the lush flower beds that were Nancy's pride and joy. "That's about the last thing I want to do."

"I know, but it's why you came out, right?"

"Yeah, mostly. I…I want to know what's going to happen. How all this is going to play out. What I have to worry about."

"What about the paternity issue?"

"You seem really hung up on that, Pete. Are you sorry he's not your kid?"

"No, of course not. But if there was any chance he was, I'd want to know. I'd want to know my son. Wouldn't you?"

"I don't know. I just don't know."

"I don't get that, but okay," Pete said and he shrugged. "Shall I call him? Set something up? Or should we wait until Leeder comes back?"

"No, let's not wait. Let's do it and do it soon. I want to get it over with."

Pete got up from the table, took the phone, and went into the back of the house. "12:30," he said when he came back out. "There's a new tavern on Division. I told him we'd meet him there."

"Okay," Derek said. "I'm going to get a shower then."

13

The Woodsman was more restaurant than tavern but they found a table over to one side and out of the way. Derek ordered a craft beer and Pete ordered a cup of tea. Derek laughed when the china cup and pot came but Pete shrugged. "Hey, this is Portland," he said. "Anything goes."

Derek didn't feel like talking and he was glad Pete didn't seem to either. He sipped his beer and tried to keep his mind blank and his expectations low. Then he felt Pete straighten up in his chair and he looked up towards the tall young man coming their way. Within five seconds, his nervousness dissipated. He saw nothing of himself in this kid. No facial features, no stance, no gestures. This wasn't his son. There was relief. He was responsible for none of this, no matter what the kid tried to pin on them. He gave a noisy exhale that made Pete look over at him.

The kid stopped at the bar and brought a draft beer over with him. He sat down without speaking to either man.

"We'd have bought you a beer," Derek said, looking the kid in the eye.

"That's not what I want from you guys."

"What do you want?" said Pete.

"Besides knowing which one of you scum bags is my ever-loving, always-there-for-you dad?"

Derek felt his jaw clench. A strange mix of anger and shame roiled through him. "Yeah, besides that," he said.

"I don't know yet." He looked straight at them, one after the other. "Which one are you?" he said to Derek.

"Walsh."

Kirchner tipped his head as if in agreement.

"We want something from you," Pete said after a few seconds had passed.

"Really? And what would that be?"

"We want to know who's on the list you got from your mother."

Kirchner put his glass down on the table. "Let me get this straight. You guys raped my mother and you don't remember who was there?"

"Keep your voice down," Derek said. "We didn't rape your mother. We had sex with her. It was—"

"I didn't have sex with her," Pete said.

Derek nodded. "Some of us had sex with her. It was consensual. She accepted our invitation and agreed to be there."

"That's not what I heard."

"Well, that's what happened. We were there. You weren't." Derek chugged the rest of his beer and signaled the waitress. As he did so, he realized he'd just admitted to being there. His gut did a flip flop.

"Look, son," said Pete.

"I'm not your son. You know it and now I do too."

"You mean the DNA test..."

"Was negative. Just like you said."

Pete blew out his exhale in relief.

"Why are you so relieved?" said Kirchner. "Did you lie to me?"

"No, no, I didn't lie. But old memories aren't always so reliable. That's what I wanted to say. That your mother's memories, our memories are old. It's been 27 years. We'd mostly forgotten about it." Pete leaned forward when he saw the kid clench his jaw. "I'm not proud to say that. But it's the truth."

"And you, Professor?" Kirchner nodded at Derek. "You have a faulty memory too?"

"How do you know what I do?" Derek didn't like this kid.

"I know a lot about you guys. I know where you live. I know where you work."

"Then you can tell us who's on the list," said Derek.

"Why would I want to do that?"

The waitress came over with two beers and another pot of hot water on a small tray and put it on the table. Derek handed her a $20 and told her to keep the change. He pushed a draft over towards Kirchner, who left it sitting there.

"Why wouldn't you want to? Again, I ask, and I'm trying to be courteous here, what do you want from us?" Derek tried to keep his voice even.

"I haven't decided," Kirchner said, finishing the beer he'd bought himself.

"Great," said Derek. "That's just great." He pushed his chair back. "Let's go, Pete. He's not going to tell us."

"Hang on, Derek. Let's try again," said Pete. He leaned into the table again. "We want to know who's on the list so we can confirm for you whether you've got the names right. As I said, it's been a lot of years—a whole lot of years—and your mother didn't know us all that well. She may not have gotten it right when she wrote the list. Can you see that that's a possibility?"

Kirchner crossed his arms over his chest, leaned back in his chair, and bounced his left leg up and down. "Okay, you tell me who was there and I'll tell you if the name is on the list."

"Don't do it, Pete. You may give him a name that he doesn't have."

"It doesn't matter, Derek. If he doesn't have the name, then my memory's faulty and maybe yours is too."

The talk stalled then. Derek could feel Kirchner watching them but he didn't know what he was waiting for.

Kirchner spoke finally. "She didn't make the list."

"What?" said Pete.

"I said, my mother didn't make the list."

"Then who did?" said Derek.

"One of you."

"Bullshit," said Derek. "None of us would have done that. Come on, Pete. Let's go. This is all just a scam. I don't know what your game is, kid, but I'm not playing."

"But, Derek…" said Pete.

"No, Pete. You and I both know that none of the brothers would have given anyone the names. That just didn't happen. I don't know how he got our names but this is over. Here and now."

"But you've both admitted to being there." Kirchner pulled out a tape recorder from his jacket pocket. "Want me to play it back?"

"Doesn't matter," said Derek, standing up. "It's inadmissible. And all I admitted to was having sex with a woman you now claim was your mother. Big deal. I've had sex with a lot of women. They all consented, just like your mother did—that is, if she is your mother. And they all enjoyed it too, just like your mother did."

At that Kirchner sprang up out of his chair and lunged across the table at Derek, who moved sideways and out of his way. The untouched glass of beer fell over and the beer ran into Pete's lap. He jumped up too and then suddenly the waitress was there and the bartender was telling them to take it outside. Pete went back to the restroom to clean up and Derek got out his wallet and handed the waitress another $20. He let Kirchner leave and then he went back to find Pete.

14

The two friends were silent on the short drive back to the house. As Pete pulled into the driveway, he slapped his hand against the steering wheel. "Shit," he said, "Nancy's here."

"You want me to leave for a while? I could take your car or walk to some place and get a sandwich." Derek wanted to give Pete some space and he also didn't want to have to explain or discuss any of this with Nancy. They'd always gotten along pretty well, but he figured that might not be true anymore. "She does know I was involved, right?"

"Yes and no. It will be a lot easier for me if you're there." Pete looked over at him.

"Okay. But if it gets too tense, I'm taking a walk."

"I'll probably come with you." Pete smiled but there was no levity in it.

The house was quiet, only a low sound of running water. Pete went down the hall to the master bedroom and then came back out. "She's in the shower. Do you want some lunch?"

They fixed sandwiches and then went outside to eat. Pete picked up his sandwich and then put it back down. "Do you believe him? That one of the other guys gave him the list?"

"I don't know. I didn't give it to him and you didn't and Jim certainly wouldn't have, since he claims he wasn't there."

"That leaves Lonnie and Fred and Murcheson."

"Lonnie was too timid to say anything about anybody. Fred might have boasted about it but he was a pretty loyal Delt. And his bragging would have been about himself. Hell, he'd have said there were a dozen of us or two dozen, whatever would have made him look better."

"And Murcheson, wasn't he a law student? He'd have known better than to say anything. It was his place," Pete said.

"I don't really remember him. I only met him a couple of times." Derek could see that Pete was grasping at straws. He felt the same way. "Do you think we ought to contact the other three guys? Create a united front?"

"You mean now that you've admitted to Kirchner that you were there?"

Derek nodded. "That was so stupid."

"Actually I was glad to see you tell the truth."

"It's always best to tell the truth." Nancy stood at the end of the table. Her long dark hair was wet and curly. She wore a simple sleeveless dress in a deep green cotton that set off her eyes. It had been a couple of years since Derek had seen her and he could tell that she was aging well. Of all the wives of his friends, this was the one he would have enjoyed the most.

She sat down next to Pete and took a bite of his sandwich. "Where's the third musketeer?"

"He's out—" Derek said.

"—visiting his sister," Nancy finished the sentence.

"Yes," said Pete with a bit of a grin.

"And you two?" Nancy took a second bite of Pete's sandwich.

"We've been to see Kirchner," Pete said. "Do you want me to make you a sandwich?"

"Sure," she said, and Pete got up and went into the kitchen. She looked at Derek. "This is a royal mess you've gotten us all into."

"Me? That night was not my idea."

"Things are never your idea, are they, Derek? You just fall into opportunities. Isn't that what you told me once? You take advantage of opportunities that come along. Like sex with your friends and a drunk co-ed?"

The venom in her voice surprised Derek, even though he was expecting it. He held his tongue. Lashing out at Nancy was the last thing that would help him here. He needed to get her on his side, for his sake and for Pete's. And she was never going to understand why he had done it.

"Nothing to say for yourself?"

"What can I say? We were young, we were drunk, we were callow and selfish."

She didn't respond right away, just looked at him, but he could see her eyes shift a little from the hot look they'd held.

"Thank you," she said finally. "At least that's honest."

Pete came back with two more sandwiches cut up on a plate and placed them in the middle of the table. He'd brought a glass of water for his wife as well.

"What happened with Kirchner?"

"We went to ask him about the list," Pete said. "We wanted him to tell us the names he had. But he wouldn't give them to us."

Nancy frowned. "Why do you need the list? You both know who was there, right?"

"We do," Pete said. "But Jim…" He looked at Derek.

"What about Jim?"

"He's saying he wasn't there," said Derek. "And he's pretty convincing."

"Well, that's convenient." Nancy looked at him and then at her husband. "But you guys are sure he was."

"Absolutely," said Pete. "I drove him home to the frat house afterwards and then went right back for Derek and Lonnie. I remember thinking I'd have to wait a while in the car—I wasn't going back in, that's for sure, but you guys were already outside on the curb when I got back. And that surprised me."

"Is that how you remember it, Derek?" said Nancy.

"Yeah, we were outside waiting for Pete."

"And you left the girl inside?" Nancy said. "How was she going to get home?" She looked at the two men and Derek saw the anger back in her eyes.

"Murcheson, I guess," said Derek after a moment. "I honestly didn't give it any thought."

"Of course not," Nancy said and she shook her head in disgust. "You'd gotten what you wanted."

Derek turned a little away from her in his chair. He felt uneasy again.

Pete told Nancy what Kirchner had told him about the DNA test. She didn't say anything in response, just finished the water in her glass and shooed a yellow jacket away from the sandwich remains on her plate. "What about you, Derek? Are you going to give Kirchner your DNA?"

Derek shrugged. "I haven't decided."

"Why am I not surprised?" Nancy said and without another look at the men, she went indoors.

When Derek went in for another beer and the bottle of sparkling water for Pete, Nancy wasn't in the kitchen or living room. He went to the front window and saw that her car was gone from the driveway. Not a good sign.

15

Jim Leeder had had a frustrating day. He hadn't made connections with either Chelsea or Suzanne, his current favorites, and had ended up instead with Melissa, a regular fallback. When they'd first known each other, they'd had some very hot times. She was funny, pretty enough, eager to please. Now she was close to 50 like he was and while he didn't like to think of himself as one of those guys who only liked young women, he was…well…one of those guys. Trouble was the younger women weren't so interested in him anymore, not in the daytime anyway.

He'd shown up unannounced at her apartment a little after 10 with two lattes and two pints of mint chocolate chip, her favorite. She scolded a moment, like he knew she would, then invited him in. They'd smoked some dope, talked about music and films they'd seen, friends they used to know. Then she'd jumped him right there on the couch and eventually they'd gone to the bedroom. When they'd finished for the third time, she teased him about the "little blue pill," but he denied it, said he was just aging well. She hadn't pushed it. Good thing too because she was benefitting from it as much as he was.

She'd invited him out for the evening. She had theater tickets with friends and could get one more, but he said no as he always did. Said he had plans with his friends, and that was true.

When he left at 2:30, the buzz had worn off. He considered lighting up in the car and then decided against it. He was smoking more and more and it wasn't a problem, but he didn't want it to become one. He wasn't quite sure what to do with himself. He could hit a couple of bars on the way back, see if another of the women could meet him for tomorrow or later tonight, but in the end, he decided to go on back to Pete's.

He didn't want to talk about that night in Salem with them anymore. He had made it clear he hadn't been there, had no memory of being there, and they ought to just believe him. If they were really his friends, they'd believe him. He'd believe them if they said that. Besides, Derek had already sorted out the legal stuff and there was no prosecution going to be happening for any of them. All they had to do was pretend to listen to this kid and he'd go away.

In his business, he'd become an expert at shining people on. People were always coming to him with requests and ideas and demands. He'd learned early on to tell them whatever they wanted to hear and then forget about it. Pete and Derek should just do this with the Kirchner kid. Or sic him on Murcheson. He'd never much liked Murcheson. Something cold in those lawyer types.

Pete's block had cars parked up and down both sides now, and little kids were running around in the yard across the street. There were balloons along the driveway to that house and a big banner that said "Happy Birthday, Kyle." He pulled in behind Pete's car. He opened the glove compartment and took out the two remaining joints and put them in his shirt pocket and then got out of the car. The tall guy was standing right next to him when he turned around.

"Jim Leeder?"

"Who wants to know?" He looked at the guy. Late 20s maybe, tall, light brown hair, fair skin. Jeans, a blue t-shirt. Nope, he didn't know this guy.

"I'll take that as a yes," the kid said. "You're one of the scumbags who raped my mother."

"What the fuck? Look, kid, you've got me mixed up with someone else."

"No, I haven't. You're Jim Leeder, the only Jim Leeder who was a student at Willamette Western in 1972. Jim Leeder, the Seattle music man, the star maker."

The kid sneered and in his mouth those titles Jim had worked so hard to earn sounded like swear words.

"Is that what you promised my mother, that you'd make her a star, just so you could get in her pants?"

"I don't know what you're talking about. Now let me by." And he moved past the kid towards the house.

"You do know what I'm talking about. You know you do. And I want to know if you're my father."

Jim stopped and turned back. "Why? You think there's some big inheritance waiting for you? Well, not from me, kid. Everything I have is mortgaged to the hilt. Call my lawyer. He'll confirm that for you."

Kirchner took a couple of steps toward him, then stopped. "It's not money I'm looking for."

"Then what? My famous name? Too late for that. I'm a has-been at this point. That boat sailed a long time ago."

"I want justice. For my mother. And for me."

"I can't help you with that. I wasn't there. And that's not going to change." He turned again and headed up the walk to the house. For the first time, he noticed Pete standing on the porch. Without a word, he brushed past his friend and went into the house.

Pete stepped down off the porch and went partway to where Kirchner remained. "He's on the list, isn't he?"

Kirchner nodded.

Pete nodded back and turned and went into the house.

16

Jason waited a few minutes to see if any of the men would come out again. He knew he could go to the door, he could push this now, but there were three of them and only one of him. There was always only one of him. He set off down the street and around the corner where he'd left his truck.

None of this was playing out the way he wanted. The first part had been so easy. The woman at the alumni office had been happy to give him the names and addresses of all six guys. The research librarian at the downtown Portland branch had been helpful too. Both women had bought his story about being a journalist doing profiles on successful men from working class backgrounds. That had given him a wealth of information on Walsh, Chandling, and Leeder.

Then Chandling had been so easy to intimidate. He'd given up his DNA without a fuss even though it had been negative. Jason knew it would be. He believed the guy when he said he hadn't had sex with his mother. There was something sincere about him, trustworthy in an odd way. And the looks were, well, so far off. But Walsh and Leeder both looked a bit like him, at least in coloring and size. And they were refusing to cooperate. He was pretty sure it was one of them and that they both had participated. But his word against theirs wasn't going to get him anywhere. Maybe Chandling was the key. Maybe he could be shamed into giving up the others. Confessions were what he needed, what he wanted.

He felt ashamed of what had happened at the tavern and then with Leeder in Chandling's driveway. He was angry and he'd been angry a long time. He was convinced he had a right to be. But he wasn't a bully or an asshole, and yet he'd come off that way with them. If Walsh was his dad or Leeder was, he wasn't making a very good impression. But was that the point? To make a good impression. Wasn't it just the truth he wanted, the truth of who he was? It was all so complicated. It was all so unfair.

As he reached the truck, a pale green Honda sedan pulled up and parked on the other side of the street. A dark-haired woman in a green dress got out and came across to him. What the hell did Chandling's wife want?

17

"How the fuck does that guy know where we are?" Jim slammed the front door and blew into the kitchen.

"Take it easy, Leeder," said Derek. "What's going on?"

"That kid, Kirchner, waylaid me as I drove up."

"What?" Derek turned to Pete as he came into the kitchen.

"Yeah, he was out there," said Pete. "What did you say to him, Jim?"

"Never mind that. How does he know where we are?"

"I guess he could have followed us from the tavern." Pete got a glass out of the cupboard and filled it with ice water from the freezer tap and held it up. "Either of you want one?"

Neither man responded. Derek got up from the table and got a couple of beers from the fridge. He handed one to Jim.

"What did you say to him?" Derek said.

"Nothing. What could I say? I wasn't there. I can't tell him anything."

"You're on the list, Leeder. The list he has."

"We don't know that, Derek. He wouldn't tell us who was on the list." Pete looked from Derek to Jim.

"He told me just now," Pete said.

"He just up and volunteered that information?" Jim paced across the floor.

"No. I asked him if you were on the list and he said yes."

"Why would you ask him that?"

"Because we know you were there, Jim," Pete said. "We were there with you."

Jim stopped pacing and looked at them for a moment. Then he sat down at the table, put his beer down in front of him, and smiled. "I know what's going on here. You guys feel so guilty about what you did that you want me—no, you need me—to share in it with you, to take some of the burden of guilt off you, to share this experience with you."

"You did share it with us," said Pete.

"You got any proof of that?" Jim was bristling now.

"You're on the list," said Derek. "That means someone else remembers you were there besides us."

"Someone else with a faulty memory, that's all. You going to trust that girl over me?"

"Rhonda," said Pete.

"What?" Jim looked at him.

"Her name is Rhonda. We can at least show her a little respect."

"That sounds like Nancy talking," Derek said.

"Well, I agree with her." Pete leaned forward. "Why don't you guys just give Kirchner the DNA? Jim, if you weren't there, it will come back negative."

"Yeah, but it's admitting I was there. And I wasn't."

"And I'm not admitting anything," said Derek. "Lawyer's orders."

"I think you guys are making a big mistake."

Derek could see that Pete was nervous saying this, positioning himself as the outsider, but part of him admired that.

Pete went on. "Just come clean about it. Find out if he's your kid. It's the right thing to do."

"That's easy for you to say, Pete. He's not your kid."

"Yeah, but I was willing to find out, wasn't I? Just in case my memory was faulty, like Jim said. Come on, guys, hasn't this bothered you over the years?"

"No," said Jim. "Because I wasn't there. How many times do I have to say it?"

"How about you, Derek? Hasn't the memory bothered you?"

Derek shrugged. "I have to say I haven't thought about it for years, decades even. I don't remember feeling bad about it afterwards. I assumed she was willing. We were all consenting adults."

After a moment, Pete said, "Did you write about it?"

Derek looked at him.

"In that journal of yours?"

Derek shrugged.

"Do you still have it? The journal?"

"What would that prove?" Jim said. "He's admitted he was there."

"It might prove you were, Leeder," said Pete. "Written right after the fact, if your name is in there, why would Derek make that up?"

"Just to screw with me," said Jim after a long moment.

"His name is in there," Derek said. He looked at Pete, not at Jim.

"You found your journal," Pete said.

"I did."

"And Jim's name is in there. As being there."

"Yes."

"It doesn't prove anything." Jim looked at Derek.

"It does to me," said Pete.

"It does to me too," said Derek. "But you don't have to admit it, Jim. It's not up to me to tell you to do that."

"Come on, Derek. Don't encourage him to lie about this," said Pete.

"What difference does it make, Pete?" said Derek. "Each of us can do this as we wish. I'll admit it to you guys but not to anyone else. And if Jim doesn't want to admit it to us, that's his business."

"You don't have to defend me, Derek," said Jim. "I wasn't there. If I was, I would remember and I don't."

"There are lots of reasons you might not remember," said Derek. "Too stoned, too drunk, too…too ashamed."

"Why would I be ashamed?" said Jim. "From what you guys have said about it, you didn't do anything wrong. She agreed to go to the apartment, and she agreed to have sex with whoever. She said yes, you said yes. It didn't mean anything. It still doesn't. She didn't accuse you of rape, she didn't even accuse you of taking advantage of her. In fact, she hasn't talked to any of us, any of you, has she? How do we even know who this guy is? There's nothing that connects him to any of us."

"There's the list," said Pete.

"I haven't seen any list," said Jim. "Have you seen a list?"

The other two shook their heads.

"So all we have," Jim said, "is a young guy who got our names from who knows where and is giving us some cock-and-bull story about paternity and rape. It proves nothing. It's our word…your word…against his. In fact, this could all just be a giant prank from Fred Landon. Let's just forget about it, okay?" He looked at Derek, who nodded. Then he looked at Pete.

Pete shook his head. "I believe him. I believe Kirchner. It was a real event, guys. I won't deny that it happened. It's the thing I was most ashamed of when I did my 5th Step with my sponsor. I'm willing to take whatever consequences there may be. I have to."

"So you've told someone else about this besides Nancy?" said Derek.

"Yes, my sponsor."

"And did you tell him about us?"

"What? No, well, I don't think so. I know I said there were five other guys, friends of mine. But I'm sure I didn't name you."

"How sure?" said Jim.

"Oh come off it. Harv isn't going to say anything. Our conversations are confidential."

"But not legally so," said Jim.

Derek spoke up. "I told you there is no legal case here. Kirchner can't sue us. Only the girl can do that. And the statute of limitations ran out long ago. It's over."

They were quiet for a moment. Then Jim looked at Pete and said, "Why in the fuck did you tell Nancy?"

Pete looked back at him. "Because that's the kind of relationship we have. One that I suspect you wouldn't understand."

The air grew thick then and the two men stared at each other for what seemed a long time. Then Jim slapped his hands down on the kitchen table and pushed his chair back. "I'm done with this. We going out or what?"

"Not me," said Pete. "I don't much feel like it."

"Walsh, you coming?" Jim stood up.

Derek could feel something shifting among the three of them, a choice rising up. He didn't like it when Pete and Jim were at odds. He didn't want to choose. But he too stood up, put their beer bottles in the sink. Once out of the kitchen, Jim said, "Get your stuff. Mine's already in the car. We're not coming back."

"Whoa," Derek said. "Let's not leave it like this."

"Yes," Jim said. "Let's leave it exactly like this," and he headed out the front door.

18

Jason followed Nancy Chandling's Honda several blocks over to a neighborhood coffee shop. Although it was a summer Saturday, it was mid-afternoon and the place was pretty empty. They ordered iced coffees and found a table out on the sidewalk. It would have been cooler to sit inside but she just put her bag down on one of the outside tables and he didn't object.

"Why did you want to talk to me, Mrs. Chandling?"

"Nancy. Please."

He couldn't call her that. They weren't friends and weren't going to be. He repeated his question. She didn't answer right away, and his left leg began jiggling up and down and he pushed on it with his hand. There was a relief in having something physical to do.

"I'm concerned for you," she said at last. "I want to know how you are doing with all of this."

He looked over at her. "You're just concerned for your husband." He could hear the whine in his voice and he didn't like it.

"No. I'm disappointed in him. And I'm angry that he participated in such an awful thing. But he's done the right thing now. He's admitted he was there. He's given you what you asked for, and…he's not your father. So I'm not concerned for him. But I am concerned for you."

"Why would you be concerned about me? You don't know me. You don't care about me."

She smiled. "You're right that I don't know you, but you're wrong that I don't care. I'm a nurse. I care about the suffering of strangers.

For some reason I don't really understand, that's what's important to me in life."

He didn't know what to say. That sounded good, but all the case workers he'd ever had sounded good too and nothing ever came of it. Well, with one exception.

"Look," she said. "You don't have to tell me your story...unless you want to. You don't have to ask for my help...unless you want it. I'm just offering. That's all. Offering to listen, offering to help if I can. What they did was wrong. Terribly wrong. Despicable. And if I can do anything...if Pete and I can do anything to help you and your mother, we will."

He shook his head. "I don't need your help."

"I didn't say you did. But if you *want* it, if there's something I can do, I'll do it." She paused and then said, "What do you want to have happen out of all this?"

Again he didn't know what to say. He looked out at the parking lot and hoped she'd speak again, hoped she'd ask some specific question that he could answer. But she didn't and he couldn't. They sat there in silence for a while, maybe five, maybe ten minutes. Then he got up and got in his pickup and drove away.

19

Jim was still fuming as they pulled away from Pete's. He muttered under his breath, slammed his hand a few times against the steering wheel, and finally pulled one of the joints out of his shirt pocket and handed it to Derek. "Light us up," he said.

They drove around stoned for a half-hour or so. The music blared out of the sound system and there was no need to talk. Derek had been afraid Jim would just get on I-5 and head north but for some reason he didn't.

Finally Jim pulled into the parking lot of a tavern way out in East County. "Let's get wasted," he said.

"Okay," said Derek, "but not here." The parking lot wasn't crowded but the vehicles that were there were pickups with country music station bumper stickers and gun racks. He knew that Jim was looking for a fight, the one he couldn't have with Pete or Kirchner. "Let's find a jazz club and drink some great whiskey. There isn't anything we want here."

Jim shrugged. "Just a pitcher and a game of pool. We're already here. Let's see what it's like."

"Leeder, you already know what it's like. We've been in taverns like this a thousand times. Music you'll hate. Men you won't like, women you won't want. Let's go somewhere else."

Jim pulled the key from the ignition. "I'm going in." And he did just that.

Derek sat there a moment, and then he called Pete, who listened for a moment and then said, "I'm on my way."

20

Nancy left right after Kirchner. She drove home thinking about him, a lost and unhappy 20-something who could be her son if she'd been the girl in that apartment. And she could have been that girl. She'd smoked a lot of dope in college, got drunk some, gone to frat parties. But she'd had girlfriends who looked out for her, who looked out for each other. Four of them who'd lived on the same dorm hall sophomore year. Annie, Ginny, and Trish. They'd taken turns being the designated driver, the lookout who drank soda and kept an eye on the others. They'd had safe words, only they hadn't known to call them that, code words that meant "get me out of here" or "does this guy seem on the up and up?" They'd kept each other out of trouble or at least minimized the harm so that the worst thing that happened was a hangover.

Jason's mother hadn't had that, not that night anyway. And one of the guys had been stupid enough or malicious enough not to use a condom. Maybe none of them had. She wondered if that was careless or deliberate, like the guy in that film *Kids* from the 80s, who knew he had HIV and slept with young girls so they'd always remember him. She knew the comparison was a cruel one and none of the three musketeers were cruel like that, but she didn't know the other three guys who'd been there that night and maybe one of them was that cruel.

She was relieved to see that Jim's SUV was gone and Pete's car was still there. She wanted to talk to him about this, wanted to work things out together. She'd meant what she said to Jason. She wanted them to help him.

Pete opened the door as she got to the porch. "Hey," he said. "I'm just leaving. I didn't expect you to cool off so soon." He grinned at her.

She couldn't help but smile back. "I hoped you might be alone and we could talk. I just left Jason Kirchner."

"What? Did he contact you too? I don't like that." His frown was so familiar.

"No, honey. I actually followed him from here. I wanted to talk to him. Somebody needs to do some saving."

"About what? I don't need saving." He was still frowning.

"I know you don't. But Jason does." She smiled at him again. Rescuing was something they had in common, part of the glue of their marriage.

"You're probably right. But I've got to go." He told her about Jim's anger and Derek's phone call.

"And you need to bail them out, is that it? They're middle-aged and they can't take care of themselves?" She looked at Pete and then sighed. "How about this? You give me 15 minutes and then if you still want to go, go with my blessing." She leaned over and kissed her husband. "But don't bring Jim back here. I've had enough of him for one weekend."

They went inside, got glasses of iced tea, and went out to the deck. She told him her impressions of Jason Kirchner. His defiance, his distrust. How little he was willing to tell her. "He could be my son. Your son. He seems so alone."

"Nance, we don't know anything really about him. Leeder thinks it's all a scam."

"Do you?"

He shook his head.

"I don't either. So what can we do for him?" Nancy took a sip of her tea and set the glass back on the table. "I think he has a right to know who his father is, don't you? I think that whichever of the others is his father should own up and at least be honest with him." She sat thinking a moment. "Maybe we could get some of their DNA."

"We can't give that to Kirchner. That's such an invasion of privacy."

"I wasn't thinking that," she said. "I could ask Kirchner for a sample and we could get his sample tested against Derek's and Jim's. Then we'd know if either of them was the father and we could talk to whichever one it is. They'd have the information without having to admit being there, which is Derek's whole thing, right? Not admitting anything?"

"That's an idea," Pete said. "And then if neither of them is the father, we can all just let it go, because it has to be Fred or Murcheson then."

"What about the sixth guy?"

"Lonnie? Derek said that he never went in the bedroom."

Nancy sighed again. "At least one guy with some sense." She looked over at him. "So we need a sample from each of them."

Pete sat thinking. Then he said, "Just a minute," and he got up and went into the kitchen. In a few minutes, he came back with two beer bottles in a zipped plastic bag. He put them on the table next to her. "I don't know whose is whose, but it's their DNA. Do you know someone who will run it for us?"

"Jane Archer might do it. She works in the lab at the hospital. I can ask her," she said. "Do you have Kirchner's number?"

"Yeah, I can give it to you."

"Great." She kissed him again. "Thank you," she said.

"No, thank you."

"No, thank you."

"No, thank you." They grinned at each other.

"Are you going to go rescue them?"

"Yes, I am."

"Just be safe."

He nodded and left her sitting there on the deck.

21

The tavern was way out Division, a flat part of town with real estate so cheap that the parking lot could hold 50 pickups although there were only a dozen or so this early on a Saturday night. Pete found it without a problem because the neon was all lit up. He also found Jim's SUV. It was the only one in the parking lot among the Ford and Chevy trucks, several with monster wheels. That didn't bode well for what could be going on inside.

He was right although the fight, such as it was, was just about over. The bartender had his bat in hand. Two guys were being pulled off of Jim, who leaned against the bar. His upper lip was bleeding and swollen and he'd taken some kind of upper cut to the right eye, which was closing up on him. Derek had apparently stayed out of it.

Pete went over to stand by Derek, who nodded in greeting, just as the bartender tapped Jim on the shoulder rather gently with the bat. "Out now," the bartender said. "You don't belong here." He looked over at Pete and Derek. They stepped over to the bar and took a position on each side of Jim, who growled and shook them off.

Derek gave him a tug on the arm. "Come on," he said, and Pete asked the bartender if they'd paid the tab.

He nodded, then said, "Don't come back."

Pete nodded in return and headed out to the cars. When he got to the SUV, Derek was trying to keep Jim from getting in the driver's seat so they both hustled him around to the passenger side and belted him in. Jim's nose had started to bleed and they rummaged around in the car for something to staunch it with. Derek found some paper towels on the floor of the back seat and handed them to Jim. Then he and Pete stepped over to Pete's car.

"Does he need to go to the ER?" Pete said.

"I don't know. It wouldn't hurt to have someone look at his eye. Maybe Nancy could do it."

"Actually, no, that's not going to work. Jim is not welcome at my house at the moment."

"Okay then," Derek said.

"Yeah. *You're* welcome to stay there and I can even get you to Seattle if you need me to. But Jim has to stay somewhere else."

They mulled their plans over a few more minutes and decided that Derek would drive Jim to one of the new urgent care centers and then he and Jim would figure out a place to stay.

"I'll let you know what's going on," said Derek, as he got into Jim's car. Then he drove away and Pete got in his car and went home.

22

Jason didn't know what to think of Nancy Chandling's offer to help. When he drove away from the coffee shop, he didn't drive far. Just got out of the neighborhood and then pulled over on a side street in the shade, rolled down his windows, and sat there. He'd expected her to read him the riot act, as one of his foster mothers used to say. Or to defend her husband. Or to tell him to get the hell out of their lives. Instead she'd been kind, concerned even. He didn't know what to do with concern. It made him feel more ashamed. And that made him feel angrier.

What's more, her question had stopped him. What *did* he want to have happen out of all of this? He thought he knew. He should have been able to tell her, right there and then. But he couldn't. And he'd been embarrassed that he couldn't. Or maybe he'd been too embarrassed to say what he wanted. The impossible. To have had a different life.

He'd told only one person about his life. Sandy. They'd been lovers for a year, and she was talking marriage one night after too many beers and she'd asked him "to share his whole self." He told her about living in eleven different homes before he was 16. Eight different schools. Told her that two of the homes had been good places and he had been sorry to leave them, especially the one with the cocker spaniel. He had loved that dog.

He told her that two of the homes had been very bad, the others he was too young to remember. He told her about the foster father who beat him although he could see that she didn't understand when he said that it hadn't been personal. The man had beaten all of them, young and old, girls and boys. The foster mother, Belinda, hadn't stopped him. Told them they were sinful and that her husband was saving their souls. The social worker hadn't believed any of the kids until one of the girls went to the hospital with a broken collar bone. Even that probably wouldn't have been enough, but one of the boys had been to the same hospital with a broken arm just three months before. They'd all been taken out of that home. He'd never seen any of those kids again. He told Sandy about the uncle in the second bad family, who had babysat the three foster kids and molested them all.

But he wasn't sure all of these things were true. The numbers were true. The eleven homes and the eight schools. That had happened all right. But maybe not all of the rest of it. Not to him anyway. These stories circulated among foster kids when they linked up in school. They related their sorrows to each other, sometimes with pride that they had survived so much. He'd embellished his stories and knew that the others had embellished theirs too. Foster-kid bragging rights. They had to prove their toughness to each other.

After a while, it was hard to know what had really happened, he'd told the stories so often. And once he left the system, he put all the bad memories behind a wall in his mind and told himself that his foster families had mostly been benign, unless you counted the crushing indifference they had shown to him. Little affection, little attention. They were harried people with too little money and even less time. He was clean, he was fed, and for the rest, he had learned to take care of himself.

Like many kids in the system, he had waited a long time, hoping his real parents would come and get him. No one seemed to know why he'd been put in the system. He knew he'd been adopted right after he was born but why that hadn't worked out, he didn't know. He hadn't told Sandy—or anyone else for that matter—about that. Being adopted and then unadopted was the worst thing that could happen. His real mother and father hadn't wanted him. His adoptive parents hadn't either.

Sandy had wanted him to read a bunch of crap about abandonment issues and healing yourself and other kinds of self-help bullshit. The only part of it that made any sense to him was that you could only count on yourself and he'd known that since he was 8. So he'd told Sandy to give up trying to help him and they hadn't lasted together very long after that.

He couldn't tell Nancy Chandling any of this. It would seem a ploy for sympathy and he didn't want sympathy from another stranger. It was nice that Chandling's wife was concerned, but she wasn't anybody to him. What's more, pity was worse than indifference, and pity wasn't going to get him that different past or a different future. And he couldn't tell her that he wanted justice. For himself, for his mother, for all the other kids in the system whose parents couldn't be bothered, for all the kids who were alone, who'd always been alone and would always be alone.

He shook off the self-pity, started up the truck, and headed up Powell to 205. He always thought better driving. Once he hit the freeway, he headed south toward Salem. He drove a ways, a long ways, without thinking too much. Then he knew what he could ask for. Not from her, for she didn't hold the key. But from him, from Pete Chandling. He could ask for an introduction to the rest of them, the three he hadn't yet talked to. Chandling could help him find them, maybe go with him to talk to them. And if Chandling refused, maybe he could get Nancy to make her husband do it. He'd learned early on to only ask for what he was sure he could get. And he was pretty sure he could get this.

23

Derek got back to Pete's neighborhood about 9:30. They'd been at the urgent care place for a quite a long time. It was Saturday night and a lot of people seemed to be in trouble. Once Jim got called into an examining room, Derek went through the contacts in Jim's phone looking for 503 area codes, Jim's Portland contacts. He recognized only two or three of the women's names but he got lucky. Melissa answered her phone and when he explained what had happened, she laughed. He turned on the charm and she flirted back and then said yes, of course, Jim could stay with her. She was on her way to the theater but would leave a key under the mat.

Jim looked pretty rough when he came back out. He'd gotten a couple of stitches above his eye and his nose was taped. "Cracked it," he said when Derek asked.

The doctor had given Jim a prescription for Vicodin and so they drove to a 24-hour pharmacy and Jim stayed in the car and slept while Derek got it filled. Then he drove Jim to Melissa's and left him there.

He drove back to Pete's house, not in any hurry to be there either. He wanted a drink and a quiet place to think, but the liquor stores were closed and he didn't know the places in Portland that would sell a guy a bottle for the asking. Then he remembered whose car he was driving and he pulled over and rummaged around. Sure enough, in the pocket on the back of the passenger's seat there was an unopened pint of bourbon. Not his favorite brand but it would do.

The half-dark of the well-lit city was settling in when he walked into the neighborhood park near Pete's. It was a warm night and people were still out walking along the paved pathways, some with dogs. But their voices were hushed and their laughter quiet. He found an empty picnic table under some trees and sat on the bench facing out to the walkway. He poured some of the bourbon into a plastic cup he'd found on the back seat of the SUV and rested his back against the table.

Pete and Jim had been at odds many times before. Their beliefs, their relationships with women, with work even, were not compatible. What held them all together was the past. The college years, sure, but since then they'd also shared a lot of good times: backpacking in the younger years, trips to the beach, nights of dope and scotch spent discussing politics and economics. And always the music. Rock and roll had been made just for them, for their generation, and they shared their discoveries, their latest top-of-the-line speakers and turntables whenever they got together. And then there were the decades of concerts. Following the Beach Boys, then Petty and the Boss. Derek had spent one summer going to every American concert on a Springsteen tour. He'd made three-way calls with Jim and Pete all along the way so they could share in it too.

But things between Jim and Pete had not been close since Pete took up with Nancy. It wasn't like she left Jim for Pete. They'd broken up several years before. Jim had moved on to a secretary in his office. What was her name? Dani? Darby? Darcy, that was it. And somewhere in there Pete had divorced Tina, his first wife. But in so many ways, Nancy was perfect for him and Pete was perfect for her. A much better fit than Jim had ever been. Pete had the kind of loyalty and fidelity that women loved. And Jim? He was a restless soul, a man for a night, not a lifetime.

Jim had given his blessing to Pete when Pete told him he was seeing Nancy and that it was getting serious. But Derek knew that the blessing was half-hearted, for Jim had told him so. "I know it's irrational," Jim had said. "Nancy and I are way past done. And I want her to be happy. But not with Pete. Or with you, for that matter. It needs to be a stranger. Not someone I have to compare myself to."

That comparison thing had always been in the way even though it made little sense, at least on the surface. Jim had the height and the looks, Pete didn't. Jim had the glamour job while Pete was now regional director of a national office machines distributor. But Pete had a solidity about him, a groundedness that Jim couldn't find anywhere in his life. And Jim's heavy use of drugs and alcohol—"I'm just this side of addiction," he'd boasted from time to time—was a big part of it and he didn't want to hear that.

Now Derek was afraid this whole Kirchner affair was going to split his friends further apart and that he would be caught in the miserable middle. He didn't want to have to choose. He finished the bourbon in the cup and picked up the bottle to pour another shot.

"Got enough to share?"

Kirchner stood a few feet away, light from a nearby pathway lamp shining on his features.

A small jolt of anxiety washed over Derek. He wasn't afraid of Kirchner—not exactly—but he'd felt a lot more comfortable at the tavern when Pete was there too. But he shrugged and said, "Sure," and moved over on the bench so Kirchner could sit on the other end. He poured two fingers into the plastic cup and handed it to Kirchner, keeping the bottle for himself. "You stalking me?" he said.

Kirchner shook his head. "Just wanted a chance to talk with you alone, just the two of us."

"Okay," Derek said, keeping his voice as calm as he could. "Here I am."

Kirchner sipped at the bourbon and looked out into the park. "I'm hoping you've reconsidered giving me your DNA so we can find out if we're related. I want to find my father. That's all."

"Why don't I believe you?"

"I don't know. What else would I want?"

"Justice? Revenge?"

Kirchner looked over at him. "Is that what you'd want if it had been your mother?"

The question, unexpected as it was, hit Derek in a deep place. He saw his mother on her sickbed, a brain tumor from metastasized lung cancer, dead at 54, barely older than he was now. They'd had a special bond, an emotionally intimate relationship that he'd been trying to reproduce ever since. Her death had broken his heart. "I'd want revenge," he admitted, looking over at the kid.

Kirchner nodded and raised his eyebrows. It made his eyes look wide and deep. He took another sip of his drink. "Was she a good woman, your mother?"

"Yes, yes, she was. A very kind and gentle person."

Kirchner nodded again. "What would she want you to do about the DNA?"

Derek's inner conflict lasted only a couple of seconds. "She'd want me to protect myself," he lied. And telling the lie made him angry.

A small smile visited Kirchner's lips and then vanished. "Well, I guess that means we're at an impasse," he said.

"Yeah, I guess so," said Derek and he shrugged. He put the lid on the bottle and stood up. "I've got to go." He stepped out onto the path. Then he turned back to Kirchner and said, "Give it up, kid. You're not going to get whatever you think we have that belongs to you. Even if we had it, whatever that is, we wouldn't give it to you. We don't owe you anything."

He didn't wait for a response, just went on to his car although the anxiety he'd felt was still strong and he listened for Kirchner's footsteps behind him but there was nothing.

The lights were still on when Derek pulled up in front of the house. Nancy's car was in the driveway with Pete's car behind hers. He'd hoped somehow she'd be gone again. She was just about the last person he wanted to have to talk to. He sighed and got out of the car, took his bag from the back, and went up the walkway.

The house was quiet. He put his bag down near the door and went into the living room. Pete looked up from the magazine he was reading. "Get Leeder squared away?"

"Yes, he's going to have quite the shiner and his nose is cracked, but he got drugs and I left him at Melissa's."

"Do you need a beer or a cup of tea or anything? Did you get any dinner? There's food in the fridge."

"Thanks," Derek said, and he went out and rummaged around and brought a beer and a cold plate of food back in with him. "Nancy asleep?"

"No. She's reading in the bedroom."

Derek sat down on the couch and put his plate on the coffee table. "Did you guys get things sorted out?"

"Nance and me? Yeah, we're good."

"And you and me?"

Pete nodded. "Yeah, we're good too."

"And Leeder?"

Pete gave a short laugh but Derek knew he didn't mean it.

"That's another story," Pete said. He was silent a bit and then said, "I won't choose him over Nancy."

"No one's asking you to."

"Oh yes, they are. Leeder wants that. He's wanted that since before I married her. Come on, Walsh, you know it's true."

Derek looked at his friend and then gave a quick nod.

"That doesn't mean I'm not concerned about him," Pete said.

"Concerned about whom?" Nancy stood in the archway in jeans and a t-shirt, her long hair pulled back in a pony tail. She looks so young, Derek thought, and the surge of attraction returned.

"Leeder," he said. "We're talking about Jim."

"Well, you guys should be worried. He's 49 years old and acting like he's 20. He's got problems I don't think you guys want to look at."

"Is this the medical professional talking?" said Derek.

"Partly," she said. "And partly it's knowing him as well as I do—or did. These aren't new problems. He's been drinking too much for a long time. But his denial of being involved in this whole thing, I don't like it. You guys believe he was there, right?" She came into the room and sat on the arm of the big overstuffed chair that Pete was sitting in.

Both men nodded.

"Then it's not good. He's lying."

"And is this lie some kind of sign of a medical problem?" Pete said.

"No," she said, and an even sterner note was suddenly there in her voice. "It's a moral problem. He's not willing to take responsibility for his actions. And if he's not taking responsibility for this huge thing, what's happening with the little things in his life?"

They were all silent then for a few minutes. Derek finished his food though he felt odd continuing to eat after that big pronouncement, as if it would insult the truth of what Nancy was saying. At the same time, he was relieved that she wasn't focused on him and his refusal to give Kirchner a sample. He got up and took the plate into the kitchen, washed it, and put it in the drainer. He wanted another beer but didn't want to appear to need it. Then he shook his head at himself and got one out of the fridge.

When he came back, Nancy and Pete had moved to the couch and were sitting close together. Derek took the overstuffed chair across from them.

"Tell me why *you* did it, Derek," Nancy said.

Derek looked over at her, stalled for time. He wanted to pretend that he didn't know what she was talking about but he did know. He knew only too well. "Curiosity," he said finally. "That probably sounds lame but that's what it was."

"Curiosity about what?" Nancy said. "About committing rape?"

"No. Hell no. I never thought about it that way. I still don't. She agreed. I wouldn't have done it if she hadn't been willing."

"So what were you curious about?"

Derek looked at her again to see if she was winding him up but the look on her face was serious and somehow open. A look she gives her patients, he thought. "Well, sex with a stranger. I hadn't done that before. I'd only had sex with girlfriends, women I cared about." He wasn't about to mention the Mustang Ranch. "I wanted to see what it was like with someone I didn't know."

"Ever the sociologist," she said. It sounded like a swear word. Then she said, "You could have done that with a prostitute."

"That wasn't so easy back then," Derek said.

"You're telling me there were no prostitutes in Salem in 1972?"

"No, of course there were, but I…I didn't have the nerve for that."

"But you had the nerve for this."

Her tone had changed and Derek could see that her eyes were no longer curious or welcoming. He glanced at Pete, who tilted his head in warning.

"Yes," Derek said and he looked Nancy in the eye. "I did. Look, the situation was just handed to me, to us. We didn't dream it up or connive or finagle it or anything. We didn't force her into a car, drag her into that apartment. Fred said she was game and I believed him. Maybe she was curious too."

"About having sex with a bunch of guys?"

"Yeah, why not? Aren't women ever curious about those kinds of things?"

"Not the women I know," she said.

"Pete, what do you think?" Derek said. "Aren't women curious about this sort of thing?"

"Well, I think some women might fantasize about this. But I don't really know." Pete didn't look at either of them as he said this.

"There," said Derek, as if that proved something. "I'm sure there are women who fantasize about that sort of thing."

"Like your wives, Derek?" Nancy sat forward. "Have they wanted to be Rhonda? Have they been Rhonda?"

"I don't know. I haven't asked them."

Nancy paused in her attack, and Derek could see that it was to gather more steam.

"Anyway, fantasy and actually doing it are two very different things," she said. "How many of those women fantasizing about it are actually going to do it? And how many of them are 18, or whatever she was, when they do? Do you think gang rape was on Rhonda's bucket list?"

"It wasn't rape, Nancy. How many times do I have to say it? It wasn't. And you're not going to convince me that it was. Rape is sex without consent and she consented." Derek could feel he was about to get in way too deep here and the best thing to do was to shut up, but he couldn't do that. This issue was just as important to him as it was to Nancy but from a whole other angle.

Nancy didn't stop either. "Did you ask her when you got into bed with her? You were what? Number 4?"

"Number 5 actually. And I did talk to her. I didn't say 'Is this what you want to do?' in so many words but I made sure she was okay with me being there." He tried to find that place in his memory. He could see himself getting into bed with her, and she was awake. That he was sure of. He didn't remember his words to her. *Are you okay?* Maybe. Or *does this feel good?* She'd murmured something. He was pretty sure of that too. He'd taken it for agreement. She certainly hadn't fought him or pushed him away or anything. He would never have touched her if that had been the case. But he didn't want to explain all of this to Nancy. The intimacy of that moment was none of her business.

Nancy shook her head in disgust. "What I don't understand," she said, "is why none of you used a condom."

"I don't know that the others didn't," said Pete.

"Were you going to use one?" she said, turning to look at him.

"No, it…it didn't occur to me. But thankfully it didn't matter."

"Yes," she said. "That didn't matter. What about you, Derek? Why weren't you prepared?"

"I was drunk, I guess." He was lying but there was no help for it. His curiosity had not really been about sleeping with a stranger, although that was sort of true. The most memorable thing, the thing he had written at length about in his journal, was not something he was going to admit to Nancy or Pete or anyone. His real curiosity had been about what the girl would feel like inside after the others had been there. That's why he'd been so okay with being fifth. He wanted to experience that sensation, to remember it, so he would know if his girlfriend or his wife had slept with someone else. Not that would he mind, necessarily. He wasn't the jealous type. But he'd want to know. And he had known. And that's why he hadn't used a condom, even though there had been one in his wallet. There was always one in his wallet.

Nancy shook her head. "That irresponsibility changed two lives, maybe more, and you guys don't seem at all sorry."

"That's not fair," Pete said. "I am sorry, sorry I went along, sorry she got pregnant although it feels odd to wish Jason Kirchner had never been born. I can't wish that on him. He's entitled to his life."

"I'm sorry if things didn't turn out well for her," Derek said, "but I'm not responsible for her choices. Her choice to come to the apartment with Fred, her choice to not say no—she did not say no to me in any way—her choice to not use birth control, her choice to have the child, her choice to give him up. And I don't believe he is my son. Kirchner doesn't look like me. If he looks like anybody, he looks like Leeder."

He feigned a yawn and looked at his watch. "I need to sleep. Thanks for letting me stay another night." And with that, he got up and took his bag from the entryway and went down the hall to the guest room. As he got into bed, he realized he hadn't mentioned his conversation with Kirchner in the park.

24

Jason followed Derek to Pete's house and sat outside for a long time. There were lights on inside until after midnight, three shadows against the living room shades. He hoped they were talking about him. It would be so much easier if the Chandlings could convince Walsh to give him the DNA, but after the conversation in the park, he didn't hold out much hope of that happening.

He wished it didn't matter. He didn't think Walsh was his father. He couldn't see himself in the man at all. But he knew that that wasn't the only consideration. There were plenty of people who didn't look much like one parent or the other even though usually some features got passed on. He'd already seen photos of Walsh on the college's website and he was pretty sure he wasn't the match, but it pissed him off that the guy was so uncooperative and insulting to boot. There wasn't any call for that. And he still wanted to know. And he wanted Walsh and all of them to take responsibility for what they had done.

Well, they would discover that he wasn't somebody to dismiss. Walsh would discover he wasn't going to just go away quietly. He had a Plan B and he was going to use it.

25

Derek was the first one up Sunday morning. He'd read late into the night, heard Pete and Nancy go to bed about an hour after he did, then finally slept. He got a shower and shaved and took Jim's car to a French bakery that he'd passed on the way back from the park the night before. He got some pastries and a *New York Times* and drove back to Pete's. No one was in the kitchen but he could hear the shower running in the back of the house. He put the pastries on a plate, started some coffee, and sat down to read the paper.

He was partly through the international section when Pete joined him. Pete poured three cups of coffee, gave Derek one, left one on the table for himself, and took one with him. He came back and sat down, but he didn't pick up a section of the paper. After a minute of silence, he cleared his throat so Derek would look at him.

"Can we talk?" Pete said.

"Sure." Derek put down the paper, his uneasiness from the night before surging up again.

"Leeder called. He'll come and get his car this afternoon and head back to Seattle. You need to be here at 3 if you want to ride with him."

"How is he?"

"He didn't say. He left a message while I was in the shower."

"He sound okay?"

"I guess. Not all that friendly though."

Derek nodded. "Do you want to try to patch things up with him before we leave?"

"No, I don't think so. Maybe later. I'm pretty disgusted with him. And there's Nancy too."

"I get it."

"But that's not what I want to talk about." Pete picked up his cup, tipped it so he could see inside, and then put it back down on the table.

"Okay," Derek said. "What's up?"

"I got on the Internet this morning and looked up Murcheson. He's still in Salem, believe it or not. Got his own law firm. I called him and he'll meet us at noon if we drive down."

"Did he remember you?"

"I don't know. He said he did."

"You tell him about Kirchner?"

"No. I just said you were in town, we had some time free, thought we'd drive down for a beer." He looked at Derek.

"You hoping to find out something we don't already know?"

"I don't know. I think we should warn him at least. I would have liked to have had some warning."

"Okay. Did you look up the others?"

"No, I started with Murcheson and since that panned out, I stopped there. He should know about Fred, don't you think? They're cousins."

"Maybe, although I know nothing about the lives of my cousins."

"You wouldn't, Walsh. You just wouldn't," and Pete chuckled.

It was one of the few times Derek had heard Pete really laugh since he'd arrived.

They left soon after. Nancy didn't come out and Derek wondered if she was avoiding him. He'd told her as much of the truth as he dared. He would have told her all of it, but he knew it wouldn't work out well. He thought about the day ahead. He didn't really want to go back to Seattle yet. Leeder would go to work the next day and Derek found Seattle a hassle to get around in. He much preferred

Portland, but he was pretty sure he was wearing out his welcome at Pete's. Maybe talking to Murcheson would give him some direction although he wasn't even sure he'd recognize the guy.

They listened to tunes on the way down, Pete working hard to convince Derek that Rascal Flatts and the Dixie Chicks were real musicians. It was a safe thing to banter and argue about, and Derek began to relax a little, to feel some of the old friendship coming back around. By the time they'd made the 45-minute drive to Salem, they were feeling pretty good.

It took them a while to find the hotel that Murcheson had suggested. "I never come to Salem," Pete said in way of explanation.

"Well, it's certainly changed a lot since our day," Derek said.

Pete stopped the car at a 7-11 and Derek went in and got directions and about five minutes later they were pulling into the hotel parking lot. They spent a couple of minutes trying to figure out which big expensive car belonged to Murcheson, settling on a black Town Car with tinted windows. Derek wondered if Pete was as nervous as he was.

The hotel had seen better days. The lobby was on its way to shabby and a pall of old cigarette smoke and industrial cleaners followed them into the lounge, which was empty except for a woman about their age who was setting up behind the bar. "Come on in, fellas," she said. "Sit anywhere."

"You okay to be here in the bar?" Derek said to Pete. "We could wait in the lobby."

"That's okay," Pete said. "I'm fine." After a brief pause, he added, "Thanks for asking though."

They found a table over to one side and sat down. The woman brought over a bowl of peanuts and two cocktail napkins. Pete ordered decaf coffee and Derek ordered a beer. They watched the woman as she got their drinks and brought them over. She didn't linger at the table but went back to doing the setup.

Derek did recognize Murcheson. He'd been a big guy before, the kind with that sloppy, soft weight and now he was on his way to obese. The height helped some and he still carried himself pretty well but he dwarfed them both. His hair was unnaturally black and thin and combed back. His skin had the ashen look of too much time indoors. He grinned though when he saw them.

"Walsh," he said, "and Pete Chandling. How the hell are ya?"

Derek had to sift through his memory to find the first name. He should have asked Pete but then he found it. "Tom," he said and he put his hand out for the ritual.

The waitress came over with the coffee pot and filled Pete's cup. Derek passed on another beer but Murcheson looked at his watch and then ordered one.

They exchanged a few pleasantries. Where they lived. What they did. Murcheson went on at some length about his law practice. Accidents, workers' comp, a few petty criminals pro bono to stay in good with the local judges. The big money, he said, was in industrial accidents at some of the big farm corporations where safety was a policy seldom followed or enforced.

"That your Town Car out there in the parking lot?" said Derek.

"Yeah," Murcheson said. "How'd you know?"

Derek grinned. "Just a guess. Seems like a good car for a lawyer."

"So is this really a get-together for old times' sake or is one of you in trouble? When I hear from old pals, it's usually about the law."

Pete and Derek looked at each other. "We may all be in trouble," Pete said.

Murcheson frowned.

Pete spoke. "Do you remember a night in '72 when Fred brought a girl over to your place?"

"Fred?"

"Fred Landon. He's your cousin, right?"

"Oh, that Fred. What night are you talking about? Fred kind of came and went from the place. He fancied himself quite the Lothario."

"It was a night in late May. 1972, like I said. Some of the rest of us came too and we…" Pete hesitated.

"We took turns having sex with the girl," said Derek.

Murcheson's face gave nothing away but he said, "Oh yeah. I remember that. What of it?"

Pete said, "The girl—her name was Rhonda—got pregnant and gave the child up for adoption. Now that kid has come looking for whichever one of us is his father."

Murcheson shrugged and his face remained impassive. "Sounds like a simple paternity issue."

Derek and Pete looked at each other again. "Maybe," Derek said. "But I think the guy is looking for more than that."

"What do you mean?" said Murcheson.

"I think he wants revenge."

"Are you guessing or has he told you this?" Murcheson's posture had changed. He'd been lounging back in his chair, fiddling with the beer glass, but now he pulled himself forward, all business.

"We talked about it briefly."

"When?" Pete said. "He didn't say anything when we saw him yesterday."

"Last night. He…I talked to him last night in the park near your house."

"You made an arrangement to see him?" Pete sounded miffed, almost jealous.

"No. I went to the park after I dropped Leeder off. I needed a place to think."

"And Kirchner just happened to be there too?"

"No," Derek said. "I'm sure he followed me."

"Leeder? Jim Leeder?" Murcheson said. "Is he involved in this too?"

Derek nodded. "Tom, do you remember who was there that night?"

The lawyer thought a moment and then shook his head. "I've never thought about that night again. I vaguely remember some of you watching TV with me until late and waiting for you all to get done so I could go to bed."

"Do you remember if Leeder was there?" said Derek.

"No, why?"

"Pete and I remember him there and he says he wasn't."

"Sorry, can't help you with that one. Is it important?"

"Only if Leeder is the father, I guess," said Derek.

Murcheson signaled the waitress. He pointed to Pete's cup. "You not drinking?"

"No," Pete said. "Eight years sober."

"Good for you." He turned to Derek. "Another round?"

Derek nodded and Murcheson told the waitress, changing his own drink to a double scotch on the rocks.

"So you think this is just a case of paternity?" Derek said to Murcheson.

"Yeah, I would guess so. Why?"

"Kirchner is accusing us of gang rape."

"Ouch," said Murcheson. "That's tough for you guys."

"What do you mean 'us guys'? You're on the list too, Tom," said Derek.

Murcheson sat back in his chair, drained the beer glass. "There's a list?"

"Yes," said Derek.

"Have you seen it?"

"No."

"Then how do you know I'm on it?"

"We don't," said Pete. "Not for sure anyway. But you were there. Why wouldn't you be on the list?"

"Any number of reasons," said Murcheson. "The girl never knew my name. How would she put it on a list?"

"She didn't make the list. One of us did. That's what Kirchner said. He got the list from one of us."

Murcheson looked at Derek, who nodded. "I take it he didn't get it from either of you or Leeder. And he sure as hell didn't get it from me." He took a sip of the fresh drink.

"What about Fred?" Pete said.

Murcheson choked on his drink and started coughing. Pete clapped him on the back and the waitress came over with a glass of water. It took Murcheson a minute or two to clear his lungs.

"I'm taking that as a no on Fred giving up the list," Derek said.

"That would be correct," Murcheson said. "Fred has never taken responsibility for anything in his life."

"How is Fred? Where is he?" Pete said.

"Don't really know. Last I heard—and that was years ago—he was living in Reno and dealing blackjack in an after-hours club. But like I said, that was years ago. We were never that close." Murcheson sipped his drink. "So where did the list come from?"

"It had to be Lonnie," said Derek after a minute.

"Who's Lonnie?" Murcheson said.

"Lonnie Tillstrom," said Pete. "He was a Sig Delt a year behind us. He was the sixth person there that night."

"Why would he give anybody the list?"

Derek shrugged. "Guilty conscience, the best I can figure."

"He that kind of guy?" said Murcheson.

"I didn't know him well at all. What do you think, Pete?"

"I didn't either, really. But I remember him as soft-spoken. Kind of a gentle guy." He paused. "Tell him the rest, Derek."

Derek looked at Pete and then at Murcheson. "Lonnie didn't take his turn in the bedroom that night."

Murcheson's eyebrows went up. "So..."

"So I think he changed his mind or felt bad and maybe he got approached by the kid and decided to give us up."

"But how did the kid find out about Lonnie? The girl would have to have known him enough to remember him," said Murcheson. "And she was with Fred that night, right? Why wouldn't she have given the kid Fred's name instead?"

Pete nodded. "You've got a point."

Derek's impatience had been building. "Can we get back to the real point here? What are we going to do about the rape allegations?"

Murcheson settled back in his chair. "There's no legal ground anymore. The girl would have to have sued us in the first six years after. Statute of limitations ran out in," he paused to calculate, "'79."

"Yes, that's what my lawyer said."

"So you've seen someone about this."

"I thought it best to find out where I stood."

"What else did he say, this lawyer you saw?" Murcheson perked up suddenly, showing more curiosity than he had in the rest of the conversation.

"Not to admit to anything."

"That's exactly what I'd tell you."

"But what about helping the kid find out which one of you is his dad?" said Pete.

"You're not a candidate?" Murcheson turned to Pete.

"Pete gave his DNA and it wasn't a match," Derek said. No need for Murcheson to know about Pete's impotence that night.

"I didn't see it as an admission of any kind of guilt," Pete said. "I was just wanting to help the kid out. If he was my son, I would want to know."

"Admirable," said Murcheson. "But not very wise. Hey, I'm hungry. Let's get some lunch," and he signaled the waitress.

26

Nancy poured herself a bowl of granola and cut a banana into it. She'd waited until the men left before coming out to the kitchen. She didn't have the patience to deal with Derek and his clinical detachment about women and sex again this morning.

She'd always held back when Derek was there and for a long time, she wasn't quite sure what it was that seemed off about him. Both Jim and Pete loved him. There was something deep and admirable about their relationship that she didn't want to interfere with. So many men she knew—and knew of—had only their partner or spouse to confide in, and that seemed a very lonely way to live. She knew she didn't want to be the only person Pete could talk to. But the longer she'd known them all, the less she was sure of how good they were for each other, or more specifically, how good Jim and Derek were for Pete.

In her years together with Jim, his habits and behaviors had driven such a wedge between the two of them that she had broken it off, and none of those behaviors had changed much in the intervening years. In fact, the years had just exacerbated them—the fly-off-the-handle anger, the permanent buzz, the inconsistencies. In the beginning, she'd loved and wanted Jim enough to put up with the music world lifestyle, but then she caught him in lie after lie and she grew up and kicked him out. Later, after she and Pete were married, she had tried to convince Pete and Derek to hold an intervention for Jim on his drinking and drugging, but they wouldn't—or couldn't—agree to cut off contact with him if he didn't go to treatment, so she dropped it. Now she planned her girlfriend getaways for the times the three men were in Portland together, and she saw Jim rarely.

Because Derek lived in Virginia, Nancy saw even less of him. Pete had lots of vacation time and she encouraged him to fly out and visit Derek when he went to see his elderly parents, who lived in Kentucky, where his father was a professor emeritus at a small religious college. At the same time, over the years, she had met Derek's several wives, who grew younger as those years went on. They all talked about how sweet and romantic he was, what a kind lover and friend he was to them. Or at least until he met someone else that he wanted to be kind and sweet and romantic to. When she'd ask them about his legendary *Playboy* collection and his adoration of free love and Hugh Hefner, they'd change the subject or say it wasn't a problem. But she didn't believe them. Karina, Derek's current wife, was number four, and Nancy hadn't met her yet. All she knew was that Karina was in her early 30s and a teacher. Pete said she was lovely. Nancy didn't doubt it.

She got up and started another pot of coffee. Pete had left Jason's number for her and had put the beer bottles in her trunk. She dialed the number and when she got voice mail, she left him a message, asking if they could get together at the same coffee shop at 1. She could have invited him to the house—he clearly knew where she lived—but she didn't want him to be there if the guys came back from Salem sooner than she expected.

She didn't like the clandestine aspects of this. She had long ago let her interest in drama fade. Her work at the hospital with sick kids was dramatic enough for several lives. But she wanted to help Jason find his father, and she didn't agree with the dogged determination of Jim and Derek to shirk their responsibility in this. At the same time, she hoped neither one was the father. Not because they didn't deserve it, but because she didn't trust them to do well by Jason. She wouldn't have wanted either of them to be her father.

When the phone rang at 12:30, it was Jason. He'd be there at 1. She went to get dressed.

27

The three men tabled the conversation while they waited for the sandwiches to arrive. They talked about sports, about other brothers from the frat that they remembered. Murcheson had kids in California, two daughters, one of them in pre-law. He was divorced from their mother and didn't see them all that often. Pete only briefly mentioned his corporate job, instead talking about his interest in photographing wildlife and a trip he'd taken to Alaska to shoot bears and moose.

"And what about you, Walsh? What do you do?" Murcheson began to plow through his French fries.

Derek put his sandwich down. "I'm on the faculty of a women's college in Virginia. I teach sociology. Been there nearly 20 years. I like it there and I like teaching. No real hobbies, but I collect rare records, rock, jazz, some blues. Summers I go to a lot of rock concerts."

"You guys used to do that back in the day, right? I'm remembering Fred trying to get me to go to Seattle with you to do some concert. Moody Blues? Van Morrison? I don't remember. I didn't go."

"Yeah, we did a lot of road trips. Used to leave mid-afternoon, drive up to Seattle, go to the concert, drive home. Follies of youth."

"You married, Walsh? Or are you one of those guys who likes to keep his options open? Didn't you have a bit of a reputation for that back in school?"

"Yeah, I guess. And yes, I'm married."

"To one of your students? Isn't that the tradition? Is that why you ended up at a women's college?"

Derek paused, then said, "That's not why I teach there but yes, she was a student there years ago although not one of mine."

Murcheson nodded as if that explained everything. Derek didn't like it.

They finished their sandwiches, pushed the burger baskets to one side of the table although Murcheson went on eating the French fries the others had left. Pete went up to the bar and ordered three coffees and came back and sat down.

Derek was asking, "Will you meet with Kirchner if he contacts you? I'm guessing he will."

"I don't know. What's the chance I'm the dad? One in six?"

"Well, actually, one in four," said Pete. "I'm not and, as we said, Lonnie can't be."

"Hmm. Does he look like me?"

"Not obviously," Derek said. "He's tall, brown hair and eyes, but when I saw you today, I didn't think 'Wow, that's Kirchner's dad.' Did you, Pete?"

Pete shook his head.

"Do you think he might be your son?" Murcheson said to Derek.

Derek shrugged. "Doesn't matter. I'm not finding out."

"Unless the rest of us prove negative," Murcheson said.

"Well, yeah, I guess so," Derek said. "I hadn't thought of that."

"So, guys, are we done here?" Murcheson licked his fingers. "Anything more we need to discuss?"

"I don't think so," said Pete. "We wanted to know if you remembered the event, if you remembered Leeder being there, if you gave Kirchner the list."

"Yeah, well, I wouldn't give anybody a list that implicated others in anything unless I was under oath. Not personally, not professionally. I do have some ethics."

"Sorry," said Pete, "I didn't mean anything by it."

Murcheson laughed. "I'm just pulling your leg." Then his look turned dark. "You know the fact that this kid has no legal recourse doesn't mean he doesn't have other ways to get at us."

"My lawyer said that too," said Derek.

Murcheson nodded. "We all have vulnerabilities, reputations, people this could hurt. Not the paternity so much. That happens more often than you think. But the rape allegation. That's a bigger complication. And ironically the fact that it's so far in the past hurts more than helps us." He pulled out his wallet and put two 20s on the tray and pushed it over to the other two. "Twenty-five years ago, the culture wasn't all that sensitized to women's rights but today it's a different story. A lot of publicity about this would not be good."

"So what do we do?" asked Pete.

"It's one argument for giving him the DNA." Murcheson looked at Derek. "Cooperation can go a long way towards soothing that kind of anger. And if he finds his father and is happy with who it is, it might all just blow over."

"But if I give him DNA, I've admitted being there that night. You said that admitting nothing was the best way to go."

"Yeah, in most cases that's true, but now I'm not so sure. Will you refuse to acknowledge him if he's your kid?"

"No. Well, I don't think so," Derek said. "I just don't want to be implicated in a rape that wasn't a rape. She consented. She agreed to be there and I haven't committed any crime."

"But that right there is the big argument for giving him the DNA." Murcheson took a sip of his coffee, grimaced, and pushed the mug aside. "I agree that it wasn't rape and nothing *legally* indicates that rape occurred. She never reported it, as far as we know, and no evidence was ever collected or filed. And I can check to see if that's true. But reputation is all about perception, and public perception of such events has changed drastically, and that won't play out in our favor. Certainly, not yours, Walsh. You have the most perception-sensitive job of any of us—professor at a women's college."

"Gee, Derek, I never thought about that," said Pete.

"Well, I have," Derek said. "I thought about it right away. They're not going to think of me as a stupid 19-year-old kid who did this with a fellow student. They're going to think that it's me now, the middle-aged college professor, who did this to one of his much younger students. The facts, the truth, will all disappear in a media shit storm. How have I suddenly got the most to lose? The whole thing wasn't even my idea."

"Luck of the draw," said Murcheson.

Derek flashed back on the torn paper, the little strip he'd pulled that had made him number 5. Then he said, "So, Tom, your advice to me now is to give him the DNA?"

"If there's no crime involved, then taking responsibility for finding out about paternity would put you in a more favorable light. You would be erasing one irresponsible action—not using a condom, which is not illegal—with a serious acceptance of responsibility."

"So you will give him DNA as well?" Derek said.

Mucheson nodded. "Yeah, obviously it makes the most sense for all of us. Especially if we agree that no crime was committed."

"Why wouldn't we agree to that?" said Pete. "It's the truth."

Murcheson shrugged.

"You're thinking about Fred, aren't you?" said Derek.

Murcheson nodded. "He can be a loose cannon."

"What do you mean?" Pete said.

"He's been in trouble over the years. Nothing major. Selling dope, carrying a firearm without a license. There were even pimping charges a while back but they couldn't make the case. Let's just say he lives on the fringes."

"Well, wouldn't he want to cooperate to stay out of more trouble? We'd all testify it was his idea, that he set it up that night. Surely he wouldn't want that," Derek said.

"If we caught him at a time when he wasn't drinking, he'd probably agree. But from what I've heard, those times are few and far between."

"Oh God. Well then, for Kirchner's sake, we have to hope that Fred isn't his father," said Pete.

The others didn't respond. Then Derek said, "What do we do? How do we protect ourselves?"

"We give Kirchner our DNA," said Murcheson. "If one of us is the father, we own up and move on with that. If we aren't, we have to hope that satisfies him." He stood up and took out his wallet again and handed Derek a business card. "You can give this to Kirchner. Tell him I'm willing to meet him and give him the sample."

Derek and Pete stood up as well. Pete got out his wallet and took the bill over to the waitress to settle up. Derek said, "Is this all going to go to shit for us?"

"I don't know," Murcheson said. "I'll call you if I learn anything from Kirchner when I see him. Have you told your wife?"

"No."

"That may be a good idea. If Kirchner decides to push this, he might well start there, with a letter or phone call to your wife. It's where I'd start if I was looking for revenge."

Derek's heart sank. He did not want to have to tell Karina about all this.

Pete came back over and the men walked out through the hotel lobby to the bright, hot parking lot. They shook hands and Murcheson went over to the Town Car and drove away. Pete and Derek got in Pete's car and headed out to the freeway and back to Portland. There seemed nothing more to say and they rode in silence for a long time. It wasn't until they'd reached the turnoff for 205 North just south of Portland that Derek thought to check the time. It was 3:30 and he knew Leeder would be long gone.

28

Nancy Chandling arrived at the coffee shop a little before 1. Kirchner was already there. He'd taken the same sidewalk table. On it were two large iced teas. "I took the liberty," he said, pointing to the tea.

"Thanks." She took the other chair but didn't drink from the tea. Her thoughts jumped around. Had he drugged the tea? Had he poisoned it? She was ashamed of these ideas. She was trusting by nature and railed against those of her friends who showed the least paranoia. She knew these thoughts had come unbidden, probably influenced by the conversation the night before with Pete and Derek. She took a sip of the tea. It was sweet and she was relieved. She stood up with the glass in her hand. "I don't like sweet tea," she said with a smile. "I'll go get an unsweetened."

"I'll do it for you," he said, rising from his chair.

"No, thanks. I can get it. Shall I leave this one for you too?"

He shook his head. "One is enough." He looked her in the eye and she couldn't tell if he could sense her suspicion. She smiled again and went into the shop.

She hoped she was wrong about Kirchner. If he was dangerous, she shouldn't take this any further. If she gave him the DNA information and he did something awful, would she be an accomplice? She shook her head. This was crazy thinking. He had been nothing but courteous to her. He was a young man who was suffering in his life, and she could do something about that suffering. That was her job, her purpose. She paid for the iced tea and went back outside. "Tell me about your life, Jason," she said. "And tell me about your mother."

His first real memories were of a bicycle when he was 7. It had belonged to a kid down the block from his foster home. He didn't know if it was the second or third or fourth placement. He'd coveted that bike and borrowed it to ride one afternoon after school. He'd ridden it up and down the block and felt like he was flying. It was an amazing sense of freedom especially when he took his hands off the handle bars. Then he'd hit a curb and gone flying. Broken his arm, wrecked the bike. His foster father had waited until his arm healed, then beaten him badly for his carelessness and their expense at replacing the bike. He'd run away for the first time a few weeks after that. But he got caught and was returned to the same family for a little while and then moved to another.

He was now a thief and labeled an incorrigible, and they moved him to a group home, mostly boys who were also already in trouble. It wasn't a bad place. There were a lot of rules, he said, but if you followed them and stayed out of trouble, they left you alone. "We had food, clean sheets, clean clothes. We went to school and we did chores. It might have been like a real home, but I don't know. I don't have anything to compare it to." He was there a year or so. He didn't really remember. Then he had a bunch of other foster homes. He didn't tell her the stories of being beaten or molested. There didn't seem to be any point. He spent the junior high years in another group home. He stayed there until he started high school, stayed out of trouble too.

"Were you happy there?" she asked.

He shrugged, took a sip of his tea. Then another family. Two kids of their own, two other foster kids. He was there about a year. The foster father was ex-military, all about muscle and strength. Made them lift weights, run miles after school, work on weekends in his lumber yard. He got strong but he hated the guy for it. He ran away as soon as he had stolen $200. Lived on the street in Eugene, Albany, Salem. Up and down the I-5corridor, hitch-hiking, doing odd jobs.

"Drugs? Alcohol?" she asked.

"No drugs. I could see what happened to the kids who got hooked. They let the code go, did anything for that next fix."

"Code?"

He looked at her to see if she really didn't know. Apparently she didn't. "Kids aren't completely lawless on the streets, you know. We aren't barbarians. There's a code. You don't steal from each other, only from Regulars."

"Regulars?"

"Regular folks. Folks with jobs and cars and houses. They have extra. We didn't."

"What else is in the code?"

"Don't sleep with someone else's girl. Don't go through someone else's stuff. Things like that. Help each other out. Don't snitch. Whatever you do, don't snitch."

"A kind of family then."

"Yeah." He could feel her looking at him. Her interest seemed sincere but he was wary nonetheless.

"How long were you on the street?"

"Till I was 15. I ended up back in Roseburg where I'd been as a kid and I went to see my case worker from two years before. I know. It sounds odd. But I was really tired of being on the street. The group home wasn't great but I missed a bed, showers, three squares. And this will probably sound odd as well. I wanted to go to school. Kids who grow up on the street, they only know the street. And after a while, they're just homeless, the dregs, the invisible. I didn't want to be invisible. I wanted some other kind of life. With a dog and a truck."

"You wanted to be visible?"

"Yeah. To be somebody. We all want that, don't we?"

She nodded. "We do. So he helped you, this case worker?"

"She. Mrs. Crosby. She found me a group home, a small one. Six guys and a couple of counselors. It was a house in Monmouth. Do you know where that is?"

She nodded again.

"It was pretty okay. We went to school, we had jobs after school. I worked in two churches as the janitor. The counselors were cool. Especially this guy Alex. He was about 25. He liked to read and he'd drive us to the library and check things out for us that we liked. He trusted us to bring them back. And he'd talk about anything. He'd lived in his car for a while to save money. Joined a gym so he could shower every day. Cheaper than rent, he said. He taught us there are lots of ways to solve problems, not just one or two."

"Did you graduate?"

"No. I'd missed too much to make that happen, but I got a GED and went to community college. Alex told us about scholarships and other stuff to help kids from the system. I got my associate's and training in electrical stuff so I could always make a living."

He looked at her again. She was still watching him but he began to feel uneasy, that maybe he had revealed too much. He stood up. "I need to use the restroom." He didn't wait for her response, just went inside.

When he came back, she stood up too. "I'll be right back," she said, and she went inside. When she came back, she had two glasses of water and two sandwiches on a tray.

"Roast beef or turkey?" she said.

"Ah, turkey, I guess." He took a sandwich and they ate in silence. He began to relax a little.

She asked him then about his work. Not much to tell. Did he have a pet? Not yet. Did he have a girlfriend? Not at the moment.

There was a long pause, and he reached over and put her trash on the tray, then his own. It seemed time to go. But she put her hand on his arm. "May I ask something else?" she said.

He paused, unsure. There wasn't any more to talk about.

She didn't wait for his reply. "How did you find your mother?"

His heart clenched. He shouldn't have been surprised. Of course, it was a logical question. Logical too for her to be curious about that. But it was way too intimate a thing to bring up and he felt sorry he had told her anything. Something dark and familiar settled in.

"I'm sorry," she said. "Is that the wrong question?"

He still didn't respond.

She waited, then spoke again. "What is the right question?"

29

Jim Leeder showed up at Pete's house at 2:30. The cars were gone, a bad sign. He knocked but there was no answer. He knew he was early but he wasn't going to wait around for a half-hour. He felt like shit from the drugs and the beating, and he didn't have the patience to wait. Walsh could get Chandling to drive him back to Seattle or he could take the train. Jim headed out Division east to 205 and the link-up with I-5.

He wasn't angry with Walsh. Derek's refusing to give his DNA was the smart thing to do. And Derek hadn't pushed him when he'd said he hadn't been there. That had been all Chandling. Pete, the righteous. Pete, the goody two-shoes. Always keeping his nose clean. And his dick as well apparently. Holier than thou. Except of course that he'd agreed to go along, to have sex with the girl. How righteous was that?

Red tail lights ahead. Why couldn't these assholes get off the road? It was Sunday afternoon, for Christ's sake.

Nancy flashed across his mind. Damn, she looked good. Always had. He thought about the night he met her. A staff party for a recording studio. She'd come with a guy he knew vaguely, a drummer. What was his name? Andy something. Something French or Canadian. He played with a band based in Minnesota of all places. He was a short guy too, just like Pete. Maybe that had been their problem. That he was too tall for her. Too good-looking. Pete certainly wasn't and that drummer hadn't been either. She'd worn a red dress. Way different from the other women who'd been in jeans and sweaters. Every man there had wanted her. And she'd left with him. Left that drummer in the dust. He smiled at that.

The traffic thinned after he crossed the bridge into Washington. He got in the left lane and set the cruise control for 75. He wanted to get home but he didn't need a speeding ticket.

He'd loved Nancy right from the start although he kept his distance for a few months, seeing her intermittently, continuing to sleep with a couple of the others. That girl in the accounting office. And the singer, Sheila. Whose career never went anywhere hard as he tried. He got her some good material but she didn't have what it took. She didn't have that spark, that presence. She was just a nice girl with a good voice and great tits.

Nancy had that presence. She'd have made a great performer but she didn't have any music in her. Or any interest in having any. Yet he'd loved the presence that she had. That sense of self. That strong knowing of who she was and what she wanted. And she had wanted him. For a long time she had wanted him. And then she didn't anymore.

He knew it was his fault. He'd held back. Didn't commit. Wouldn't move in with her. Wouldn't talk about marriage. He didn't ever say so but he needed to keep his options open. Shit, he was 30 then. He was a music man. What did she expect?

They'd had a lot of good times over those years. He was always proud to be seen with her, to introduce her to people. She was his public partner and he wanted that to be enough for her. That pride, that acknowledgement. But she wanted everything. All of his time, all of his attention. And he felt trapped at the idea of that. So he'd pulled away and she didn't come after him. There was never a big argument, not even anything that could be called breaking up. He thought about the last time, dinner out for her birthday. She'd said she was moving to Portland, taking a better job as a supervisor on a pediatric floor. They'd recruited her and she was really pleased with that. What could he say? Don't go? I need you here? I need it all to stay the same? But he couldn't, so he congratulated her. Ordered champagne to celebrate. Gave her the ruby earrings. Put her in a cab. Called the girl from accounting.

The Kelso exits came up and he looked at the gas tank. Low but okay. He'd get something to eat in Olympia.

He wondered if she was happy with Pete. He knew Pete was happy with her. He could see it in his friend. In the way he was. Happy in his life. Not like him. And not like Walsh, no matter how much Derek talked about his job and his wife. He knew unhappiness when he saw it and Walsh was unhappy. The new wife was cute, blonde, curvy, and probably smart. Walsh liked them smart. But he'd had a string of these women and it never lasted very long. And for all his own smarts, Walsh kept marrying them. Which meant he had to divorce them and be tangled up in alimony and the legal system. So much better to hang loose the way he did.

Like this whole paternity mess. If Walsh was the father, then he'd have to involve his wife in whatever decisions he made. Not like him. He'd be free to ignore the kid and no one would have any say.

30

Nancy watched Jason's profile, the jaw that clenched reflexively, the lips that smiled so rarely. Anxiety? Reluctance? Sadness? Men were so much harder to read than women. They had so much practice in keeping it all hidden. She saw that on the pediatric ward, the pain of the mothers written all over them, the pain of the fathers hidden deep inside. She waited. Jason would tell her what he was going to when he was ready.

He shifted in his seat, looked over at her, looked away. Then he started to talk again.

He'd looked first for the couple that adopted him as an infant, the ones that gave him to the system. He wanted to know what had happened, why they'd only loved him for two years. How bad could a 2-year-old be to let him go like that? That's what he'd thought. That something in him had changed, some bad seed had come to light. A woman he'd known, a sort of girlfriend, had told him he was crazy to think that. That before he decided that was the truth, he should find out the circumstances, he should be sure it was his fault. So he'd gone back to Mrs. Crosby in Roseburg.

It took her a couple of days to find the file as he'd been out of the system for six years. He spent the time driving around the homes he'd lived in, schools he'd attended. He hated Roseburg. It was full of ugly memories.

On the second day, he went back to see her at closing time. She met him outside the building. There was a bench on the sidewalk and they sat down there. She didn't have the file with her. He was disappointed for he'd hoped to read it for himself. "I was afraid she wouldn't tell me the truth, that she'd make up something to make me feel better."

The social worker gave him the name of the couple who'd adopted him. That was a matter of public record. She could not share what was in the file without a court order. But she could tell him that the woman still lived in the area, out in the little town of Drain. Sharon Morrissey was her name now, and she handed him the address.

He drove out to Drain. He'd never been there before. It was a strange little crossroads on the way out to the coast. A rundown store, a dead gas station, a few houses, and an old sawdust burner from a long disappeared sawmill. The only thing of interest was a huge Victorian house all freshly painted. Tours from 1-3 daily, the sign in the yard said. There wasn't much in the way of street signs but she lived on Main and he found the house. More of a cottage, it was, and set back off the road a little bit. The house was shabby but the yard was full of flowers and he had a sharp memory of color like that.

She answered the door. He could smell bacon frying. He didn't recognize her. Nothing about her was familiar.

"I'm Jason Kirchner," he said. "You adopted me in 1973."

For a moment, her face was blank. Then it crumpled and she began to cry. No sobs, no noises, just tears running down her face. She opened the screen door in the same silence and he followed her into the kitchen where she turned off the stove and sat down with him at the table. It wasn't a very long story. She and her husband had divorced just after his second birthday. She had gotten custody. The husband wasn't interested. Then she got ill. MS. She didn't have much money and so she moved in with her parents, who could take care of her. Only they didn't want the baby.

"She said they'd opposed the adoption in the first place. Said her dad was a hard man. He didn't warm to me because I wasn't blood kin. She began to cry again. Said she couldn't take care of me and her parents wouldn't. 'I know you won't understand but I had to let you go,' she said. 'I wanted to give you up while you were still little enough to be adopted again. That seemed the best for us all.' That's what she said." Jason looked over at Mrs. Chandling.

"She got up then and got us coffee as if we were neighbors having a chat," he said. "I couldn't stand the casualness of that. I thought of the most hurtful thing I could say and then I said it to her. 'I didn't get adopted again.'"

He sat in silence for a moment. "I hurt her. I could see it in her face. She cried some more and I didn't know what to do so I left." He looked over at Nancy. "She tried to touch me but I couldn't have that. She started apologizing, saying she loved me, but I couldn't handle that either. I got out of there as fast as I could."

"That all must have been very hard to hear," Nancy said.

"Yeah, I've been through that in my head a million times. Maybe if I'd been her birth child, it would have been different."

"Maybe," Nancy said. She waited to see if he would say anything else about it. Then she said, "When did you start looking for Rhonda?"

He looked over at her as he heard the name. Then he shrugged. "Not until a long time later. Years and years later. I heard it wasn't easy and I wasn't sure what difference it would make to know. She'd given me up at birth. That's a pretty obvious story. And she hadn't come looking for me." The bitterness in his voice was so sharp, so adolescent that Nancy winced.

"But you changed your mind."

"Yeah, I did. Curiosity mostly. And the urging of a friend who was an EMT, talking about how I needed to know my genetic history for health reasons. Especially if I wanted to have my own kids."

"Makes sense to me," she said.

"The timing was in my favor. Do you know what Measure 58 is?"

She nodded. "Open adoption records."

"Yeah. Oregon is one of a handful of states that lets you find out."

"So you found out."

He nodded. "I applied for a copy of my birth certificate and there was her name, my birth date, and the location. Good Samaritan Hospital in Portland. What the certificate didn't have was the name of my father. That was blank. And I couldn't figure out why. What harm would there have been in saying who he was even if she never planned to tell him. I'd already assumed she was unmarried. That's the reason most women give up a baby, isn't it?"

He looked at Nancy, who nodded.

"So why not list the guy?" He paused, cleared his throat.

"Do you want some more tea or water?" she said.

"Water." And he got up quickly and went into the café. He was gone a moment and she gathered all that she'd heard and tucked it away. Sad stories about families were a dime a dozen in pediatrics, and she'd always maintained a great deal of distance from the particulars as she cared for the kids and communicated with the families. Their lives, their stories were more than she could carry and do her job well. But she found she couldn't separate herself from Jason in the same way. Maybe it was because of the role Pete had played in this whole story. He hadn't had sex with Rhonda but he had done nothing to stop the others from doing something he knew was wrong. She knew that guilt was motivating him to help Jason. And maybe she had some kind of misplaced maternal instincts for him. She was Rhonda's age. Or maybe it was just the caregiver in her, the savior of lost dogs and sick kids.

He came back with two glasses of ice water. "Thanks for thinking of me," she said.

He didn't acknowledge her words, just drank most of his water and then put the glass on the table. "It's not as easy to find someone as people think. Even with the Internet. Especially if it's a woman."

"Because women get married and change their names."

He nodded.

"Not all of us do that anymore."

"Maybe not. But my mother did."

"How did you find her?"

"I thought at first the hospital would give me the address she'd given when she had me but they wouldn't, so I searched phone directories, called Information. Nothing. The birth certificate showed her as born in Salem so I looked for her family there. There were some Ordways in the obituaries in the Salem paper but I didn't know if they were related or not. And there were no Ordways with phone listings in Salem. I tried Eugene and Portland but no luck. Then it occurred to me to try Roseburg. I assumed I'd been in foster care there because of the adoption but maybe I'd been given up for adoption there too. So I lucked out. I found a cousin of hers in Roseburg. Said I was an old friend of Rhonda's, wanted to connect with her. And she gave me her married name and an address in Portland."

He paused and Nancy let the silence hang there. Then she said, "What happened when you went to see her?"

He looked over at her. "I didn't go to see her."

She waited.

"I sent her a letter. Explained who I was and included a copy of my birth certificate. After my experience with my adopted mother, I couldn't stand to witness another meltdown. I told her I was looking for health information for both birth parents. I offered to meet her to get the information."

He paused, finished his water, tossing if off as if it had been whiskey. Maybe he wished it was, she thought. She waited.

"About two weeks later, I got a letter back. But not from her. From her husband." He reached into his backpack and pulled out an envelope, then handed it to her.

She took it, looked at him, and pulled out the sheet of yellow lined paper and read the handwriting.

Dear Jason,

Thank you for contacting my wife. Below you will find the medical information you requested for my wife's family. There's not a lot on there as she seems to come from pretty healthy people who live a long time. I hope that is good news for you and your family.

We cannot give you the name of your birth father. That is a complicated story but if you would like to hear it, I'd be happy to meet with you and share it with you.

Sincerely,
Paul Trevino

"She didn't write to you herself."

"No, she didn't."

Nancy could hear the bitterness again. "I'm sorry," she said and put the paper back in the envelope and pushed it across the table to him.

Jason shrugged. "Whatever. It doesn't matter. She didn't want me then. She doesn't want me now."

"It's most likely not that simple at all, Jason. It's heart-breaking for women to give up their baby. It's almost never a case of not wanting you. It's usually a case of very difficult circumstances. Do you know how old your mother was when you were born?"

He didn't say anything for a minute, then looked at her. "Eighteen."

"That's really young. And if her parents wouldn't help her, then she may have had no choice."

"But why wouldn't she want to meet me now?"

"I can't say. Guilt? Shame? It's very complicated. But what I can say is most likely she's never stopped loving you."

They were quiet a long moment after that. Then Nancy spoke. "Did you meet with her husband?"

"Yes. We met on a Saturday afternoon about a month ago in a coffee shop." He picked up his glass and saw that it was empty. He put it back down. "He was old, old enough to be my grandfather but in pretty good shape. Said he'd been a fire fighter and a logger. I didn't care. It wasn't him I was interested in. Then he told me what happened to her—meeting the guys in the tavern, being invited back to an apartment for a party, saying yes to one guy, not realizing she'd said yes to the five others. Said she didn't know how to get out of it once she was in it. Is that possible?" He looked at Nancy.

"Yes. Sad to say it is."

He sighed and went on. "Then she got pregnant, so she dropped out of school, came up to Portland to have me, and put me up for adoption. 'It was the only thing she could do,' he said."

"There you go. That's most likely true," Nancy said. "She was in a pretty impossible situation."

"I don't want to believe that."

"I can well imagine." She put her hand on his arm and then pulled it back. "But when you're young and have no money and no support, you make the best choice you can. I suspect she thought you'd find loving adoptive parents and live happily ever after."

"Well, we know how that turned out."

"But she couldn't know that. She still doesn't know that."

They were silent again. Then she said, "Did he tell you anything else?"

"Yes. Towards the end of her pregnancy, she ran into one of the six guys. He said that he was being eaten up with guilt and he wanted to tell her how sorry he was that they had done that to her. He gave her $200 and the list of names. Just in case she needed to know for some reason."

"Did the husband say which one visited her?"

"No. I asked him but he said she wouldn't tell him. That it didn't matter."

"So then he gave you the list."

Jason nodded.

"Did he say anything else?"

"No, but you know what? He wanted to take my picture, outside as we were leaving. I said no. My mother won't come meet me but she wants a picture? No way in hell."

Nancy sighed.

"He never asked me a single question about myself or about my life. Like I didn't matter at all."

"Perhaps to him you don't. He doesn't know you. But I can tell you that you matter to your mother. Women don't forget the children they lose. They just don't."

"But she doesn't want to know me, to have a relationship with me."

"Not yet."

"You mean she might?"

She could hear a little bit of hopefulness in his voice. "I wouldn't be surprised. She knows how to reach you, right?"

He nodded, and Nancy smiled at him. "Then you never know. Thanks for telling me all this. I want to help you. Pete and I want to help you." She hesitated and then said, "We have access to the DNA of Derek Walsh and Jim Leeder. I can't give it to you, but if you want to give me a sample of yours, I'll have the test run where I work. It's got to be expensive to run the test."

"Yes, it is."

"This seems the least we can do. And if you get samples from the other guys, I can have those run for you too."

He was quiet a moment. "I don't mean to sound ungrateful but what will keep you from just telling me they don't match?"

"Because I believe in your right to know. Pete and I both do. And because I think they need to take responsibility for what they did. All of them."

He paused again and then reached into his bag for a swab kit, used it on his mouth, and handed it to her. "Why are you helping me? I'm nothing to you."

"No, you're not nothing. I'm married to Pete, and Pete did you an injustice. Besides, I think it's important that you know that not all women are going to abandon you. I'm not going to abandon you." She put her hand on his arm again for a long moment. He didn't pull away.

"I can bring you the DNA results. We could meet here when I have them."

He shrugged. "Okay, thanks." He stood up. "I've taken too much of your time."

"It's all right." She stood too.

"Thank you."

"You're welcome." She went over to him and gave him a brief hug and then walked to her car and drove home. He hadn't returned the hug but neither had he pulled away.

31

Jim stopped in Olympia. He ached all over and wanted to get home and crawl into bed, but the car needed gas and he needed fuel too. There was a Denny's across from the first gas station he came to, but he needed a drink and he didn't remember if Denny's served beer. So he got gas and asked the kid at the cash register where he could get pizza and a beer. The closest place was a mile on into town and that's not what he wanted to do, get mired in Olympia. He thought about buying a six-pack and drinking it in the car but it was too risky. He'd already had a run-in with drinking and driving last year. Fortunately, he wasn't drunk. The test came back way under the limit, but they had cited him for an open container in the car. His insurance was already high and he didn't need more grief, so he drove the mile down the road.

The sausage pizza was surprisingly good and it came fast because the place was empty. It was 4:30 on a Sunday. He drank two beers, ate most of the pizza, and felt a lot better when he got back on the road. He thought about taking another Vicodin but decided against it. Just another problem if he got stopped.

He wondered if Walsh was mad that he hadn't waited. He knew Pete and Nancy would be. He didn't care much what Pete thought, but he didn't like it when he and Nancy were on the outs. He still cared about what she thought of him even though he didn't want to. He also wondered if they had noticed the same thing he had. That Kirchner looked like him. It wasn't an obvious match, but the height, the dark hair and eyes, the shape of the face. They were very similar. But he also didn't remember what Murcheson looked like and he didn't remember Lonnie whoever at all. Even Fred was a hazy memory. So the kid could look like one of them and this faint resemblance to him could be just a coincidence.

He'd often wondered if he had a kid or two out there in the world somewhere. He'd slept with so many women—wannabe stars, groupies, partygoers, secretaries, models. Every guy's dream, right? It had been fun, a lot of fun at first. And it continued to be fun afterwards, bragging, sharing his exploits with Walsh and Chandling, watching the envy in their eyes, especially Walsh with his inventories and his journals of his conquests. He knew he had Walsh way outnumbered.

He hadn't been careful, not until AIDS came along. He always figured the woman would be prepared. If she didn't want to get pregnant, she'd make sure it didn't happen. There was that one girl who hit him up for money. Marched into his office six months along. He barely remembered her or how they met. She swore it was his kid. He gave her a thousand bucks and then it turned out that the kid was black. She wasn't and of course he wasn't so that was the end of that. He'd thought about asking her for the money back but in the end he let it go. Live and learn.

It had never occurred to him that he'd gotten Rhonda pregnant. Not that night at the apartment with the other guys or later when he'd seen her again. They'd gone out for three or four weeks after that night. He'd seen her a lot. He'd liked her, maybe even loved her a little although he'd never said that to her. Then the summer had come and she'd gone home to Roseburg and he'd gone home to Pullman where he could get good pay working in the wheat fields. She'd written to him for the first month or so. Lots of letters, Sweet letters. At first, he'd written back. And then he hadn't. Just not his thing. In the early letters, they'd talked about him taking the bus to Roseburg. But that never happened. Then she'd written that Dear John letter. I met somebody else. Blah, blah, blah. He didn't believe it at first but why would she lie to him about something like that? When he went back to school in the fall, he hadn't tried to find her. He figured he'd run into her somewhere, but he didn't and there were plenty of other girls. And then he forgot about her.

He'd never told Derek or Pete that he'd seen Rhonda after that night at Murcheson's apartment. He didn't trust them to understand and he didn't want to explain. Their teasing would have been merciless. They'd all figured she was a slut to have agreed to it. And why would he go out with a slut when there were so many nice girls available? He and Rhonda had never talked about that night at Murcheson's either. It was as if it hadn't happened.

He wasn't sure why he'd denied being there that night. It was a jolt listening to Walsh read that letter in the car. He hadn't thought of Rhonda in years and years, not even a passing memory, but it had only taken a few seconds for him to realize he had a better chance of being the father than any of them. But to admit that, he'd have to explain it all and he couldn't imagine doing that.

He wished he had Nancy to talk to about this, but she'd made her stand pretty clear. That wasn't surprising. She'd always had a strong sense of ethics. That had been a problem between them when they were together. He worked in an unethical business, where payoffs and favors were a part of the game. She'd hated that and as their years together went on, he'd stopped talking to her about everything he did. And that silence had been a big part of their undoing.

Now he'd been silent again. Not just silent but in overt denial. But he couldn't find a way to tell them all about his relationship with Rhonda. It wasn't their business. And it left him with no one to talk to about any of it.

The Seattle skyline finally came into view. Home ahead. Whiskey, painkillers, sleep.

32

No one was there when Nancy got back to the house at 4:30. She'd gone first to the hospital and taken Jason's sample and the two beer bottles to the lab. Jane worked there on weekends. Sunday afternoons were usually slow, and she hoped Jane might have time before her shift was over. If not, she'd find time later in the week. And she wouldn't ask any questions.

Jane didn't ask questions about why she wanted the DNA tests run, but she was not eager to run them. "I'd like to do it for you but I don't know, Nance, this is so against regulations. You need a doctor's orders for this."

"Even in your off-time?"

"It's still the hospital's equipment and testing materials."

"Yeah, you're right," Nancy said. She hesitated, then told Jane what was going on.

"Wow," Jane said. "That's quite a story."

"I know. I'm just trying to help this kid out. Is there a way I can pay for the materials?

"I don't see how."

"Is there a private lab that does this kind of thing?"

"I'm sure there is," Jane said. "Let me find out what I can."

"Thanks, hon. You're the best."

From the hospital, Nancy had gone to the grocery store and then stopped by the bank ATM for cash on her way home. Pete had left her a note on the kitchen counter. "Taking Derek to the train." So she put the food away, changed her clothes, got a jug of cold water from the fridge, and went out to the garden. Pulling weeds was always therapeutic.

She was pretty sure that Jason was Jim's son. It wasn't really the physical resemblance although there were some similarities there—body type, coloring, and something about the eyes. But none of the features matched up in any straightforward way. However, there was a way about him, an aura, a sense of self that was so much like Jim. A fragile lost soul. It's what she had loved about Jim, that vulnerable boy in the man's body. Her mothering self now wanted to reach out to Jason, to protect him, to shore him up in that same way.

She didn't understand why Jim kept denying he'd been there. She knew that Pete and Derek wouldn't keep insisting that he had been there if it weren't true. It was possible Jim had been in a blackout. That happened and people could not remember what they had done because nothing got processed into memory. In Pete's memory of that night, Jim wasn't drunk but that's hard to judge in another person and it had been a whole lot of years before so Pete might not be remembering clearly. Or maybe all the drinking and drugs since then had impaired Jim's memory. Or maybe it had meant so little to him that he hadn't bothered to remember it.

All of these possibilities made her sad. To not be fully present for the conception of your child. To do it in lust or indifference and not in love. To be careless about the life of a human being, of two human beings. She wasn't naïve or unrealistic. She knew this happened all the time. Men were often heedless about their penises and what they did with them, and women most often paid the price. But she didn't want the men she cared about to be like that.

She had the power now to confirm that Jim was Jason's father. But she wasn't sure what good that information would do any of them. Jim would have to admit he'd been there. And then what? That wouldn't make him willing to acknowledge Jason or to care about him in any kind and real way. And she wasn't sure Jim was capable of any real fathering. She'd never wanted to have a child with him for that very reason. And if he wasn't the father, he'd skate. No consequences for something so despicable.

The more she thought about all this, the more she realized she'd gotten involved not just so she could offer some solace to Jason Kirchner as she'd told Jane but so she could punish Jim and Derek for what they had done and, most of all, for their lack of remorse. That was the hardest thing for her to deal with. She could forgive them the act; everyone does stupid and cruel things. But to not be sorry, to blame Rhonda? That was despicable. She tore at the weeds in her anger and frustration.

"Do you want some help?"

Nancy looked up to see Pete beside her. He smiled at her in such a kind and loving way that her heart eased some.

"No," she said. "I'm about done. Want to start some dinner? There are veggies for a stir fry and some chicken. I'll finish up here and take a quick shower."

He nodded, smiled again, and went inside. She dumped the plastic tub of weeds in the recycle bin in the driveway, put away her tools, and went in as well, stopping to kiss Pete, who was already chopping peppers and zucchini. She was hot and sweaty from the yard, and the shower was cool and helped her shift her mood even more. Dinner was ready by the time she'd dressed and she poured sparkling water in two wine glasses with slices of lime and took them out to the patio where Pete had set the table.

"Derek got off on the train okay?"

"Yes," Pete said. "We were late coming back from Salem, and Jim obviously didn't want to wait."

She nodded. "How was your meeting with Murcheson?"

He told her as much of what had been said as he remembered. "The bottom line," he said, "is that Murcheson convinced Derek to give Jason his DNA for testing. That he was far better off doing that than pissing Jason off."

"Did he give you a sample?"

"What do you mean?"

"Derek, before he left, did he give you a sample?"

He shook his head. "We didn't think of it."

"Do you think he's going to do it?" She put down her fork and looked at Pete.

"I would think so. He seemed convinced."

"But how and when?"

"Honey, we can't control that."

"Well, actually we can. We do."

"You're right. The beer bottles. You can give them to Jason."

"I've done better than that," she said. "I got a sample from him, and I took it and the bottles to the lab at work and asked Jane to run the tests for me."

He looked at her for a long moment without saying anything.

"What?" she said. "We agreed on doing that."

"I know, but that was before we met with Murcheson. Don't you think it's better if Derek gives the sample himself?"

"Yes, but when? You know Jim isn't going to encourage him to do that, probably the opposite. It should have happened here before he left." She wanted to express her frustration but decided not to.

"I agree. But it didn't. He didn't leave the sample."

Nancy sighed. "Should I ask Jane not to run the tests? I don't want to do this if we aren't in it together."

Pete thought for a moment and then shook his head. "No, let her do it. We don't have to do anything with the results."

33

Derek found a window seat on the train. He was looking forward to the quiet and the movement of the train. He hoped it would give him time to think. But the train was full of revelers from a preseason Huskies game, many of them several sheets to the wind. There was raucous laughter and stumbling around in the aisle and flasks passed hand to hand. The Café Car was just as bad, but he bought a beer and found a seat off to the side. And when the woman bartender refused to serve some of the alumni because they were drunk, the car emptied out and he found the silence he was looking for.

He felt undone by the weekend and realized he hadn't been registering all of the tension he'd been holding until now. He didn't know what to do with Jim's denial that he had been there. Like Pete, he didn't remember Jim as being drunk that night. In his remembering, they hadn't been at the tavern very long before they ran into Fred and the girl. Enough time for a game of pool, a beer or two each. They'd smoked a joint on the way to the tavern and then shared a few hits on the joint outside Murcheson's apartment. Then another beer as they waited out on the sidewalk. Not enough to get any of them drunk and not enough for sure to get Jim into a blackout. How could Jim not remember that night? It didn't make any sense.

He looked out into the late afternoon sun. The Cascade Starlight ran along the Columbia River and then headed inland through the lower Washington central valley. The fields were green and yellow, the mountains blue in the distance. Even though most of the land was farmed, it was still wilder than in Virginia, where everything seemed owned and managed. He missed the wildness, the pioneer feel of the Northwest. His roots.

His beer was gone and Derek got up for another. He spent a few minutes flirting with the bartender, asking her about the work, where she lived, what she did for fun. He liked to keep his hand in. You never knew where it might lead. He'd never had sex on a train. She was older, not pretty, but friendly. But he could tell nothing was going to happen and he went back to his seat.

Murcheson's advice to give Kirchner the sample had made sense at the time. But it contradicted what Bruce Houghton had said, which also made sense. What worried Derek most about giving the sample was the finality of it. Words he could take back. The sample would be forever. The truth was he didn't want a kid. He'd never wanted a kid. The wives of his friends had changed after their babies were born. The kid had become the priority, not the husband. There was less sex, less fun. His friends loved their kids but missed their wives. He wasn't willing to do that. He wanted to be the priority.

He'd made it abundantly clear to every woman he had been with that children weren't an option. And in his early 30s, he'd had a vasectomy. Although he had a steady girlfriend at the time, he was having sex with a lot of women on the side and he didn't trust them to be on the pill or have an IUD. He kept his extracurricular activities separate from his relationship with his second wife until Julie, until he married her, and he didn't want a pregnancy ruining the arrangement that he had worked so hard to construct.

Of course, having a 27-year-old son in his life would not be the same as having a baby. But he still didn't want it. Kirchner wasn't that much younger than Karina. What if she connected with him, preferred that younger, stronger body? History, literature, hell, sociology were all full of such stories, of wives having sex with their stepsons. As long as he didn't give the DNA sample, he wouldn't have to know, wouldn't have to figure out what to do about all that.

They'd been following the edge of Puget Sound for a while now and the bartender gave a last call. There was still more than an hour of the trip and a third beer sounded good, but he didn't get up. He was hoping that Jim would want to go out when he got there. There were some great whiskey bars in Seattle. And maybe he could pry out of him why he wasn't remembering the night with Rhonda.

For the first time, he thought about her. Rhonda. He wondered what that night had been like for her. What kind of sex she had with each of them and if she'd had any orgasms. He wondered if he could get women to talk about those kinds of experiences with successive partners. It would make one hell of a paper for the annual sociology conference.

34

Tom Murcheson didn't go home after his meeting with Walsh and Chandling although it was a Sunday afternoon and he usually spent them in bed with Marie Elena, drinking margaritas and watching old movies in Spanish. Salem had more and more Latinos doing the agricultural grunt work of the big farms, and he had hired her to tutor him and improve the Spanish he had studied in college so he could get some of their legal business. The migrants of course had no money but the farm managers and the shop and restaurant owners did. And they all needed somebody to go up against the insurance companies and the rest of the system for them. Marie Elena was a good teacher and they'd become good friends.

Instead he went to his office. It was in an old Victorian house not far from downtown. He had the whole first floor for his offices. There was an extra room where he could hold meetings, and the paralegal who came three days a week had her desk in there. He went into the small galley kitchen and started a pot of coffee.

He didn't know what to think about the whole Kirchner affair. Fred had borrowed his apartment for sex with his girlfriends a lot because he lived with his folks for the first two years of school and couldn't always borrow a car. But inviting the other guys to come along, that was a first. The other guys, he barely knew. They'd all been pledges living in the dorm when he was a senior in the frat house. The most time he'd ever spent with them was that night while they waited to take their turn.

He poured a cup of coffee, took into his office, and sat down at his desk.

He remembered now he'd been pissed at Fred that night because he'd left right after he was through with the girl. He'd expected his cousin to at least come back later and take the girl home, but that didn't happen. And none of the other guys offered to take her home either. They just packed up and left.

He'd waited a few minutes after the last of them were gone, thinking the girl would get dressed and come out. But she didn't and he'd been more pissed. He had an early class the next morning and he needed to sleep, but it was too late to call Fred's house. His parents would be asleep. So he'd gone into the bedroom for his alarm clock and some clean clothes and planned to sleep on the couch. He didn't care that the girl was in the bed but he wasn't sleeping in those sheets.

He opened the door. The lamp on the nightstand was on, but someone had thrown a t-shirt over it to dim the light. He moved to the dresser and pulled one of the drawers open.

"Are you next?" He remembered that voice in the darkened room. Small, like a child.

"No," he'd told her. "We're all done." He grabbed his clothes and stood a moment with his back to her. A wave of uneasiness had washed over him then and it washed over him now in memory.

"Do you need a ride home?" he'd asked finally.

"What time is it?"

He looked at his watch. "Twenty to 3."

"I can't go home now. I…"

"It's okay. Just sleep there. I'll sleep on the couch." He grabbed the clock, turned off the lamp, and headed to the door.

"Where's the bathroom?" she'd said.

"Just down the hall," he'd said and closed the door behind him.

He didn't remember hearing her use the bathroom. He'd gone right to sleep. When he'd come back at 10:30 from his class, she was gone. That was the last time he'd let Fred use his apartment.

They'd been so stupid. Of course, she could have gotten pregnant, but it never crossed his mind. He didn't know her at all. Fred brought her in, introduced her, took her into the bedroom. It wasn't until the other guys showed up that he'd figured out what was going on. Then, well, it was a done deal. When Fred came out—and he was in there a pretty long time—it was obviously his turn. And he took it. He didn't remember thinking about it, debating whether he should do it. He just got up and went in and took his turn.

In his memory, it had been dark in the room—someone must have turned on the light later—and he never got much of a look at her. He hadn't said anything to her, just took off his clothes, and got in the bed. He didn't remember the sex. Nothing about it. Then he'd gotten up, put on his clothes, and gone out to the others.

Means and opportunity for sure. Motive? None. Just means and opportunity. Not much of a defense. There was no defense. He hadn't asked her and she hadn't consented. No defense. If she had reported it, if she had pressed charges, they'd all have lied. He was sure of it. But she hadn't reported it. Instead, she'd taken all the consequences on herself.

For the first time in all this, he thought about his daughters. Imagined one of them in that bed. Not that it would have been him, but some other callous guy at 24, not remembering, not caring.

The office suddenly became unbearably hot and he turned on the air conditioner in the window. It didn't help. He was burning with shame.

35

When the phone rang Monday morning, Derek was in Leeder's kitchen, debating on a beer for his hangover. It was just after 10 and he hadn't been up long. Leeder had picked him up at the train station and they'd gone out to a half-dozen bars. It didn't take tasting too many flights of whiskey for them to forget all about the weekend and Kirchner and the squabbles with Pete and Nancy. They'd talked mostly about music. Jim had bragged about the two up-and-coming bands he was investing in. He played a demo of one of them as they drove between bars. Derek came up with an idea to write an article on the social implications of late adolescents working out their gang nature through rock quintets. Getting a piece in *Rolling Stone* would be a huge feather in his cap and might even impress the promotion committee at the college.

He didn't answer the phone—Leeder's business—and he opted for a very tall glass of ice and orange juice and took it out to the backyard, which wasn't much. Leeder had no green thumb and no interest in developing one so it was grass and a few rhododendrons and azaleas. The lawn was green and wet and he remembered hearing the sprinkler system come on in the early morning. It was a gorgeous morning of blue sky and cool, and he marveled again at the lack of humidity and the lightness of the air, so different from the Virginia summer. He heard the phone again but there was no sign of Leeder.

The sugar in the orange juice began to take effect. So did the three ibuprofen he'd taken. Some breakfast and he'd feel pretty human. There wasn't anything much in Jim's fridge though and he searched his memory for a café that he could walk to in the neighborhood. Leeder lived in Seattle proper but in a dense neighborhood of small houses. He hadn't noticed anything the night before but they'd come back very late.

He went back into the kitchen for a refill on the juice and the phone rang a third time. It clicked to the answering machine and he could hear Karina's voice. By the time he got to the phone, she was gone so he called her back, but the phone just rang and their own answering machine came on with his voice. He debated listening to Leeder's machine. He didn't want to invade his friend's privacy but it had clearly been Karina's voice and he could skip over messages that weren't for him.

As it turned out, all three messages on the machine were from Karina. The first two were brief. "Derek, call me back." Her voice was strained and he immediately began to worry. Karina was the unflappable type. Everything rolled off her. Not this apparently. The third message had more information. "Your dean called. Said she needed to talk to you and that it was urgent. I told her you were away for a few days and she said she suggested you come back right away. Derek, she wasn't pleasant on the phone. Call me and tell me what's going on."

Bernadette Lachland was tough, and she and Derek had already had a couple of unpleasant exchanges. His third marriage had been to one of his students—just after she graduated—with a 20-year age difference. When she'd left him five years later, there'd been rumors and gossip that he would marry another student. Several girls in his freshman writing class claimed he was sleeping with them, and he'd had a hell of a time convincing Dean Lachland that it was just gossip and that he was happily involved with a flight attendant based in DC. But things really hadn't quieted down until he'd married Karina, an alumna from the college with a substantial inheritance and ten years from her own graduation. Still the rumors circulated.

But what could he do? He was a popular professor with a fan club. He wondered who'd been talking about him now.

He called the switchboard at the college and asked for the dean. Her secretary put her straight through when he said his name.

"Dr. Walsh, I need to see you right away. I understand you're on vacation but this is urgent."

"Bernadette, I'm in Seattle and not planning to return until Thursday. What's this about?"

"It's not something I can discuss on the phone. When can you be here?"

"Well, if I can get a flight today, I can be there tomorrow."

"That will have to do. Please call my office when you know your schedule and I'll clear my calendar." With nothing further, she hung up.

He called the airlines. He could get a flight at 3 to Atlanta and a flight home through Charlotte first thing in the morning. He could be on campus by noon. He called the dean's office back and the secretary scheduled him for 1 pm the next day. Then he called home and left Karina a message. Told her not to worry but he was coming back early and would be there when she got home Tuesday night.

Then he left Leeder a note and set off to find a café or a grocery store. His head was pounding and he needed breakfast.

36

Jason took off work early so he could miss the rush hour traffic heading south on I-5. His boss wasn't any too pleased but he placated her with the promise of coming in early on Tuesday to make up the time. He'd had a message Sunday night from Nancy Chandling that Murcheson had agreed to give him a sample. He wanted to confront the guy before the man had a chance to change his mind.

Walsh had apparently changed his mind several times. Nancy said that he too had agreed but that he had gone back to Seattle without leaving a sample. Jason was disappointed but his Plan B was already in motion. Of the ones he'd met, Walsh was the biggest jerk. He hadn't liked Jim Leeder much either, but Leeder had seemed sincere in his denial of being there. Maybe he didn't remember. There was a lot he himself didn't remember from his past. And he had to admit that he had no way to verify if the list of six was accurate. Maybe Leeder hadn't been there after all. If the other guys' DNA didn't pan out, he could pursue that later.

Brake lights just past the 217 exit made him turn his attention to the road. It wasn't until he got past Wilsonville that the traffic thinned and he could think again.

He was afraid that Walsh was his father. He wanted it to be Pete Chandling, mostly because he liked Nancy. But Pete wasn't it. That ship had sailed. And if it was Walsh, there was never going to be any apology or amends or any real relationship. He wasn't someone Jason could trust. He wasn't a standup guy. Jason had learned about that very early on—who you could trust and who you couldn't. In foster care it was a matter of survival. The system didn't look out for you. They put you in a home and left you to it. And whatever happened to you there was your fault. Never the adult's fault. Never. And Walsh? He was definitely a not-my-fault kind of guy.

He thought about his conversation the afternoon before with Nancy. It was more than he'd ever told anyone else and most of it was true. He'd thought about telling her more about his meeting with his mother's husband but he might have broken down if he'd talked about the disappointment, and the last thing he wanted was for her to feel sorry for him. But he liked the way she had listened.

He looked out at the flat fields rolling by, the hills further away. Wondered what it would be like to live in a farm house and grow stuff. Have a dog. Have a wife. He couldn't see it happening.

The Salem exit came up and he drove the long miles into town. It took him a while to find the house with Murcheson's office, and when he finally found it and went inside, there was only a middle-aged woman there.

"He's in court this afternoon," she said. And then she asked his name.

When he gave it, she nodded and handed him a manila envelope. "He said to tell you he'd be back by 6 today if you wanted to see him."

He thanked her and went out. He could feel the DNA sample kit in the envelope and when he opened it, that's what it was. There was a momentary surge of anger, that he was being dismissed, but he talked himself out of it. He hadn't had an appointment with Murcheson, just an agreement to give him a sample. And the guy had offered to see him later on. The question now was if he should wait to see him.

37

When Murcheson drove up at 5 after 6, there was an unfamiliar pickup in the small parking lot. He cursed. He had hoped that Kirchner would take the sample and go. He knew himself well enough to know that shame made him insecure and insecurity made him angry. He didn't want to lose his temper with this kid, but he already felt trapped and they hadn't said two words to each other.

He got out of the car, went around to the passenger seat, and gathered up his briefcase and a thick file holder. Behind him he heard the door of the pickup open and the crunch of gravel. For a tiny moment, he felt uneasy, maybe just a little afraid. Then he took in a deep breath and straightened up.

Kirchner stood a respectful distance away. His hands were empty and Murcheson exhaled in relief. You just never knew. He nodded at the kid and walked over to the door, freeing one hand so he could unlock it. He moved through the door but held it open for Kirchner. Then he headed to his office.

"Excuse me," Kirchner said.

Murcheson turned around.

"Is there a bathroom I can use?"

Again Murcheson felt uneasy but he let it go. "Sure, second door on the left." He went on ahead to his office, put everything down on a side table, and moved behind his desk. He needed the power position. He unlocked the right bottom drawer, turned on the tape recorder, left the drawer open a little. Then he settled into as meditative a place as he could get to. Finally he heard the door open down the hall, the sound of the flush. And then Kirchner was in the doorway.

Murcheson pointed to one of the chairs in front of his desk but the kid shook his head and remained where he was. So Murcheson got up and went over to a cabinet on the far wall. He opened the door and pulled out a bottle of bourbon and gestured with it to Kirchener, who again shook his head. The lawyer poured himself a drink and took the glass and the bottle over to his desk and sat down again.

There was silence for a long moment, Murcheson looking for similarities. Maybe the kid was too. The nose and chin weren't similar, but there was something about the eyes that reminded him of his mother or maybe her sister, his Aunt Helen. Murcheson could feel the kid examining him too. Finally, the lawyer spoke. "What I can do for you, Mr. Kirchner?"

"Did you have sex with my mother?"

Murcheson sighed. "I was there that night. I had sex with the girl who was in the bedroom. If she is your mother, then the answer is yes." He drank down the bourbon.

"Did you ask her permission?"

Murcheson picked up the bottle and poured another three fingers in the glass. He looked at Kirchner and shook his head. "No."

"Did you talk to her, get to know her at all?"

"No."

"Did you get her drunk?"

Murcheson thought for a moment. "No, there was beer in my refrigerator but I didn't give her one or even offer it."

"Was she drunk?"

"I don't know. She didn't seem drunk. But I don't know."

"Was she conscious? When you…when you had sex with her?"

"Yes, of course. She was not only conscious, she was responsive."

"What does that mean, 'responsive'?"

Murcheson could feel the anger rising as the shame kicked back in. "It means she participated. We had sex with each other, not just me on her." He paused. "I know you don't want to hear that. That isn't the story you've been told or been telling yourself."

"You don't know what I want. You don't know anything about me."

Murcheson paused, then said, "You're right. I don't know what you want. But I can guess you don't want to hear that she participated, at least with me. I suspect it doesn't square up with what you've been believing." He saw Kirchner's jaw clench, saw the fist close. "Look, it wasn't a good thing—what we did. It wasn't right. I'm not saying it was. But it wasn't rape either. We didn't kidnap her or coerce her in any way. She willingly came to the apartment, willingly went into the bedroom, willingly stayed there. When I was with her, she didn't say no, she didn't fight me. Like I just said, she participated." He felt like he'd been talking a mile a minute and he sat back in his chair.

Kirchner hadn't moved and his fist was still tight. "Was she in her right mind?"

Murcheson sighed again. "I can't answer that, Mr. Kirchener. I didn't know her. Do you have reason to believe she wasn't in her right mind? No, don't answer that. It doesn't matter. She consented to be there and she was of legal age. That's what matters."

"What woman in her right mind would do something like that?" Kirchner's voice was suddenly much younger, almost querulous.

Murcheson shook his head. "I can't answer that either. Maybe out of curiosity. I don't know."

"Is that what drove you? Curiosity?"

"No. Testosterone. I had a lot of it."

Kirchner stepped forward into the room. "Do you think you are my father?"

Murcheson looked at the kid's hands. They had relaxed. "I don't know," he said. "I obviously could be."

"Do you have kids?"

"I do."

"How old?"

"19 and 23."

"Sons?"

He shook his head. He looked at Kirchner, who looked back at him. "So you have daughters the age of my mom when you had sex with her."

"The irony of that has not been lost on me, Mr. Kirchner."

The younger man nodded, turned to go. Then he turned back and hesitated. Then he said, "One more thing. If you are my father, will you see me again?"

Murcheson didn't hesitate. "Yes."

The kid turned again then and left. Murcheson waited until he heard tires bite the gravel and then the shift in gears as the pickup hit the street before he moved. He called Marie Elena, begged off with a headache, and took himself home.

38

Derek Walsh spent a restless night near the Atlanta airport. It was after 1 in the morning when he got to the hotel and even though he'd had several drinks on the plane, he was pretty wired. He took a shower hoping it would relax him, watched ESPN for an hour. Nothing seemed to help but he turned the light off just before 3 and willed himself to sleep. He was mostly mad. Mad to have cut his trip short at considerable expense: changing the ticket, this hotel room, the cab to the airport when Leeder couldn't take him. He saw now that he should just have stayed at the airport. He had to be back there by 7 and he certainly wasn't sleeping. Karina, of course, wouldn't begrudge him the money or a few hours rest but still it was annoying.

On the long flight, he'd figured out what the dean was going to ask about. Mary Alice Tatum. The flirting between them spring term had gotten out of hand. She'd come by his office on the weekends while he was grading papers and wanted to "chat." She hadn't really forced him into the two make-out sessions they'd had, but when he played the wife card, the monogamy card, she'd just laughed. Between his divorce from his third wife and his marriage to Karina, he'd spent the years of his middle 40s blissfully single. Different women most weekends, some of them recent graduates who'd stayed in town for one reason or another. He'd thought about marrying two of them. And while he'd never had sex with a student while she was a student, his reputation for affairs with students had become legendary anyway, something he was secretly proud of. The fact that he never cheated when he was married didn't seem to make it into the legend, hence Mary Alice's assumption that their flirtation would go somewhere and her rancor that it hadn't. He suspected she might have talked to the dean. Women lied when it served them.

He had a bloody Mary once he got back to the airport, then another. He just couldn't seem to relax. He made sure there was a lot of spice in the drinks so it would cover the vodka on his breath although he didn't meet with the dean until after lunch.

He was disappointed Karina wasn't at the airport to pick him up even though he knew she was teaching. Coming home to no welcome always made him sad. He got another cab—another unnecessary expense—and was home just before 11. He took a long shower, shaved, lay down on the bed for a bit in hopes of recouping some energy, but the long night and the return to the heat and humidity wouldn't let him go. He heard the phone ring, the machine kick on, Karina's voice, but he stayed where he was and watched the clock until it was 12:30. Then he brushed his teeth, got dressed, and walked over to campus.

39

Jason watched Pete Chandling pull out of the driveway at 7:15. Then he waited another five minutes before he headed up the walk. He had to ring twice before Nancy opened the door. She'd cinched a terrycloth robe around her waist and a towel turbaned her hair. She didn't seem surprised to see him.

"Hey, Jason." Her smile seemed genuine.

"Hi. I saw Mr. Murcheson last night and he gave me this." He handed her the swab kit.

"Great. I'll take it to the hospital this morning."

"Do you have results on the other two samples you said you had?"

"Not yet. But when I take this in today, I'll ask about them." She looked at him and smiled again. "How are you doing?"

"I'm tired of this. I want to know and move on."

"I can see that," she said. "I'll call you tonight or tomorrow when I get results."

He turned away and she called after him, "How about coming for dinner some night?" but he pretended not to hear and went on to his truck.

When he called his answering machine from work at noon, there was a message from her. "Jason, I've got bad news. My friend Jane at the hospital lab lost the samples I gave her on Sunday. It's complicated. She couldn't label them and run them through our system because I'm not authorized to request DNA work. She was just going to do me a favor. Anyway, to make a long story short, the samples were on beer bottles and they got recycled. I'm so sorry.

Tell you what. I'll get Pete to call Derek and Jim and remind them to send the samples. It may take a few days and I know that will be frustrating but it's all I can do. Again, I'm really sorry."

One step forward, two steps back. Anger rushed through him. Complications, missteps. He should have gotten the samples from them himself. And he should have run the tests himself. Letting Nancy Chandling do it had been a mistake. It took all the energy he had to go back to work.

40

The dean didn't greet Derek when he entered her office, just gestured to a chair on the other side of the desk. The academic hot seat. This wasn't good.

She handed him a piece of paper. He took a quick glance. It wasn't what he'd expected—a letter from Mary Alice or, worse yet, a letter from her parents. It was neither. It was a press release.

PRESS RELEASE

August 14, 1999
Portland, Ore.
Virginia College Professor Implicated in Rape

Derek Wilson Walsh, professor of sociology at Thorn Haven College for Women, has been implicated as a participant in the gang rape of a young college student in Oregon. Five additional men, all members of the same fraternity, are also being questioned. The girl, aged 18, whose name has not been released, was lured to the apartment of one of the fraternity brothers, where she was allegedly assaulted by each of the men in turn.

"We are devastated by this event," said a close family member, who wished to remain anonymous pending legal outcomes. "We are asking all of these men to come forward and take responsibility." An investigator, Jason Kirchner, reported that Walsh had been uncooperative and had fled the jurisdiction.

Five of the men were students at Western Willamette University in Salem, Ore; the sixth was a recent graduate and a student at Western Willamette Law School. The girl was a freshman at a neighboring college with family in the Roseburg, Ore., area.

Anyone with information on this case is encouraged to contact Mr. Kirchner at 503-555-3344.

Derek read through the press release twice. He knew everything that was on the page, yet he couldn't make sense of a word of it. In the same way, he knew something terrible was happening but he couldn't feel anything. He looked up when the dean cleared her throat.

"Dr. Walsh, I was hoping when I got this yesterday that it was a prank. It would have been a terrible prank as it came as a fax and faxes are handled by student workers as well as my staff but we can always quash a prank." She looked him in the eye. "But I took the liberty of phoning Mr. Kirchner, who told me he met with you in Portland last week and he described you in a way that convinced me he was telling the truth."

Derek made a noise of objection and the dean raised her hand to silence him. "He also gave me the names of two of the other men." She consulted her notes. "Mr. Chandling and Mr. Murcheson. I have not yet reached Mr. Chandling, but Mr. Murcheson told me he has admitted participating and that you were there as well. He also told me he has cooperated fully with Mr. Kirchner and he advised you to do the same." She sat back in her chair.

Derek waited a moment to see if she was through. Then he did his best to gather himself together. His mind was splintered, bits of words and ideas swirling around.

41

The intercom buzzed. "Peter Chandling's on the phone for you," his secretary said.

"I gave the kid the DNA yesterday," Murcheson said by way of greeting.

"That's great," Pete said. "Thanks."

"Why are *you* thanking me? It makes me think you're orchestrating this."

"No, not at all," said Chandling. "It's just that Nancy—my wife—has taken a serious interest in this guy and his story and she wants to see it all turn out well."

Murcheson said nothing in response and Pete went on. "Did you meet him?"

"Yeah, he came by last night. Asked me questions, probably the same ones he asked you. But he didn't tell me anything much about himself."

"He hasn't told me either. Leave it to a woman to get the truth out of him."

"How do you know it's the truth?"

"Why wouldn't it be?" Chandling sounded confused, maybe disappointed.

"People don't always tell the truth, especially when they want something." He knew he sounded like the skeptic he was. And why was he warning Chandling anyway? He didn't owe the guy anything. He barely knew him.

There was a pause. Then Chandling spoke again. "Do you think he's your son?"

"I don't know. My daughters both inherited my nose and my chin. If they both did, it seems likely a son would too. But his eyes, well, maybe they're a bit like my mother's. As I said, I don't know."

"What questions did he ask?"

"He wanted to know if we raped her. I said no, told him she was awake, didn't say no, didn't fight me. Actually she seemed into it."

"It?"

"Having sex with me. He didn't want to hear that, I don't think."

"Do you blame him? This is his mother we're talking about."

"No, I don't blame him." He didn't know if he should tell Chandling how sorry he was about the whole thing. How he didn't like the part of himself that had participated. He decided to keep that to himself.

"Tom, did he ask you about Fred, about how to find him?"

"No, he didn't mention Fred at all."

"Do you know how to find him?"

"Maybe. But I'm not sure involving him is such a good idea. If he's the father…well, I wouldn't wish that on Kirchner as we talked about on Sunday."

"You don't think he'd give his DNA?"

"Oh, he would. In a heartbeat. Something more to brag about. He's a guy who keeps score, if you know what I mean."

"Yeah, I do."

There was another pause. Then Murcheson said, "Do you want me to see if I can find Fred for you?"

"Well, yes, but not for me, for us."

"No, for you. I don't want to have anything to do with him. If you meet him again, you'll know why."

"Okay, thanks for the warning. Let me know when you find out something. And you don't by chance know the whereabouts of Lonnie Tillstrom?"

"Who's that again?"

"The sixth guy."

"No, I don't remember him at all. That one's your puzzle."

42

"I'm waiting, Derek."

He looked up from the press release. The dean's scowl was deeper than usual. Their relationship had been sour for most of her tenure. As she was twice-divorced herself, he'd thought that would be a common bond, but her friendliness at the start hadn't lasted after he'd made it clear he wasn't interested in dating her. That too might have smoothed over, but his reputation as overly friendly with students and his liberal West Coast politics had also alienated her. Their relationship survived through professional courtesy and Southern good manners.

"Don't you find this a curious document?" he said finally.

"What do you mean?"

"What organization sent it? Usually a press release is on letterhead, isn't it? So who is Kirchner investigating for? He doesn't seem to have a legal affiliation. And why aren't the other men named? Why is the press release only about me? Doesn't that strike you as suspicious?" Derek hoped his tone held as much curiosity as righteous indignation.

"I hadn't looked at it that way."

"Of course not. Because it's about me."

She frowned and drummed her fingers on the desk top. Then she held her hand out for the paper and he handed it to her and waited while she looked it over.

"I see your point," she said slowly.

"Has this been in the papers?" he asked. "Or on TV?"

"Not that I've seen," she said.

"Me either. Reporters aren't calling me. Have they called you?"

She shook her head.

"Don't you think they would?"

"Yes," she said. Her mouth was still tight but the fierceness of her body language had eased.

"Of course they would," he said. "A scandal this juicy."

They looked at each other for a long moment. Her phone rang and she picked it up. "Not now," she said. "I need 15 minutes," and she put the receiver down.

"Do you know what is going on here? Do you know Jason Kirchner? And…" she looked again at her notes, "Chandling and Murcheson?"

"Yes. I knew Chandling and Murcheson in college. I met Kirchner for the first time last Saturday."

"What did he want?"

"It's a private matter that doesn't concern the school."

"Mr. Kirchner seems determined to make it public. And Mr. Murcheson admitted his participation in this." She held up the paper.

"What exactly did Murcheson admit to?"

"What do you mean? He admitted to participating."

"He admitted to rape?"

The dean looked at him and Derek could see the tables starting to turn.

"No," she said. "Not in so many words." She began to play with the simple gold chain around her neck. He'd seen this "tell" of hers before.

"What did he admit to?"

"He said he had been there that night and you'd been there too."

"And what else?"

"That was it."

"So he didn't describe what happened that night?"

She paused. "No, he didn't."

Again they looked at each other a long moment and as if on cue, the phone rang. The dean picked up the receiver. "Not now," she barked. "Reschedule the next appointment."

Derek felt himself relax as he gained control. "Did Kirchner tell you that the night in question occurred in 1972?"

"What? No. I assumed this was recent…last week."

"Wow, you really do have a low opinion of me."

She said nothing so he repeated the point. "The night in question took place in 1972."

"It doesn't say that here." She gestured to the press release.

"No, it doesn't. Although the verbs are in past tense."

"What?"

"The men *were* students, not *are*. The girl *was* a student, not *is*."

"I see that now." She read through the paper again. "Is any of this true?"

He felt caught. He didn't want to declare any part of this, but he didn't see how he could divert this any further. He asked to see the press release again, read through it again, and then said, "To the best of my knowledge, none of these allegations are true."

They looked at each other and the dean nodded. The phone rang again, and she said, "I have to go. I'll let you know if I need anything further. Thank you for coming in."

It was his turn to nod and he stood up and left.

43

Jim Leeder made two phone calls on Tuesday morning. The first was to Nancy. He knew she started work at 11 and that Pete went in before 8, so there was always a good window of time to talk to her in the midmorning. She answered on the second ring. It did something to him to hear that voice. Its warmth still had the power to touch him.

"Hey, it's me, Nance."

"Hey back." Their old love code. Did she remember that?

"I'm wondering if you would give me Jason Kirchner's number."

She didn't say anything.

"Nance?"

"I'm here. Why do you want it? I thought you weren't there that night."

"I was unkind to him on Sunday when he approached me in your driveway. I was rude and insensitive."

"Yes, I imagine you were."

"Yeah, well, don't rub it in. Can I have the number?"

"Sure, why not? Hang on."

He could hear her rustling through her purse, a noise he'd heard a million times. Another pang of longing went through him and then he let it go. She came back on and gave him the number. She didn't ask any more questions and he didn't volunteer anything. Instead he said, "Please don't tell Pete I called you, okay?"

"Why?"

"I can't explain. Please just don't. Promise me?"

"Okay, I promise. But I'm going to ask you about this again."

"Okay, thanks," he said and hung up. He'd cross that bridge when he came to it.

The second call was to Kirchner. Jim got voice mail, left his name and number. It was noon when he got the return call. There was no greeting.

"You going to give me the sample?"

"What? No. That's not why I called."

"I don't have anything else to talk to you about."

"Wait. Don't hang up." He waited for the click but it didn't come. "Do you have your mother's address?"

"Why in the world do you want that? You don't know her. You said so yourself."

"I do know her. I mean I did know her. And I want to speak with her."

"Give me the sample and I'll give you the address."

Jim hesitated.

"Yeah, right," said Kirchner. "This is bogus."

"No, wait. Okay, I'll do it. But I'm in Seattle."

"And I'm in Portland. How about tonight? I'll meet you in front of your friend's house."

"Chandling's?"

"Yeah, 7 pm." Then Kirchner was gone.

He put down the phone and sat there a moment. He didn't relish another drive to Portland but what the hell. He needed to connect with Rhonda and, if he told himself the truth, he needed to know if Kirchner was his son.

44

Tom Murcheson cancelled a lunch date with the local district attorney, who was his best buddy, and cleared the early afternoon calendar as well. Then he headed up I-5 to Woodburn to visit his mother. When he'd first made real money, extra money, he'd bought his mom a small house in a wooded development up there. She'd settled in, made friends in her gregarious way, and though he could afford something much nicer for her now, she refused to move. Her only complaint was the lack of proximity to her granddaughters.

He parked in front. Her silver blue Riviera took up most of the driveway. The lawn needed mowing and he wondered if he'd have enough time to do that before he left. Then he gathered up the bags with Chinese takeout and went around back to the patio. His mother sat in the glider, iced tea in her hand. The round plastic table wore a bright yellow cloth and was set for two. He emptied the bag on the table, placing chop sticks on each plate. Then he poured himself an iced tea and settled in next to her on the glider.

His mother was still a club woman and she forced him into a requisite period of small talk each time they met. This time it was his golf game and her sciatica, his girls, her bridge friends, and a fundraiser for college scholarships she was involved in. He promised to send a check by the end of the week.

They moved over to the table and began to eat. He knew to wait until they were through before asking. Finally she put down her fork and he put down his chop sticks, and she looked at him and smiled. "Do you want to tell me what you came for?"

"Can't I just want to see my old mom?"

"Of course, but I do suspect there's something else on your mind, dear."

"I need to get in touch with Fred. Do you know where he is?"

She frowned and shook her head. "Why in the world would you want to do that? He's a—propriety stops me from an appropriate label." She looked at her son. "Hasn't he already gotten you into enough trouble?"

Murcheson flashed on the night in the apartment. No way his mother knew about that. "What do you mean?"

"That stolen car ordeal."

"Oh, that." A joy ride in a neighbor's convertible. Fred had hotwired it, picked up a couple of girls, and come around to their house. He'd gone along, not knowing who the car belonged to. His dad and his uncle, Fred's dad, had reamed them each a new one and then paid the neighbor for his trouble. Not long after that, Fred's family moved to Medford and they saw each other only at family gatherings until they'd both ended up at school in Salem.

"You've got a great memory for ancient history, Mom."

"Well, thank God that was the end of our problems with you, but it sure wasn't the end of the problems with Fred." She launched into a litany of Fred's sins—graduating from high school by the skin of his teeth, expelled from Southern Oregon College in Ashland his freshman year for smoking dope in his dorm room, the strings Uncle Larry had had to pull to get him into Western Willamette. Unpaid parking tickets, speeding tickets, a DUI. He'd worked for Tom's dad for a while at his appliance store, but Fred took whatever he felt like out of the till so that didn't last long.

Murcheson only half-listened. He'd heard all this before. When his mother wound down, he said, "Any news about him recently?"

"I don't know," she said, placing her napkin on the table. "I never ask Helen about him. We find it too painful a subject."

"I need to find him, Mom. It's important."

"Well, I don't know where he is."

"Does Aunt Helen?"

She looked at him. "Why is this so important? You're not in trouble, are you?"

"No. No, not at all." He wasn't about to go into all this with his mother. "But a couple of my fraternity brothers are in a bit of a jam, and Fred, believe it or not, can help them out."

She thought a moment. "It would be nice to see him do some good for a change."

"It would, wouldn't it?"

They sat there in silence for a few minutes. Then Murcheson got up and smiled at her. "How about I mow the lawn while you call Aunt Helen and get a phone number and address for me?" He went into the house without waiting for a reply. His dad's huge overalls were in the closet in the spare bedroom, one of the few things his mother had hung on to when the old man died. He changed into them and went through the kitchen into the garage where they kept the mower.

It took just under an hour to mow the small front and back lawns. It was hot and he was sweating profusely. The damn weight he carried didn't help. He stopped a couple of times to refill his iced tea on the patio table. The lunch dishes had been cleared and there was no sign of his mother. He finished up, put the lawn mower away, took a shower, and changed back into his own clothes. The house was cool, the central air a relief from the heat of the yard. He found his mother on the sun porch, watching a soap opera. She glanced up at him and handed him a piece of paper.

"Thanks for doing this," he said, leaning down to kiss her cheek.

"You're welcome. Thanks for the lawn and lunch. And bring the girls next time." She turned back to her show.

45

By the time he got home from the dean's office, Derek was fuming. Only his quick wits and Kirchner's ineptness had kept this from being a complete disaster, and he wasn't at all sure that he was out of the woods with the school. And he was going to have to tell Karina now and he wasn't looking forward to that. It was too hot to go for a run but he had to do something with his anger so he called Pete.

There was no answer, just the machine with Nancy's voice. He got even madder. He hung up and then changed his mind and called back to leave a message. "Your pet project has really done it now. He's threatening my job. We need to put a stop to this." He was about to say more when the machine cut him off. He called back, madder than ever, and left a few more cryptic words about the dean. Then he threw down the phone and went into the kitchen. He knew he needed to calm down, to start thinking, start figuring out a plan, but he couldn't see how to do that.

He got a beer out of the fridge and went up to his office. There was a stack of mail to go through and even more emails, mostly about the upcoming faculty workshop and the start of the new semester. The beer was gone in no time and he went down and got another and poured himself a scotch at the same time. He knew he should eat something. He'd had nothing but a scone at the airport but he didn't have the patience to fix anything. He went back upstairs.

About 4, the phone rang. He let the machine take it even though it was probably Karina. She didn't have to know that he was home.

But curiosity got the better of him and he went down for another drink and to listen to the message. It wasn't Karina. It was Mary Alice Tatum. "Professor Walsh, we know you're back from vacation. Some of us are down at Malone's cooling off after work. Come cool off with us. And tell your wife she's welcome to come too."

He had to admire her bravado. Inviting Karina was a clever touch. He looked at his watch. At least two hours until Karina got home, maybe a bit more. He had plenty of time to go down to Malone's. He started out the door, then went back and erased the message from Mary Alice.

46

Pete Chandling hadn't a clue about how to find Lonnie Tillstrom. His two good ideas hadn't panned out. The alumni office at Western Willamette showed Lonnie's status as inactive. "What does that mean?" he asked the woman on the phone.

"It means our mail to him comes back undeliverable," she told him. "The note on his file says 'undeliverable, no forwarding address.'"

The same was true with the national fraternity. "Mr. Tillstrom has not paid dues since 1976," the man told him. Then he'd wanted to check Pete's own records and get them up to date. "Not today," Pete had said and hung up.

He needed to get on with his work day so he turned the project over to Kevin, his assistant. "Check phone books in Oregon and Washington," he said. "Police records, maybe, or military records. I don't know. Whatever you can think of."

He had sales meetings, an executive meeting, then client meetings. Tuesdays were a miserable schedule and he usually got little work done, just talk and arguments and internal politics. He didn't give Lonnie Tillstrom another thought until he came back to his office at 4:30. Kevin had left a note on his desk: "No death certificate in the state. No white pages listing in the metro area or major Oregon cities. However, there is a Tillstrom Road out in Damascus and a Carl Tillstrom living on SE Ankeny near 20th. No phone listed but here's the address. Maybe a relative?"

He shot off an email of thanks to Kevin. Then he called home, left Nancy a message that he might be late. He also listened to the messages from Derek about Jason and the fax. He could hear how furious Derek was and decided not to call back. He didn't want to get into it with him. Didn't want to have to defend Jason or remind Derek about his refusal to give the DNA sample or how dismissive he'd been with the kid. Instead he called Murcheson and left him a message about the fax. "If you think we should do something about this, Tom, call me back." Then he headed out to find Carl Tillstrom.

The traffic was backed up as always. The commute from home to work and back had become a giant pain. Quitting and devoting himself full time to his photography crossed his mind as it always did while he waited for the line of cars to creep through the control lights and onto the freeway. His work wasn't a career, it was a job. But the longer he'd delayed leaving, the more money he made. Golden handcuffs and a comfortable life. Now it felt too late to try something else.

He looked impatiently at the cars ahead of his. Usually he could use this as a form of meditation, breathe deep, stay in the moment. But tonight he wanted to get moving, to see if Carl Tillstrom could help him find Lonnie, and he cursed the line.

He didn't take 26 all the way to town. Instead he got off at Barnes Road and wound up and down the big Burnside hill. The traffic was still slow and heavy, but it kept moving through the intersections in a way the freeway didn't. Plus it put him onto Burnside and once he got through Old Town and across the river, things opened up.

Carl Tillstrom lived right off 20th in an odd block of mixed use. Old homes, some of them quite ornate, on the south side of the street. Parking lots on the other side for the Burnside businesses with an occasional empty lot with trees, weeds, and trash. Tillstrom's house was in the middle of the block, a wrought-iron fence freshly painted black, some sort of ugly groundcover instead of a lawn, and all the windows shuttered. An old white van was parked in the driveway, the kind kidnappers always used in action films. Pete shook his head at his frame of reference.

He was glad he'd changed into jeans and a sport shirt before he left the office. This wasn't a neighborhood for a suit and tie. He figured out the gate in the fence though it was creaky with disuse and went up the porch to the front door. He rang the bell but didn't hear it ring. He knocked and there was still nothing but he thought he heard a voice murmuring inside, so he went back out the front gate and around the driveway to the back porch. A door stood open to the kitchen and the voice was coming from an old radio he could see on the ledge above the sink. He recognized the sound of NPR.

He climbed the three steps to the open door and called out, "Hello. Anyone home?" He waited a few seconds and stepped just into the kitchen and called out again. This time he heard a man clear his throat so he called out one more time.

"Hold your horses," the man said and Pete heard the squeaking of springs and then muffled footsteps. A man stood in the opposite doorway to the kitchen. He was short and heavy, with gray curly hair and a gray beard, both in need of a trim. He wore gray corduroy slacks and a brown corduroy jacket with leather elbow patches over a black turtleneck although it had to be 85 degrees in the kitchen. He said nothing, just looked at Pete, but his eyes were pale and their expression hard to read behind his thick glasses.

"Hi," Pete said. "I'm looking for Lonnie Tillstrom. Are you Carl?"

The man looked over at the radio and then looked back. He nodded.

"Is Lonnie related to you?"

The man nodded. "What do you want with him?"

"It's a complicated story."

"Aren't they all," the man said.

"May I come in?"

"You seem to already be in."

"I meant can I come in and talk to you about Lonnie?"

The man moved into the kitchen. He picked up a pot holder and opened the oven. Pete could see potatoes baking on the rack. The man forked one, made a noise Pete couldn't interpret, and closed the oven door. Then he turned and walked back into the house. "Come on if you're coming," he said.

47

The address Murcheson got from his mother was for a post box at the Seven Feathers Casino. He remembered passing the casino on a road trip to California some years back but couldn't remember the location. He found the number in information when he got back to his office and called the switchboard.

"We're located 15 miles south of Roseburg, sir," the bright young thing on the other end said, "and 25 miles north of Grants Pass."

"Do you have an employee named Fred Landon?"

"I'm sorry, sir, but I can't give out that information. Would you like to speak to someone in Human Resources?"

He was on hold for three minutes, then four, then five, debating whether to hang up. Finally a woman came on, took his question, and declined to answer. "We don't give out that information, sir."

He called the switchboard operator back. "Can you put me through to the mail room at the RV resort?"

"That location isn't staffed regularly, sir."

"But if I stay there, I can get mail there, right?"

"Yes sir, if you stay more than seven nights, you can receive mail. You can always send mail out regardless of your length of stay."

"But there's no staff?"

"No, sir, someone just picks up the mail and delivers anything that comes in."

"May I speak to that person?"

"I'm sorry, sir. There's no one person that does this. We all sort of take turns. This isn't really a very big place."

He couldn't think of any other way to reach Fred by phone so he thanked her and hung up. The casino was about 150 miles south down I-5, under 3 hours. He looked at his calendar. He had no clients but his time was scheduled for research for a deposition on Friday. He pulled out the case file to see how much there was to do. He could take the file and reading materials with him. He could be there by 8, talk to Fred, stay over and read the materials in his hotel room, then come back early and be in the office by 10.

And if Fred wasn't there? Didn't work there? Well, he'd have done what he could to find him and that would have to be enough. Plus it would be a road trip. He was always up for that.

He could hear his secretary's heels on the hardwood floor of the outer office. He'd get her to make a reservation at the casino hotel and sort out the reading for the deposition. That would put him on the road by 4:30.

48

Derek didn't get home until close to 9:30. He'd thought about not showing up until the next morning, telling Karina his flight had been delayed but even in his drunkenness, he remembered all the signs that he'd been there earlier in the day. Opened mail, empty beer bottles, his unpacked suitcase in the bedroom. He knew he was going to be in trouble. A drink or two with students was one thing but he'd been gone hours without calling.

The ordeal with the dean had fueled a lot of anger, so being worshipped by coeds had seemed the perfect antidote, and in many ways it had worked. The three girls who were waiting at the tavern hung on his every word, laughed and flirted with him. All this centered him back in his present world, his real world, not all that crap about something he'd done decades ago.

He'd left Mary Alice's summer apartment most of an hour before. He'd showered there to wash off the perfume and sex. He hadn't had full intercourse with her—so he could believe he'd kept his monogamy vows. But they'd done just about everything else. He blamed the other two girls for leaving the tavern at 6. One had a date, one had to work. If they'd stayed, he wouldn't have ordered another pitcher, he wouldn't have found himself walking Mary Alice home and being invited in and all of what followed.

Mary Alice had offered to drive him home after but he'd said no. It was two miles to campus and another half-mile home. He needed to walk, to clear his head, to dry his hair. He needed to come up with something believable to tell Karina, both about the evening and about the night in the apartment. But the walk only did so much, and then he was in front of his house with way too little to say for himself.

He decided not to go straight in and instead went around the side of the house to the back patio. The downstairs was dark except for the light over the stove and he could hear the murmur of the TV from the back bedroom above him. He settled into a chaise longue and fell asleep lulled by the night noises of the gulch.

49

Pete Chandling followed Carl Tillstrom down a dark hallway into an equally dark front room. Only one lamp was lit, a floor lamp with a velvet shade and heavy beaded fringe. There was just enough light to see that the room was crowded with furniture—heavy antiques as far as he could tell. A velvet settee, several large dining tables, an armoire that took up at least a quarter of the room. Tillstrom sat down in a wingback chair next to the lamp. Pete didn't know whether to sit or stand so he perched on the edge of the settee.

"Why are you looking for Lonnie?" Tillstrom didn't look at Pete as he asked the question. Instead he took an old-fashioned silver cigarette case out of his pocket, hesitated while choosing a cigarette, and lit it with a match. He didn't offer Pete one or ask him if he minded the smoke. Pete felt he had stepped back in time.

"Lonnie and I knew each other in college," Pete said. "I need to ask him some questions."

Tillstrom frowned. "After—what—25 years?"

"I know it must seem odd but it's important. If you could just tell me how to reach him, that would be great. A phone number or an address. We were in the same fraternity."

"Ah, the fraternity!" Tillstrom looked over at Pete for the first time. "What a despicable group you were!" Bitterness soured his mouth. "You looking to make amends?"

Confusion washed over Pete. "Me? No, I don't owe him amends. I didn't harm him that I know of."

"You were part of the fraternity, weren't you? One of those guys?"

"Yes, I guess so. Mr. Tillstrom, I don't really know what you're talking about."

"You guys made Lonnie's life a living hell."

"But Lonnie didn't do anything that night. And nothing ever came of it. Not until now."

The confusion had migrated to Tillstrom's face. They were silent a moment and then Pete said, "I get the impression we're talking about two different things."

Tillstrom said nothing, just frowned and then opened the cigarette case again and went through the same ritual while the first cigarette lay burning in the ash tray on a side table.

Pete decided to start again. "Mr. Tillstrom, Lonnie and I were friends back in college. Not close exactly but really friendly. I liked him. He liked me. We haven't been in touch over the years but, you know, people go their separate ways."

Tillstrom looked at him again. "What's your name?"

"Peter Chandling." He took out a business card and handed it to the other man although he wasn't quite sure why. "Look, perhaps you could just call Lonnie and ask him if he'd be willing to speak with me or meet with me."

"That's not possible." He paused. "My brother isn't well."

"Oh, I'm sorry to hear that. Is he here in town? Perhaps I could visit him."

"I don't think so."

They sat in silence then for what seemed to Pete a long time. Then they both spoke at once.

"You first," Pete said.

"No, you go."

"When you talked about amends," Pete said, "what did you mean?"

"For the malicious hazing that Lonnie got from the fraternity. That's the word, right? Hazing?"

"Well, yeah. All pledges to the fraternity got hazed. It's part of the deal. We all knew it going in."

"I'm not talking about that barbaric practice. I'm talking about all the malice Lonnie was subjected to during the two years he was there."

"He was only there two years?"

"Yes. I thought you said you were friends."

"We *were* friends. But I didn't remember that Lonnie left. Why'd he leave?"

"To save himself from your cruelty."

"I'm sorry but that makes no sense to me." Pete thought a moment. "Was this in the spring of '72?"

Tillstrom thought a moment. "Yes, that's about right. June or so."

"What kind of malice? And who was doing it?"

"He never gave me any specifics. Just said he felt tormented and shunned by guys he thought were his friends." Tillstrom went through the cigarette ritual again. Now there were three cigarettes burning and Pete found the smoke harder and harder to handle. He suppressed the urge to cough.

"I'm sorry about that," Pete said. "I didn't know."

"Maybe you didn't want to know."

"Maybe. I don't remember." Pete looked at his hands, then back at Tillstrom. "Look, I need to speak to Lonnie. I'd like to apologize for not knowing what was going on and I need to ask him some questions."

"About what?"

"About something we were involved in together. In the spring of '72. Did he ever talk about a night from then?"

"No." Tillstrom smoked his cigarette, blew smoke rings up towards the ceiling. His legs were crossed and he swung his ankle up and down. Pete couldn't tell if it was habit or nervousness.

They sat in silence again and Pete began to be aware of faint noises in the house. Not just the murmur of NPR from the kitchen but footsteps upstairs. Then he heard a toilet flush and the footsteps again. "Lonnie," he said.

Tillstrom didn't look at him, but he gave a large sigh. Then he repeated, "He's not well."

"Cancer?"

Another pause. "No, AIDS."

And Pete felt everything fall into place, then shame for not having figured it out all those years before. Lonnie's lack of a girlfriend, his discomfort when they'd boasted of their conquests, his refusal to participate that night. It all clicked. He did have amends to make.

"Is he dying?"

"Not yet. Just suffering. It's hard to watch."

"I'm sorry," Pete said and he hoped Tillstrom could hear how much he meant it. "May I see him? I won't stay long."

"That's not up to me."

"Will you ask him if he'll see me?"

Tillstrom looked over at him, frowned, then heaved himself up out of the chair like a very old man, and went slowly up the stairs.

50

The late afternoon was warm and Murcheson opened up the back windows to let the air in and so he could listen to the sound of the tires on the pavement. He loved that sound. He'd stopped for a mocha to carry him through until dinner and he settled in for the drive.

He loved driving. In cities, along the coast, through the mountains, even on freeways. He loved being behind the wheel. It was the one place in his life where getting to the conclusion was not the goal. It didn't matter whether he had music or a book on tape or just his thoughts. He never got bored. He never got tired of the sensation of moving along, watching the world go by. It was his one regret as a lawyer—that he didn't drive for a living.

Once he got on I-5, he began to think about Fred. It had been years since he'd seen him. His father's memorial service six years before? No, Fred hadn't been there, much to his Aunt Helen's dismay. That's what Murcheson remembered. Her anger with her son. The last time must have been eight or nine years before. In his mind's eye, Murcheson could see Fred in the backyard of the big house in Illahee Hills where his daughters grew up. A birthday party? No, the family reunion barbecue that their mothers had organized and he and Ellen had hosted.

Fred had shown up late, already two sheets to the wind. With him was a very young woman, 18 at best. He'd picked her up hitchhiking on his way from Vegas. She was very pretty and very stoned. Fortunately, she was well behaved. Certainly, better behaved than Fred, who bumbled around and said inappropriate things although Tom knew it was all an act. Nobody held his liquor like Fred. Nobody did things with more forethought and deliberation than Fred. In fact, Fred was the smartest person Tom had ever met and he'd met some very smart people.

When they were growing up, Fred had been the ring leader, the instigator of all their pranks. The shoplifting, the petty thefts, toilet paper and window-soap vandalism. If white boys in the suburbs had had gangs in the 60s, Fred would have been *capo*. Instead, he came up with schemes and invited other guys to join him. Like that night in the apartment in Salem. Fred had a kind of magnetism that was hard to explain. It wasn't charisma exactly. It was more like permission. Fred gave you permission to do whatever you were thinking. Because that's what he did—whatever he was thinking.

Fred had dropped out of school late in his junior year. Preoccupied with law school, Murcheson hadn't paid much attention, but he heard through the grapevine that Fred and a buddy had broken into the dean's office and changed the grades of a few friends and acquaintances who'd paid them to do it. Fred's father had intervened and gotten Fred a chance to withdraw rather than be expelled. Fred had refused to go to yet another college and just disappeared, resurfacing every few years at some family function, like he had at the reunion in Illahee Hills.

As he flew past the Eugene exits, Tom thought about his own motives for this trip. It wasn't really about reconnecting with Fred although he was curious to see who and what Fred had become. It certainly wasn't about warning Fred, even with the news that Kirchner had sent a fax implicating Derek. Derek could have saved himself all that grief by leaving a sample. And the Fred he knew wouldn't be intimidated by Kirchner.

No, his own motive was more about restitution. Doing what he could for Jason Kirchner. Doing what he could for that young girl whose life they'd changed without giving it a thought. The vision of one of his daughters in that bed hadn't faded, and it filled him with shame and anger each time it crossed his mind. He'd brought along a swab kit and hoped Fred would be amenable, but there were all kinds of ways to get his DNA. A glass. A cigarette butt.

Tom hoped Fred wasn't the father. He didn't know much about Kirchner, what kind of person he was, but he'd seen a straightforwardness, an honesty in him that Fred had never been capable of. More importantly, the kid had already had his fair share of shame. That was almost always true of kids who grew up in the system. Shame and the aggression that covered it. Having a conscience-less con artist for a father wasn't going to mitigate any of that.

Murcheson had wanted a son. Most men did, didn't they? Someone to teach to be a man. A better man than you were. He'd been delighted with his daughters and never sorry a minute that they were girls, but when his wife had said no to a third child, he'd been sad. Did he have that third child in Kirchner? He didn't think so. His daughters looked like him, more than they did their mother. He'd seen no resemblance in any of Kirchner's features except for the eyes. When he'd been with his mother, he looked for something similar in the shape, the shade of brown, the eyebrows maybe. It was possible. And the height. Kirchner was tall like him, like Fred. But there hadn't been any immediate connection. Not like he felt for his daughters. If for some reason he hadn't raised them himself, he was still sure he would recognize them. That the heart connection, the genetic tie would show itself.

Roseburg came and went and the casino billboards began to appear. The thick August light of evening lit his way down the nearly empty freeway. He turned on a Billy Joel CD and stopped thinking for a while.

51

The long room at the top of the stairs was darkened by black pull-shades, twilight coming in only around the edges. A small lamp was lit on a dresser near the door, but a red scarf of some kind over it softened the light to a rosy glow. In what light there was, Pete could just make out a large dark headboard against a wall and the skeleton apparatus of an IV drip. An air conditioner rumbled from a distant window.

"Come on in, Pete." The words were strong and clear, and to his surprise, Pete recognized Lonnie's voice. The voice came from the bed and as Pete's eyes adjusted, he could make out the thin body under the sheets. He moved into the room and saw that a wingback chair similar to the one downstairs had been drawn up to the bed. He sat down in it.

"Would you turn on the lamp there by you?"

Pete saw another small lamp on the bedside table and leaned over and turned it on. Then he looked over and saw that a big smile lit up Lonnie's face. He couldn't help but smile back.

"I can't tell you what a wonderful surprise this is. I thought all my old pals had forgotten all about me."

"No, Lonnie, I…we haven't forgotten you. Just didn't know you were ill."

"Well, it's not exactly something you send an announcement about." He smiled that same big smile. "You look great, Pete. Life must agree with you."

"I've been good."

"Married?"

"Twice. I've got a wonderful woman now."

"I'm so glad. You were always a good person. You were kind to me."

Pete felt a wash of emotion. He looked away to hide it and then back at Lonnie. After a moment, he gestured at the bed, the room. "I never guessed," he said.

"Why would you? It takes one to know one, and you weren't one. Besides, it's another thing that you don't announce to the world. Certainly not back then." He coughed and then kept coughing. Pete stood up but Lonnie motioned to him to sit. Eventually the spasm subsided but it took a toll and Lonnie fell back against the pillows gasping for air.

Pete gave him a chance to rest, then said. "Your brother told me that some of the Sig Delts harassed you about it."

Lonnie nodded. "Compton and Dweevers. Remember them?"

It was Pete's turn to nod. "Thug 1 and Thug 2, as I recall."

"That's right. I don't think it was about my being gay. I don't think they really had a clue, but I wasn't willing to be crude and crass with them, not willing to bash gays and women along with them, and they made it really unpleasant. That's why I moved out of the house."

Pete felt another twinge of shame. "I didn't remember that you did."

"Yeah, I shared a house on Commercial with a couple of women." He coughed again but the spasm was shorter this time. "Did you ever become a photographer?"

"You remember that?" Pete was touched. "Not professionally but I still dabble. Maybe when I retire." He felt uneasy talking about the future with someone who probably didn't have one. He changed the subject. "What kind of work have you done?"

But Lonnie didn't answer. He coughed instead and this time it went on and on. The next thing Pete knew, the brother was there at the bedside, gently patting and rubbing Lonnie's back. "Mr. Chandling, my brother needs to rest. Did you get your questions answered?"

Pete stood up. "No, no, we've been talking about old times."

"I thought that's what you came to ask about." He settled Lonnie back on the pillows, helped him sip some water.

"I'm sorry…we just got talking."

"It's okay, Carl," Lonnie said. "Give us a few more minutes. If Pete has a question, I want to answer it."

Carl looked at them both. He nodded, then said, "I'll be back in about five minutes to show you out, Mr. Chandling," and they heard him go down the stairs.

Pete didn't sit back down but moved to the side of the bed. Lonnie reached over and took his hand. Again, Pete felt touched both by shame and an odd sort of affection.

"It's about Rhonda, isn't it?" said Lonnie.

"How'd you guess?"

Lonnie shrugged. "It's the kind of thing that lives on. One of those things that binds us."

52

"She's here in Portland?" Jim Leeder held the slip of paper Jason Kirchner handed him. Jim had just swabbed his own mouth for the sample. They were standing on the sidewalk across the street from Pete and Nancy's. The early evening heat poured over them, and sweat ran into Jim's eyes as he squinted at the words and numbers of the address.

"Yeah. So?"

"I thought she'd be in Roseburg or Coos Bay or, I don't know, Medford."

"Nope. Last I knew she was at that address."

"Do you have a phone number for her?"

"No, just for her husband at work. Do you want it?"

"No, but what's his name?"

"Paul Trevino."

"Is that her name too?"

Kirchner shrugged. "I expect so, but I didn't ask." He looked at Jim for a long moment. "Why do you want the address? You were pretty clear with me that you weren't there that night."

Jim looked him in the eye and held up the slip of paper. "Thanks for this." He headed across the street to his car and got in and sat there. Kirchner drove off and still he sat there. He wanted a drink or several. The Chandlings' driveway was empty and he knew where the key was and where they kept the liquor, but he didn't want to take a chance of running into them so he drove on.

Rhonda's address was out in East County, not all that far from the tavern where he'd gotten into so much trouble Saturday night. The irony of that wasn't lost on him. But he couldn't have done it differently. He didn't need or want the others to know. It took him about 30 minutes in the last of the commuter traffic to find the address on NE 120th off Glisan. A small white house, brown grass, no trees. Identical to the other houses on the block. A not-so-new pickup truck in the carport. An even older Corolla on the street. Rhonda lived poor and it made him sad. He sat out there a while and then headed to over 82nd and Sandy where he knew there were some cheap motels and a couple of taverns. He'd go back in the morning and see if he could talk to her alone.

53

Nancy was doing the dishes when Pete walked into the kitchen. "I got too hungry to wait," she said. Then she looked over at him. "Whoa, you look like you've had a terrible day. What's happened?"

"I found Lonnie Tillstrom. He's in bad shape."

She put the knife down. "Drugs?"

He shook his head. "AIDS."

"Oh, honey." She came around the butcher block and put her arms around him. "Late stage?"

"I don't know. He's at his brother's. They don't live all that far from here. Just off Burnside and 20th. He's bedridden, IV hookup, but he was clear and cheerful, and he was so glad to see me. I felt so sad. I still do. The fact that he was gay just went right by me back then."

"It was a long time ago, honey. People were a lot more secretive then."

"I know, I just...He was so glad to see me. And I feel like I should have known. I should have kept in touch with him. It broke my heart."

Nancy pulled away and went to the fridge and took out some iced tea. She poured two glasses and took Pete's hand and they went out to the patio. It was still very warm but the swing was in a big patch of shade. They sat and rocked for a while. Then Pete started to talk. He told her about Carl and his reluctance to let Pete see Lonnie. Their reminiscing about the old days and then Carl's interruption. "I still hadn't asked about that night but when Carl left the room,

Lonnie brought it up himself. I don't know how he knew that's what I'd come about. It was all so strange." Then he told her what Lonnie had told him.

About three months after the night in the apartment, Lonnie had run into Rhonda at a new supermarket near his apartment. He'd just moved out of the frat house and was living in a house not far from campus. He was going to summer school and working three different jobs to make his tuition. Rhonda was working as a cashier at the market. He recognized her right away but although she seemed to recognize him, she wouldn't look him in the eye and he got his bags and moved on.

"I felt awful and I had to do something," Lonnie had said. "It was evening and I saw that the store closed at 10 so I went back just before closing time and waited until she came out."

She didn't want to talk with him but he pleaded with her and she finally agreed to leave her car and go across the street to a pizza place. He told her how sorry he was. How wrong it was for us to do that. How he hadn't gone into the bedroom but he was as guilty as the others anyway. She listened without saying anything. He said it was weird, like she was barely there.

Pete paused, then went on. Then Rhonda said, "I'm pregnant" and started to cry. For a long time, Lonnie just held her hand. He couldn't bring himself to ask her what she was going to do. But in the end she told him on her own. How she couldn't do an abortion. That her parents didn't know. That she would go up to Portland and find a place to have the baby and put it up for adoption. It was the best solution, she kept saying, the only solution. Lonnie offered her what money he had and convinced her to take it. And she made him promise that he would not tell the rest of us what had happened. "It wasn't a little promise she wanted from me," he said. "It was a solemn oath. And I have honored that."

"It was Lonnie's idea to give her the list of names," Pete said to Nancy. "He made it very clear to me that she didn't ask him for it.

He wanted to make restitution in some way. That was his word for it. So he wrote out the names, including his own, and handed it to her. Then he walked her back to her car. He never saw her again."

Nancy sighed and leaned over and kissed Pete on the cheek. "How sad. Sad for her. Sad for Lonnie. Sad for all of you." She looked out at the yard and then back at her husband. "Was Jim's name on the list?"

"Of course it was."

She sighed again and got up and went inside to fix dinner. She decided not to mention Jim's call asking for Jason's number.

54

"Wake up, honey, you're dreaming." Karina was leaning over him. Behind her, above her were stars and a murky moonlight. The air was cool, and the sweat of the dream and the awakening began to chill him. He waited for his heart to stop pounding and his breathing to slow.

"What are you doing out here? Where've you been?"

For a moment Derek didn't know. For a blessed moment, he couldn't remember. And then it all flooded back. The close call with the dean, the tavern with the three girls, Mary Alice's apartment, Mary Alice's warm, perfumed skin. The memory triggered a response in his body and he was glad it was dark, glad that Karina wouldn't see.

"It's a long story, babe. I'll tell you in the morning. What time is it?"

"Just after 12. Come on up to bed. I've missed you."

"Head on up," he said, swinging his feet to the ground so he could sit up. "I'll be right behind you. I need to get something to drink."

"Okay, but don't be long." She moved on ahead and he heard the screen door open and close. He pulled himself to standing and waited a moment for the dizziness to pass. He was still a bit drunk. He moved over to the edge of the gulch and waited for the erection to subside so he could pee. Then he went in and got a glass of cold club soda out of the fridge and stood sipping it in the dark.

He was in big trouble and he knew it. He was going to have to tell Karina about Kirchner. If the guy would threaten him at work, he wouldn't hesitate to contact Karina directly and tell her the whole story. And Kirchner's version of it would be a lot harder for her to understand than his would be. He could tell her so she would understand him and what he'd been going through that night, something the bare facts wouldn't reveal. He wouldn't tell Karina all of it, but enough so that Kirchner's call or letter—if it ever came— would be easy to dismiss.

Then there was the dean. He didn't have any idea whether she would pursue the matter further or if Kirchner would follow up in some way. The guy clearly had a plan and wasn't shy about making it happen. Maybe he could call Pete and get Kirchner's number and find out where to send the DNA sample. And then he suddenly realized it didn't have to be his sample. It probably had to be male. He could find out if that was clear in DNA but surely he could get a friend or student's boyfriend to give him some kind of sample. Didn't the saliva on cigarette butts work? Mary Alice could find him somebody.

Mary Alice. The third problem for sure. It wasn't going to end here. She wasn't going to let it. Could she keep her mouth shut and not tell all of her friends? Would the gossip possibility, the bragging rights be too much for her? He was going to need to talk her and do it in the morning first thing. They would have to come to some agreement, and he knew it was going to involve cheating on Karina. Of course, he could deny anything she said and it would be her word against his, but the dean wouldn't buy that and she'd find a way to get rid of him. What a mess he'd made of this!

The truth was he liked being married. Between wives, each time, he'd been elated to be free again. To date, to seduce, to bed as many women as he could. And he never really tired of that part of it. But eventually, the empty house was too lonely. He liked the familiar as well as the new. He liked having a steady source of affection, both to give and to get. He liked knowing someone was waiting, someone committed to him and committed to accepting his faults. Monogamy came with each of those marriages—he took those vows seriously and he didn't chafe under them. He could look, he could fantasize, he could refrain from touching. It was a nice counterpoint to the multiple relationships of the single times. But now he'd broken his commitment, all because of Kirchner, all because of Fred and that damn night in Murcheson's apartment.

He poured another half-glass of soda and leaned against the kitchen counter and thought about the evening. Mary Alice's mouth on him, the feel of her breasts, the sounds she made. He grew hard again. He heard Karina call to him and he put the glass down and went upstairs to his wife.

55

Murcheson pulled into the casino parking lot about 8:15. It was still broad daylight though the forest around the place cast deep shadows over the parked cars and RVs. And it was still hot. The heat radiated off the pavement in big waves, and he grabbed his bag from the trunk and hurried into the lobby of the hotel with its welcome chill. A swipe of the credit card, a signature, and he was directed to the elevator and the third floor. According to the very pretty girl at the desk, food was served around the clock in the main hall but he could have a quieter dinner in one of the two restaurants until 2 am. He decided to take a shower and then go downstairs.

He'd asked the girl about Fred, said he was his cousin, and seen a flicker of recognition cross her face, but she'd followed the party line and was unable to tell him if Fred was working there. He knew if he asked enough people, the word would reach Fred eventually. Fred wasn't the kind of guy you kept out of the loop.

It was 9:30 when he went downstairs. The casino building was like a big wheel with most of the spokes full of people gambling and smoking. He felt the familiar nostalgia for cigarettes, a habit he'd dropped a decade before when he'd had a scare about his heart. He stopped at two information booths and asked about Fred. Same line. These people were well trained. He also asked the server in the restaurant when he ordered. Another pretty girl, another flicker of recognition.

He had a scotch, then another with his meal. The food was

surprisingly good and it came very quickly. He figured they didn't want to keep people from the tables very long. After dinner, he walked around some more, watched people gamble. It wasn't one of his vices. It was repetitive and boring. If he was going to bet, he'd bet on a sports match between two great opponents, but even that he didn't fool with. It wasn't that he was particularly cautious. He just liked to be in control.

The last casino he'd been in was in Monte Carlo years before. He'd had to rent a tux to get in. It was an amazing scene of the rich and the beautiful. Gorgeous young women, well-dressed old men, and an occasional couple somewhere in between. Everything had been quiet, elegant, like something out of a James Bond movie. Seven Feathers was a very different experience. To say people were casually dressed was an understatement. Frayed jeans and tank tops on both men and women. Work boots and work shirts. A few Aryan brothers in leathers. Anything resembling well-dressed—a sport jacket, a polo shirt, a skirt on a woman—stood out like the proverbial sore thumb. These weren't the rich and beautiful; these were the poor and addicted.

He wandered through every gaming room that had dealers looking for Fred, but he didn't see him. He hung out a while near the blackjack tables, one of the more interesting games. There was at least one pro at the table, whether a plant by the casino or someone on her own, he didn't know. He could see a lot of skill and experience going into each decision she made, although she never hesitated. Her wins were modest but steady and he figured she was on her own. One summer of law school, he and Fred had both worked in Reno. He'd learned a lot, enough to convince him to never gamble seriously.

10:30 came and went, then 11. He finished his drink and headed up to his room. When he opened the door, he could see that a lamp was on and Fred was sitting in the easy chair by the window.

"Long time no see, cuz," he said.

Murcheson shook his head. "Got a key to every room, Fred?"

"Only takes one. Comes in handy." He stood up and moved towards Tom. The hug was brief, intense, and then turned into a pat-down.

"I don't carry a gun if that's what you're looking for."

Fred said nothing, just grinned.

Murcheson moved away and went into the bathroom. He came out carrying two glasses. He'd seen the bottle on the lamp table. He picked up the ice bucket.

"Not for me," Fred said. "I don't like to dilute my experiences."

An old familiar irritation washed over Murcheson, who put the ice bucket down and went over to the lamp table and poured each of them a drink. He could tell by the smell that it was gin. "*I* need ice for this," he said, and he took the bucket and left the room.

It was true that he wouldn't drink warm gin, but he also needed a chance to get himself organized. The pat-down told him Fred was in trouble. Murcheson didn't do much criminal law. The small towns around Salem didn't have a big need for that, and divorces and estate settlements were more plentiful and more lucrative. But like many of his colleagues, he was addicted to reading detective fiction and watching the law-and-order TV shows. And while they were overly dramatic, most of them contained enough realism to be instructive, so he could guess that Fred was involved in something shady. He didn't want any part of Fred's criminal activities. He didn't even want to know. He just needed to have a straightforward conversation about the girl and Kirchner and get a DNA sample one way or the other.

Fred was still there when he got back, sitting in one of the easy chairs. He sat back in the chair, looking perfectly at ease, one ankle on the other knee, sipping his gin. Murcheson put the ice bucket on the table, put a couple of cubes in his glass, and sat down in the second chair.

"How's your mom?" Fred said.

"Good. I had lunch with her yesterday. How's yours?"

"No idea. It's been a few years."

"What do you do here?"

"Blackjack mostly. Roulette if they need a fill-in." Fred poured himself more gin, gestured with the bottle at his cousin, who shook his head.

"You're not working tonight?"

"No. Is this work for you?"

Murcheson looked over at him. "No. Are you in some kind of trouble with the law?"

"Oh, probably."

"But that's not why you patted me down."

"No." He shifted in his chair.

Murcheson couldn't tell if Fred was ill at ease. Early on, Fred had perfected all kinds of masks and a measured stillness that kept his feelings hidden. He could be all smiles and seething inside. Murcheseon had seen the volcano blow with no warning more than a few times.

"Why don't you tell me why you came?" Fred said.

"Rhonda Ordway."

"Who's that?"

"A girl you brought to my apartment in 1972. Invited your Sig Delt friends along to have sex with her in my bedroom."

Fred shrugged, the same neutral look on his face. "If you say so."

"You don't remember?"

"Why should I?"

"The rest of us do."

"The rest being?"

"Pete Chandling, Derek Walsh, Jim Leeder."

"Shit, I haven't thought of those guys in years, decades even. How are they?"

"Not the point, Fred. You don't remember that night? You don't remember Rhonda?

"Can't say as I do. There've been so many nights, so many girls."
And the 15-year-old braggart was suddenly there in Fred's body
language.

Murcheson paused. He felt like he was in the courtroom. He was
going to need to trick Fred somehow. "Did you have sex with her
that night?"

"With a girl I don't remember on a night I don't remember?" His
cousin looked at him.

He remembered that look very well. It was a you're-a fool-and-
I'm-not look. Then Fred shrugged again. "If I was there and she was
willing, then I had sex with her. Why wouldn't I?" He leaned over
and poured himself more gin. "What's this all about, Tom? 1972 is a
very long time ago. Several lifetimes, as a matter of fact."

"There was a child involved."

"No, she wasn't. She was 18. I made sure of it."

"So you were there."

"Okay, what if I was? She wasn't a child."

"I didn't say that. I said 'there was a child involved.' She got
pregnant and had a son. And one of us is the father of that kid."

Fred's face remained impassive but a flicker of something crossed
his eyes. "And you know this how?"

"He found us. The kid. He found Pete, Derek, Jim, me. He had a
list with our names on it. Yours is on it too. And somebody named
Lonnie."

"Lonnie Tillstrom? Queer as they come. He was there that night?
I wouldn't have said that was his thing."

"According to Pete and Derek, he was there."

"So this kid, this guy, who's what 30-something?—is blackmailing
all of you about a prank from ancient history. No thanks, keep me
out of it."

Murcheson thought of the fax and what Kirchner had done to
Derek but then shook his head. "Only you would think immediately

of blackmail. Actually, he's looking for his father. He's convinced one of us is it."

"Did you tell him where I am?"

"No, I came to see you myself."

"What's his name? You got a picture of him?"

"No, no picture. Jason Kirchner. That's his name."

"Well, thanks for the heads-up." Fred uncrossed his legs and threw back the rest of the gin in his glass and set it on the table. "But this isn't really my problem. And since the chances are what? One in six?"

"One in four, actually."

Fred raised an eyebrow in question.

"It isn't Chandling or Lonnie."

"How come?"

"Chandling had a DNA test and it came back not a match. And Lonnie, well he never went in the bedroom."

"I told you. Queer as they come." Fred stood up, stretched his back. Then he picked up the bottle of gin. "Hey, it's my night off. Want to go out and find some girls? This place is teeming with eager women."

Tom shook his head. "Not my scene anymore. I've got somebody steady."

"She'll never know."

"I'll know. That's what's important."

"Suit yourself." Fred grinned. "You leaving in the morning?"

"Yeah, you want to have breakfast?" Tom thought maybe he could ask for the sample in the morning when Fred hadn't been drinking. If not, there was the gin glass.

"I don't get up much before 2 or 3. You'll be gone by then. Sure you don't want to come and party with us now?"

"No, thanks. I'm sure."

"Okay then." He reached down and picked up his glass. "I'll take this down to housekeeping for you." He winked at Tom. "Without company, you'll only need one."

Murcheson moved to stand up but Fred held up his hand. "No need. We already did the hug thing. Take care of yourself, Tom. Say hello to your mother." He moved towards the door and then turned. "Does he look like me?"

Tom thought about it. The kid didn't. "No, not really."

Fred nodded and went on out the door.

56

Derek glanced at the clock as he pulled away from Karina. It was 1:15. Their lovemaking had been sweet and simple. It often was when he'd been away. They had a great deal of affection for each other. In his youth, he had preferred passionate women who were as insatiable as he was. But they had always been jealous and problematic, so after Julie, he'd kept his eye out for a calm, abiding presence. Karina was one of those.

"Are you still awake?" He turned to face her.

"Yes, of course."

"I need to talk to you about something."

"The call from the dean?"

"Yeah." He turned on the bedside lamp and pulled himself up to sitting.

"This is serious then."

"Yes, I'm afraid so."

Karina sat up then too and fixed the pillows behind her back. She handed him the glass of water she always kept on the night table, and he drank part of it and handed it back to her. She held on to the glass.

"When I was in college, I belonged to a fraternity. You know that, right?"

"Yeah. That's where you met Pete and Jim."

"Yes and of course I met a lot of other guys too. One in particular, a guy named Fred, was a big prankster and a kind of schemer. He was always flaunting the rules and pushing the envelope and what he could do and what he get us to do. He got expelled finally for tampering with people's grades. In the sophomore yearbook, we voted him the brother most likely to go to prison."

"And this guy was a friend of yours."

"Not a friend exactly. Not like Pete and Jim, but I knew him and I occasionally did things with him and so did the others."

"Derek, sweetie, I'm not sure where this is going."

"This is very hard for me to talk about, okay? I'm just trying to give you some context for what I did."

"Okay," she said and settled back against the headboard.

"In the early 70s, the sexual revolution was in full swing and I was an activist. You know that too. I dated a lot of girls and slept with a bunch and got started thinking about the philosophy and sociology of sex. I didn't realize it at the time but I was doing research for my dissertation. Did I ever tell you about my trip to the Mustang Ranch in Nevada?" He looked over at her.

She shook her head.

"Well, I will sometime but Fred was the one who suggested we go, and Jim and I went with him." He paused. "Okay, here's the pertinent part. One night in the spring of '72, a bunch of us were out drinking and playing pool and Fred introduced us to this girl named Rhonda. I don't know if she was a student at our school or the other college near us or just a girl from town. It doesn't matter. We all drank together for a while and then when she went to the bathroom, Fred told us she was willing to come to his cousin's apartment and party with us."

"Were there other girls there with you?"

He paused again. "No."

"And how many of you?"

"Six, including Fred's cousin."

"I don't like the sound of this."

"We were all sort of drunk and stoned, except maybe for Pete, who was driving. Fred assured us she was willing and we took his word for it."

"And so what happened?"

"We...we all had sex with her."

"You watched each other do this?" He could hear the horror in her voice.

"No, God, no. We...each went into the bedroom, one at a time. Except Lonnie, the sixth guy. He decided he didn't want to."

Karina moved then. She got out of bed and pulled on a robe and went to stand at the window out onto the street. There was a street lamp not far down the block and he could see her clear profile and the set of her jaw. She didn't say anything for a long moment and he wanted to beg her forgiveness but he knew deep down that that wasn't going to help.

"Did she report this to the police?"

"No."

"Then why does your dean know about this?"

He sighed. "She got pregnant and her son is blackmailing me to give him a DNA sample."

"He wants to know if you're his father."

"Yes."

She turned and looked at him. "Why don't you just give him a DNA sample?"

He didn't respond and in a minute, she turned back to the window. "How is he blackmailing you?" she said.

"I'll show you." He got up and went down the hall to his office and brought the copy of the fax back and handed it to her. He watched her read it and the sympathy he hoped for didn't appear on her face. Instead, she looked confused.

"Why is he doing this? Why didn't he just ask you for the sample?"

"Well, he did. But I said no."

"Why? Why wouldn't you want to know? Or let him know?"

"Because Bruce Houghton told me not to admit anything."

"When did you talk to Bruce?"

"Last week before I went to Seattle."

"You've known about this for a week and you're just telling me now?"

"I didn't have all the facts until Jim and I went to Portland."

"You had enough facts to talk to Bruce."

"Yes, I should have told you. I don't know why I didn't."

"Yes, you do. This is just another example of…" she threw up her hands and walked out of the room.

He heard her use the bathroom and go down the stairs. He got back into bed, sitting up again against the pillows. He didn't think the conversation was over. But the minutes went by and she didn't come back up and finally he turned off the light and went to sleep.

57

Jim Leeder checked into the Cameo Motel on Sandy and 82nd a bit after 10. He'd had a burger in a sports tavern a mile or so from the motel, and he'd watched a couple of games on the big screen with a bunch of other baseball fanatics. The place had smelled of beer and cigarettes. He took a shower and opened one of the beers he'd bought on the way and got into bed. The air conditioner was a shitty window unit and it made a lot of racket, but he knew he'd be grateful later because he hadn't thought about the location of the motel at a busy intersection when he'd called and made the reservation.

He drank some of the beer, but he didn't really want it. If someone had asked, he'd have said he didn't know what he wanted. But that wouldn't have been true. He wanted a wife. He wanted a woman who loved him dearly, the way Nancy loved Pete. He wanted somebody to be there when he got home, to care about his day, to notice when he was sad or lonely. There were times he wished he'd hung on to Nancy. She had been offering what he now wanted. But he didn't want it then, not the way he wanted it now.

In his memories, his feelings for Nancy and for Rhonda were similar. He had felt so good when he was with each of them. It wasn't just the sex. In fact, the sex wasn't very important. The touching and being touched meant something else. There was a kindness to it, a warmth. Like the few memories he had of his mother before she left. When she'd hugged him or put her hand on his head, he'd felt that same warm, kind thing. He didn't have anybody in his life who touched him like that and he hadn't had it in the 10 years since

Nancy left. He'd pretended all this time that it didn't matter. That he could make do with the desire he felt from the girls he met through his work, that their desire made him somebody special. And he could fall back on the kind of good-natured sex he had with Melissa in Portland and with Kathy in Seattle, his version of a girl in every port.

He knew Walsh envied him for the life he had. And even though Derek kept getting married and divorced, so he could have the best of both worlds, from Jim's viewpoint, only the married part was the best although he'd never say that to Walsh. It was important that Walsh go on envying his freedom. It was important for their friendship that he had something to contribute to Walsh's ongoing study of the playboy life. Just as it was important to him that Pete believed that he had no regrets about letting Nancy go, that he was completely neutral where she was concerned.

He lay on his side in the dark, facing his watch. It was 11:10 and sleep wasn't coming.

He thought about Kirchner. He hadn't apologized the way he'd told Nancy. He'd just given him the sample and taken the address. The truth was, he was afraid to really look at the kid. Afraid to see himself in those eyes, in those features. And yet, what if he was his kid? His and Rhonda's. Wouldn't that be the best for everyone? Well, he'd soon find out and so would the others. There'd be no keeping it secret, at least not from Pete and Nancy and Derek. He didn't care a whit about what Murcheson or Landon or that Lonnie, whoever he was, thought. And his friends would assume that the kid came from that night, not the half-dozen other times he and Rhonda were together.

And maybe, just maybe, Rhonda would be happy that he was the father. That thought soothed him and he drifted off to sleep.

58

Murcheson took a shower as soon as Fred left his room. He felt an overwhelming need to wash off the encounter. He stood under the hot water for a long time, blessing the water heaters that hotels had. Then he dried off and shaved and brushed his teeth. He turned the lights off in his room and just sat for a while.

He looked at the clock by the bed. It was too late to call Marie Elena but he wanted to hear her voice, connect with someone honest and real. The more he thought about it though, the more he realized that Fred had probably been honest and real. He didn't care about anyone else and he had made that clear. Besides, Tom had always known that about Fred. The narcissism might not have been formally diagnosed but it was there all along.

But it wasn't too late to call Bob Willis. Bob answered right away. He always did, day or night. Tom told him briefly what he needed and asked him to call back with whatever he could find by 1 am. Then he called the 24-hour room service and ordered ice cream. He put on a robe and turned on Jay Leno and settled in.

Bob called back about an hour later just as Leno was winding up. Bob was sending all that he'd found in an email. "There's a lot, boss," he said. "This is a pretty seedy character. Do you want me to summarize?"

"No, that's not necessary, but let me turn on my computer and be sure I can open up the file. Hold on." Tom opened the briefcase and got set up, linked through to email, and found the file. "I'm good," he said. "Thanks and send me your bill."

There were nearly a dozen documents so he called the front desk and asked if a printer was available. There was, so he copied them all to a flash drive and got dressed and went downstairs. It didn't seem prudent to ask the staff to do what he needed so he printed it all out himself. He ordered some coffee and more ice cream from room service and began to read.

He knew a lot of the early stuff. Fred had bragged about some of it. He'd heard his parents talking about other escapades. There was a sealed juvenile record he didn't know about though and as Fred got older, the deeds got darker. The drug dealing didn't surprise Murcheson, but the drunk and disorderlies began to morph into assault and battery charges, usually drunken brawls in taverns although one was at the Miami airport where he punched a customs official and two were listed as domestic violence (in both cases he'd tangled with a husband who pressed charges). None of this really worried Murcheson and as he moved through the stack of papers, he hoped this would be all he'd find. But that wasn't the case.

The last three documents were the longest and they were cases of alleged rape. All three cases had been dropped due to insufficient evidence for prosecution. One dated from the late 1980s and the other two from a couple of years back. All of the girls were 18 or 19, all of them were college students, all of them claimed they'd been drugged. The last case was the most disturbing as the girl, Bethany Miller, claimed three men had taken part in the rape, which occurred in her apartment. She had met Fred at a bar near campus and he'd offered to walk her home, where he invited himself into her apartment. She said she'd asked him to leave but he wouldn't. Instead he held her down and forced her to drink whiskey. Pretty quickly, she began to fade in and out. The other two men appeared in her apartment at this point although she had no memory of letting them in or of Fred doing so. Fred then took her into the bedroom where he had sex with her. Then the other men came in one at a time and had sex with her too.

"I must have slept for a long while because when I woke up, it was nearly noon and I was alone in my apartment," she said at the inquest. She felt sick and sore and was terrified they'd come back. She called a friend who took her to the local ER and a rape kit was performed. DNA from three men was found but only Fred's was in the system so he was arrested. Bethany couldn't identify the other two men in any way that led to an arrest, and Fred's lawyer argued that she had invited him back to her apartment and had been more than willing to have sex with him. Fred claimed he didn't know anything about the other men. His fingerprints were found inside the apartment but only in logical places (handle of the toilet, the knob on the inside of the front door). There was no sign of alcohol in the apartment at all except for two unopened beers in the fridge. The prior arrests for rape were deemed inadmissible, and the grand jury refused to indict him.

Murcheson leaned back in his chair. He felt sick. He'd recognized the name of the lawyer in all three cases. Joel Prescott of Landon, Prescott, and Davies. The law firm of Fred's father. He suspected Fred's mother knew nothing of any of this and even if she did, she probably wouldn't have told her sister, so his own mother wouldn't have known.

He didn't know what difference *his* knowing now made. He just hoped more than ever that Fred was not Jason Kirchner's father.

59

The alarm on Leeder's watch went off at 5. He stretched himself awake. He'd slept better than he'd expected. He was anxious but his head was clear. He took another shower, put his gear in his car, and went next door to the pancake house for coffee to go. He was in position across the street from Rhonda's house just about 6. He was relieved to see that both the pickup and the Corolla were still there. That meant that neither of them had gone to work yet. He was hoping the husband would go to work first, so that he could talk to Rhonda at her house. But what if the husband was unemployed or she was too and they both just stayed in the house all day? He talked himself down from that and sat sipping the coffee and just watched.

At 6:45, the husband came out of the house. He carried an old-fashioned metal lunch pail and a hard hat. He looked to be a lot older than they were, 60s or so. Balding, a big man with a bit of a beer belly. He rolled the garbage and recycling bins out to the street and then got in the pickup and backed out of the driveway. He honked before he took off, and Jim saw the curtains move in the plate glass window to the right of the porch.

The sun was beginning to warm up the SUV and Jim rolled down his window for the cooler air outside. He told himself it was too early to call on a woman he hadn't seen in 27 years. But the truth was he was afraid, and the longer he sat there, the more his anxiety ratcheted up. He didn't know what he was going to say. He didn't even know for sure why he was there. He just knew he had to do this.

At 7:20, she came out of the house. She wore a dark blue uniform and dark tennis shoes and carried a big bag over her shoulder. She headed across the lawn to the Corolla and before Jim could collect himself, she was driving off. He started up the SUV and took off after her.

She turned left at the corner, right on Glisan, and then left on 122nd until she got to Halsey, where she turned right. Three blocks farther on, she turned left across the traffic onto a side street and then pulled into a parking area immediately behind a strip mall. Jim had to wait for the traffic and when he got across and down the side street, he saw that her car was empty. He parked on the street itself a ways down, sat a long moment, and then walked back to the front of the mall.

He found her in a café between a hair salon and a locksmith's. The dozen tables and six stools at the counter were mostly occupied. Rhonda was serving big platters of food to three guys at the counter. The smell of bacon and fried potatoes hung in the air. He took a small table to the back of the place, near the restrooms. It was as out of the way as he could get.

She came over to his table, put down a glass of water and a menu. "Coffee, hon?" she said and he turned the thick beige mug over and she filled it. She didn't look at him, just went about her work. He turned his chair a little so he could watch her. He felt like a love-starved teenager again, watching her, remembering her. She hadn't changed as much as he would have thought. She was still slim and not gray yet. Only her hands gave her age away and the lines around her eyes and mouth. Her voice had deepened, age and maybe cigarettes.

She came back around for his order and he spoke her name. "Rhonda, do you remember me? Jim Leeder."

Her eyes widened and then something he couldn't decipher crossed her face. He saw her take in a deep breath, something just short of a gasp. A few seconds passed and they seemed frozen there, him looking up at her, she down at him. Then a man's voice called "Order up," and she turned her head towards the pass-through window behind the counter where plates of food were appearing. Without a word, she moved to the window, picked up the plates, and served an elderly couple across the room. Then she disappeared into the kitchen.

A minute later, another waitress appeared at his table. Jim didn't know what to think or what to ask, so he ordered eggs and bacon and hash browns. He waited for the food, for Rhonda to come back, for the courage to approach her again. Rhonda came back into the room and waited on customers but not on him. She didn't come over to his side of the room at all. When the food came, it was the other waitress, who put down the plate, asked him if he needed ketchup or hot sauce, and left him to eat. He felt stymied but the food smelled good and he was hungry so he ate most of it and drank the not very good coffee. The same waitress came by with his check. Next to it though she placed a second slip of paper. When he turned it over, he saw this: "Break at 11. Mocha Madness across the street. R."

60

When Derek got up on Wednesday, it was past 9. He hadn't heard Karina leave and she didn't leave a note. She'd seemed more upset about his not telling her than the event itself, and he hoped that was true. He could more easily persuade her as to why he hadn't said anything than why he had gone into that bedroom in Murcheson's apartment in the first place.

He got a bowl of cereal and took it out to the patio. The sun was hot already but that was fine with him. Maybe it would burn the rest of the hangover out of him. He stripped down to his boxers when he'd finished eating and lay back in the sun and he was soon asleep again. From some distant place, he heard the phone ring and the murmur of a voice on the answering machine. After a while, it rang again and another murmur. And then a third time. The heat made him languid and he made no effort to fight off the fatigue.

A dark shadow fell over him and a hand ran down his belly to the waistband of his boxers. He opened his eyes to Mary Alice, who was leaning over him and stroking his sex through his shorts. He grabbed her wrist and pushed it away. Then he struggled to get up. He felt naked, vulnerable, exposed.

She grinned and pulled a chair over so she was sitting knee to knee with him. She opened her legs and wrapped her ankles around his. Her white tennis skirt barely covered her. Her lips were moving but he couldn't hear the sentences. It was like a bad phone connection

202 | Jill Kelly

that kept fading in and out. "...apology ...going with this...forget about last night."

He said "no" and then "no" again. He looked around for his clothes. He saw his t-shirt and reached for it but she tightened her legs around him.

"Don't," he said. "Don't. I love my wife."

She began to laugh. "No one will know. No one will know. No one will know." She grinned again, a Cheshire Cat grin, an unholy grin. Then she released her grip on his legs and leaned back in her chair.

"I can't do this. I won't."

"Oh, of course you can. You raped that girl."

"It wasn't rape."

"I don't care if it was." That grin again. "Inside or out?"

He shook his head. "What do you mean?"

"You. Me. Now. Inside your house or out here?"

61

The phone rang at 7:15. Pete was at the stove stirring oatmeal. He let it go but the voice mail didn't click on. Wrong number or telemarketer. He shook his head at people's rudeness. He covered the oatmeal and cut up some fruit. He knew his wife loved a nice presentation so he got a rose from the garden and put it on the table. Its fragrance quickly filled the warm room. The phone rang again. This time he answered.

"Mr. Chandling, it's Jason Kirchner. I'm not having any luck finding Lonnie Tillstrom or Fred Landon. I got a sample from Mr. Murcheson and I got one from Mr. Leeder. I'd really like to be done with this. Can you help me?"

"Lonnie isn't your father," Pete said and he told about seeing Lonnie the night before and how he'd never gone in the bedroom. He also recounted Lonnie's meeting with Rhonda and giving her the list of names.

"Why was his name on the list then? That doesn't make much sense."

"I don't think he gave her the names of who might be your father. I think he gave her the names of the guilty. He felt guilty for his part in that night. He still feels guilty."

Jason was quiet. "Would he see me?"

"I don't know," Pete said. "And his brother's a fierce watch dog. But you could try." He gave him Lonnie's address."

"So that just leaves Walsh and Landon," said Jason. "Did Walsh send you a sample? Your wife thought he was going to do that."

"Well, I haven't received anything," Pete said. "Look, I'll call Derek this morning and urge him to send you the sample. He'd agreed before he left for home and I'm sure he just forgot."

"You don't sound very sure of that."

"I'll do my best. That's all I can do."

"And what about Fred Landon? Do you know where he is?"

"No, but Murcheson is looking into that."

"Why would he do that?"

"They're cousins." He heard the words come out of his mouth and was immediately sorry. That wasn't his to divulge. "Anyway, let Murcheson handle that."

He saw Nancy come into the kitchen. She smiled at him and he smiled back. "Anything else? I've got to go."

"No, we're done. Thanks."

Over breakfast, he told Nancy about the phone call and about Jason getting a sample from Leeder. She told him about Jim's call for Jason's number. He had the good sense not to ask why she hadn't told him the night before.

62

When Leeder finished his breakfast, it was only 8:25. He had no idea of what to do with himself until 11. He couldn't sit in the café and he didn't want to sit over in the coffee shop across the street all that time. So he paid his bill and drove over to Pete's house. It was just something to do. Pete's car was gone, but Nancy's Honda was still in the driveway. He parked in front of the house, tilted the back rest down, and closed his eyes.

Nancy's voice woke him. She'd opened the driver's door and was standing right beside him. "Jim, are you all right?" There was no accusation in her voice, only curiosity and her usual kindness.

He straightened the seat up so he wouldn't feel so vulnerable. "I've an appointment at 11 and I needed a little nap. You have a quiet street."

She gave a laugh. "Come on in. It's not even 9 yet."

"Pete's not home." Since a late drunken evening the year before when he had told Derek he still loved Nancy and Derek had told Pete, Leeder had made it a point to not see Nancy when Pete wasn't around. He didn't want Pete to worry or Derek to gossip.

"It's okay," she said. "I'll call and tell him you're here. Come on in." She went back in the house without waiting for him.

He popped a breath mint, ran a comb through his hair, waited another couple of minutes, and then went in after her.

"Pete says hi." She held up a coffee mug but he shook his head. She poured herself a cup and sat down at the table. He sat down across from her. She was dressed for work, pale blue scrubs with elephants and giraffes dancing across them. Her curly hair was wet and hung down on her shoulders. She looked so much like she had when he'd first met her all those years ago, when she'd showered for him.

"What's your appointment? You're not sick, are you?"

"No, nothing like that." He knew it was no accident he'd come here. He'd known Pete would be gone and Nancy would be hanging out until her shift started. And who else was he going to tell if not her? He screwed up his courage. "I'm going to meet Rhonda."

He could see he had caught her by surprise but she recovered quickly. "Does she live here in Portland?" Her voice was calm and steady, so much more than his own.

"Yes, 120th and Glisan."

"Not far from here."

"Yeah."

"Do you want to tell me about this?"

"Just between us?"

"I can't keep secrets from Pete. I won't." She looked him in the eye. He hesitated and then nodded.

"Tell me," she said.

"I was there that night in Murcheson's apartment."

"We all know that, Jim." Her look was kind.

"Yeah, well, anyway, I ran into Rhonda about a week after that. I was in a coffee shop, talking to another girl actually, and I saw Rhonda walk by and go on down the street. I told the other girl I had to leave and I went after her."

"To apologize?"

"No, well, no. I just wanted to see her again." He looked out at the sunny morning and the patio with all its flowers. "I was attracted to her. Right from the get-go at the tavern before we went to the apartment. I liked her. She was pretty and funny. Easy to be with. And…and we'd had a good time in the bedroom. It wasn't impersonal with me. I wanted to have sex with her. I mean with *her*, not just anybody, but with her. Rhonda."

Nancy smiled at him but he could see there was sadness in it. "What happened next?" she said.

"I caught up with her a couple of blocks further down. I skipped my classes and took her to lunch and then to a movie. I saw her a lot for the rest of the semester. About a month, I guess."

"And you had sex with her."

"Of course. We were—well, I was in love with her, I guess." As he said, he knew it had been true.

He waited for her to say something but she just gave him that same smile with the sadness in it and he went on. "Then the term was over and I went home to work and she went home to Roseburg and we wrote letters and talked on the phone some and I thought about taking the bus down to see her but before that happened, she sent me a Dear John letter. 'I've met somebody else, yada, yada.' And I got on with my life."

"That must have broken your heart."

"Yeah, I guess. It was a long time ago."

"But still."

"Hey, I learned that women are fickle."

"Well, some women are. And you never told Pete or Derek you were seeing her."

"After that night in the apartment? Are you kidding? I'd have been the laughing stock of the whole frat."

"Just like Pete."

"What about Pete?"

"Never mind." She thought a moment. "And it didn't bother you that she had had sex with all the others?"

"I wasn't thrilled about Murcheson and Fred. I didn't know Murcheson and I didn't much like Fred, but the fact that she'd had sex with Derek and Pete, well, that was okay with me. And she didn't have sex with any of the others afterwards. Just with me."

"So now you know what really happened. She didn't meet somebody else that summer. She got pregnant."

He looked at her and then out at the yard again.

"Do you think Jason is your son?"

"I don't know. I guess it's likely. I had sex with her more than that one time, but I don't know."

"What do you think though? Do you think he is your son?"

"He could be."

"Are you going to be okay with it if he is?"

"I don't have much choice. He is or he isn't."

"How will you know?"

"I gave him my DNA sample in exchange for his mother's address." He looked at his watch. It was a little after 10. "I should go. I don't want to be late."

"Will you call me and let me know what happens?" She paused. "Only if you want to."

"Maybe," Jim said. He got up and went to the front door.

She followed him and stood in the doorway. "Thanks for sharing all this with me."

He turned back to her. "Don't tell Pete if you don't have to."

She smiled and nodded.

63

Derek woke sweating. His watch said 11:12. He'd had a terrible and very real dream about Mary Alice and he was relieved to find himself alone on the patio. He took a couple of deep breaths so his heart would stop pounding. He could feel the sun burning his skin. He got up as quickly as he could and went in and took a cold shower to stop the burn.

He put on a pair of jeans and a t-shirt, slipped his feet into sandals. He still didn't feel very good but he knew if he hung around the house, he'd convince himself that he could start drinking. But where to go and what to do? He came downstairs and noticed the light blinking on the phone. Three messages. That part of the dream had been real.

The first was from Pete. "Hey Derek, Pete here. Just calling to encourage you to connect with Kirchner about the DNA sample. He has a sample from Murcheson and from Leeder—not sure how he pulled that off—and he was getting one today from Fred. I also found Lonnie and talked to him. Long story there. Call me when you can." No mention of the message he'd left the day before. How was that possible? Then it struck him. Nancy had erased the message and not told Pete so he'd help her precious Kirchner. He started fuming again.

The second message was from the dean. "Derek, it's Dean Lachland. I wanted to be sure you picked up the copy of the fax we discussed yesterday. I have the original but I don't want that fax floating around and I am sure you don't either. I'm trusting you've also communicated with the source of the fax to resolve your differences if that's feasible. Do call me back right away if you don't have the copy."

The last one was from Mary Alice. "Hello, Derek, loved our time together last night. Erase this quick before your wife hears it. Hugs and kisses from your other lover."

He groaned. The shit was just getting deeper and deeper. He didn't see how he could have another heart-to-heart conversation with Karina about Mary Alice. They weren't over the last one yet. He needed Karina on his side. And he needed to stop Mary Alice now but how? He paced around for a while. Went out to the patio but it was too hot for thinking. So he got in the shower again and let the water run and run. He did some of his best thinking in the shower. When he was done, he had a plan.

First, he called the dean's office and asked for an appointment. She could fit him in at 2, her secretary said. He left a message that he did indeed have the copy of the fax and was working on a resolution but needed to talk to her about another rather urgent matter.

Then he called Pete at his office. It was just after 9 on the West Coast. Pete answered on the second ring and Derek dove straight in. "Your boy Jason has gotten me in a lot of trouble."

"Hello to you too. Are you talking about the fax?

"Of course I am. I'm in deep shit here." He went on tell Pete how he'd flipped it around and saved his own skin. He paused, waiting for Pete's compliment on his cleverness and skill, but Pete was quiet. Derek went on waiting but when Pete spoke, he said, "Are you going to give him the sample now?"

"That's all you've got to say?"

"That's what's most important from my perspective. Look, I'm not defending him or condoning what he did. But he needed to get your attention. He wants to know if you're his father and I think you should let him find out."

"And what about my right to privacy?"

"Maybe you gave that up when you went into the bedroom."

A long moment of silence followed. Then Derek said, "Whose side are you on anyway?"

Pete sighed. "I'm on the side of taking responsibility for our actions, of manning up, as they say."

"That's easy for you to say. You're not the father."

"No, but I would take responsibility if I were. It's the right thing to do."

"But the others aren't doing the 'right thing,' as you call it, either."

"Actually they are. Murcheson met with Jason and gave him a sample and apparently Leeder did too."

"You're kidding. How did that happen?"

"I don't know. I'm as surprised about it as you are, but Jason said he did."

"What about Lonnie Tillstrom or Fred?"

Pete again described the evening before. "As I told Lonnie, I had no idea he was gay. It has made me very sad. He's a great guy."

"Except that he got us all into this mess when he gave her the list."

"No, Derek, we got ourselves into this."

"And Fred?"

"No idea. I think Murcheson is the link there and I haven't talked to him."

Derek thought again. "Okay, how do I get Kirchner a sample from here?"

"You need to work that out with him." Pete gave him Jason's number. "It's the right thing to do."

"Yeah, but I'm not sure it's the best thing to do."

64

At 10:30, Jason used a pay phone to check his messages. There were six. An extra work shift was available if he wanted it. He didn't. Three from the same telemarketer. Didn't the woman realize he'd recognize her voice? The fifth message was from Derek Walsh. It was brief and abrupt. "I'm ready to give you a sample. Tell me how to send it and where."

Jason felt a flush of satisfaction. He still didn't like Walsh and he was glad he'd sent the fax since he was going to get what he wanted. He took out his wallet, got out his long-distance card, and dialed Walsh's number. He got the machine and had to leave a message. "I'll call you back this afternoon. I want to talk to your wife. I'll tell her how you can send the sample." He could be a jerk too.

65

Murcheson woke about 9 in the hotel casino. He lay there a while, hoping more sleep would come. He felt weary and unhappy about all that he had learned about Fred. He felt ashamed to be related to him although he knew every psychopath, every serial killer had parents and siblings and cousins. About 9:20 he gave up on sleep and took another shower, hoping to be revived. He felt cleaner but no happier.

He packed his things and checked out. The slot machines near the hotel desk were all in play, and he avoided looking at the haggard faces of the night owls. The morning air was fresh and cool even though the August heat wave wasn't over, and he was looking forward to the drive back. He'd stop for coffee and breakfast in Roseburg and then go straight into the office.

Fred was waiting at his car.

"You stalking me?" Murcheson tried to make it sound light but he didn't feel light. He started to wonder how Fred knew which car was his and then stopped. It was clear that Fred made it his business to know what was going on. He was a survivor and that's what survivors did.

"Nah, just wanted to thank you for coming. Nobody in the family really reaches out to me anymore. Not even my own mother." There was self-pity in his voice but it didn't ring true.

"Well, it was interesting to see you." Murcheson stowed his bag and briefcase in the back seat and turned to face his cousin. "Did you change your mind about giving me the sample?"

"Yes, as a matter of fact. You'll find another way to get it if I don't and I can save you the trouble." Fred grinned and Murcheson could see a glimpse of the boy he had known.

"Okay, then." He opened the rear door and rummaged in his briefcase for the swab kit and handed it to Fred, who used it and handed it back.

"So you don't think the kid looks like me?"

"Honestly, no, he doesn't," Tom said. "He looks more like me but there's no obvious resemblance and I can't remember the girl well enough to even know if he looks like her."

"So this could all be an elaborate hoax."

"Well, *elaborate* would be the word for it. A lot of trouble for not much reward."

"People will do all kinds of elaborate things for money." Fred lit a joint. Tom could smell the sweetness of the dope.

"He isn't asking for any."

"Not yet. He will. When he does, tell him I don't have any. If I did, I'd be in Monte Carlo, not at Seven Feathers." Fred offered him the joint.

"I'll tell him," Tom said, shaking his head at the joint.

"Okay, then. Stay out of trouble."

"You too."

Fred laughed "What fun would that be?" He turned and moved through the cars towards the front of the casino.

From where he'd parked his truck, Jason could see Murcheson leave the casino and walk to his car. He didn't recognize the man who was leaning against the car and although he wasn't very far away, he couldn't hear their conversation, just a low murmur of voices when the breeze came his way. He watched Murcheson stow his bags in the car. After a minute of talking, he opened the back driver-side door and leaned inside and then handed the guy something.

They shifted positions and Jason could only see Murcheson's back. The men stood there not much more than a minute, and then Murcheson drove away.

Jason didn't follow him. Instead he watched the other man change direction and head around the casino. He started up his truck and followed him. He was taking a chance that this was Fred Landon.

66

Murcheson thought about Fred all the way to Roseburg. He wished there was some way to get him behind bars. It didn't matter that he was family. He was a sexual predator and they didn't stop. He fantasized about an elaborate sting operation in which he'd catch Fred in the act and put him away. But he knew he wouldn't do it. Not because of Fred, but because of his family. He couldn't put his mother and his aunt through that, not on his instigation, and he knew Fred would implicate him and the others in the night in the apartment. He didn't care so much for himself. He hadn't broken any law and even the notoriety would be unlikely to impact his law practice. Hell, it might even bring him some new clients. But he couldn't be responsible for messing with the lives of the other four men and their families as well as his own.

He thought about Jason Kirchner, wondering again if he looked like him or his family. Did he look like Fred or Fred's parents? He didn't think so. He'd seen him so briefly and even though he'd tried to absorb as many impressions as he could, his feelings were running so high that he couldn't compute it all at once. The kid actually looked the most like him as he'd told Fred. But if predation was genetic and Kirchner was his son, he'd share some DNA with Fred anyway. And if Fred was the father—and that would be an awful fate for the kid—Kirchner would be his nephew.

How would he feel if Kirchner was his son? It would be weird to suddenly have this other person in his life, in his family, but it would work out somehow. He could afford to be of some help. And he could let Kirchner decide what kind of connection he wanted. It would work out. That settled, he turned his attention back to the joy of the road.

67

Derek realized he hadn't talked with Pete about Mary Alice. In earlier days, he might have but maybe not. Leeder was the one who'd be more interested in this entanglement. Like his friend Todd, Pete wasn't a rambling man. But calling and talking to Leeder seemed somehow more difficult now that Jim had given his sample to Kirchner. Derek couldn't figure out how that had come about or why Leeder would have consented. He could call and ask him but what good would that do?

He got dressed in suitably academic clothes and went to his appointment with the dean.

"What can I do for you, Professor Walsh?" Dr. Lachland didn't look any too pleased to see him again.

For a moment, he hesitated, uneasy and unsure if this was the best way to go. But he felt so stymied, so stuck in his own mess that he couldn't think of a different option. "Yes, first, thanks for being concerned about the fax copy. I appreciate your diligence with that."

She nodded.

"I've reached out to the sender of the fax and although I had to leave a voicemail, I offered to resolve this with him."

"But that's not why you came to see me."

"No, it's not. It's one of the students, Mary Alice Tatum. She has been stalking me, harassing me, and claiming I'm having sex with her."

"That's a very serious claim."

"Believe me, I know. But…well, she started coming around last spring to my office and making overtures. Of course, I just ignored them and kept the professional boundaries. Then she signed up for my summer class on the sociology of violence. She's a good student but she kept coming for tutoring, asking for one-on-one appointments. After the first one, I refused to see her alone in my office. I was holding group discussions and encouraged her to use those opportunities to get her questions answered." He paused. He wasn't quite sure how to spin all this.

"As you know, summer afternoon classes often end up in a coffee shop or café and I do like to go along sometimes and get to know the students more informally. Mary Alice was always in those groups when I went and she always ended up next to me at the table. I knew she was flirting with me, but since she never touched me, I figured I was rebuffing her in the kindest way. But when she left this message on my home answering machine this morning, I knew I had to speak to you about it." He reached down to his briefcase and pulled out the machine. "May I?"

She nodded again.

He plugged the machine in and played the message for the dean.

"I see what you mean. Please play it again."

She sat a moment and then looked at him. "What's her reference to 'last night'?"

"Yesterday afternoon about 4, I ran into her and Christie Montrose and Allyson Trondheim at Malone's. I sat and had a beer with them. Christie and Allyson left about 6 and Mary Alice asked me to walk her home as she was pretty drunk. It felt irresponsible not to do that so I did. I got her to her apartment and I left her there and walked home."

"Derek, I'm struck by the timing of this 'problem' and the fax of yesterday, both issues of sexual misconduct."

"Well, Bernadette, I didn't have control over the timing. I didn't send the fax and I didn't leave the message. I believe it's just a coincidence."

She looked at him again. He couldn't read what was behind her eyes.

"All right. Is Mary Alice a sociology major?"

"No, and I don't believe she's minoring in it either."

"Then there's no need for her to take any additional classes from you. Have you already turned in her summer grade?"

"Yes, of course. They were due August 1." He thanked his lucky stars that he could say that.

"Then I will ask you to avoid her on campus and in the community. And I will ask her to do the same."

"And if she won't?"

"Let's assume she will. That it will be in her best interest to do so. Just as it will be in yours." She stood up. "Is there anything else?"

"No, thank you." He too stood up, unplugged the machine, and put it back in his briefcase. He didn't take a deep breath of relief until he was in his car.

68

Fred Landon got into a Mercury Marquis that was parked on the very outskirts of the casino property. Jason watched him sit there a minute and then he started it up and headed to I-5 north. Jason followed him. There was a lot of truck traffic on the freeway, and Landon drove fast, pulling out at the last minute to go around the semis, darting back into the right lane. It was like a game somehow, a reckless game. It made keeping him in sight more difficult although not impossible. The car was a burgundy red that had long been out of fashion. That helped.

Landon took the Roseburg city center exit but turned left under the freeway. He drove a ways, finally reaching an industrial area where he parked his car on a rough stretch of pavement a short ways from a tavern. The tavern's beer signs were lit up, but the parking lot was empty except for a couple of pickups around the side. However, half a dozen cars were parked along the same rough stretch of pavement, all older luxury cars like Landon's.

Jason drove past the group of cars and then turned around and parked a bit further down. Landon got out of his car and went into the tavern. Jason waited, unsure what his next move should be. He rummaged in his backpack and put a swab kit in his jacket pocket. When he looked up, Landon was coming out of the tavern. He had a six pack in his hand. He walked across the lot to a small dilapidated house that sat on the edge of the tavern's parking lot. He climbed the porch stairs and went inside.

Jason stayed in his truck. He wasn't sure what he'd find in the house. A girlfriend most likely. If he waited too long, they'd be having sex and that would be even more awkward. All he wanted was a chance to meet Landon and get the sample. It didn't have to take more than five minutes, but there was something about Landon that made him wary. Maybe it was because Murcheson hadn't just called and told him where he could find Landon. Instead he'd driven down to see him himself. Maybe Murcheson knew something he didn't, that Landon was his father. Maybe he was protecting his cousin.

Well, fuck that, he thought. *I need that swab*. He got out of his car and went down the street.

<u>69</u>

Jim Leeder found a back table at Mocha Madness. He got himself a latte but he was so nervous he couldn't drink it. He had no guarantee Rhonda would come, but he also knew he couldn't hound her at work or visit her at home. That wasn't fair no matter what he wanted.

11 o'clock came. 11:05. 11:10. He felt sad that she didn't want to see him. Maybe she hated him, hated what he'd been a part of. Maybe she knew he wasn't the father and she knew who was. Maybe she'd had relationships with the others after that night as well. Maybe he had never meant much of anything to her. He got up and dumped the cold latte in the trash. He ordered a double espresso for the road and was waiting at the pickup counter when she came in.

Her smile was shy, just like it had been all those years before. Something unbearably sweet and gentle about that smile. She came up to him. "Sorry I'm late. It's not easy to get away some mornings. We were slammed."

He felt shy himself and embarrassed for his thoughts. It was an odd feeling and an old one. He didn't know what to say now so he played it safe. "Do you want a coffee?"

"No. Just some water."

He nodded and got a paper cup and filled it at the jug by the sugars and lids. Then he got his drink and followed her over to the same table where he had been sitting. Funny that she would choose that one too.

"I assume you met my son. And that's how you found me."

"Actually he found me or rather found us. But he gave me your address and I followed you to work this morning."

"That's a lot of trouble."

"It didn't seem like it. I wanted to see you."

She sipped at the glass of water and didn't say anything for a minute. Then she looked at him and smiled. Her smile too was sad and it pained him that two women he cared about smiled at him that way. "It's going to sound like a cliché," she said, "but I fantasized for a long time that you would come back."

"I believed the letter you sent me, that you'd met somebody else."

"I know. And in a sense, I had met somebody else. Jason. And that was more important than you and me somehow."

He watched her face, saw the girl he'd loved come and go across her features, then this middle-aged woman he didn't know. It was a kaleidoscope of expressions and somehow of all the women he'd known.

"Is he…am I his father?"

She looked in his eyes, seemed to search for something there. Then he saw something bitter and sad cross her face. "I don't know. I don't. If it took more than one…time to get pregnant, then you would be the father. But we both know it doesn't take more than once. So any of you could be." She paused. "And one of you is."

The reality struck him. "You were a virgin that night in the apartment. I'm so sorry."

She shook her head. "No, that's not it. It wasn't my first time. I'd had a boyfriend in high school but we'd broken up months before. So…look, you may not want to hear this, but I knew that Fred wanted to have sex that night and I was okay with that. I wanted experience. And I liked him enough. He was pretty charming and kind of handsome in his own way. And he told me we could use his cousin's apartment and that sounded a lot nicer to me than the back seat of his car."

She paused and took another sip of the water. "I wasn't in love with him. You know that. I was soon to be in love with you." She smiled that sad smile again and it went straight to his heart.

"Did Fred tell you about the rest of us?"

"No. Of course not." She looked away and then looked back at him. "This is all so hard to talk about."

"You don't need to tell me any more."

"No, I do. I want to." She opened her purse and took out a red wallet. "I need that coffee now."

He put up his hand. "I'll get it. What do you want?"

"Just a decaf with one sugar."

He smiled at her and as he left the table, he put a hand on her shoulder. She put her hand over his and they stayed like that for the briefest of moments. Then he went over to the counter and got her the coffee. It took a couple of minutes and he was afraid she would leave, but she was still sitting there when he got back. He placed the coffee and a spoon in front of her and handed her three packets: sweetener, raw sugar, white sugar. "I didn't know what you like."

She thanked him and put the white sugar in her coffee. She took a sip and something in her seemed to relax and she sat back in her chair. "When Fred and I were, well, finished, he got up right away, which surprised me. But he said he'd be right back. He put on his clothes but I'd expected that because his cousin was in the front room watching TV. And he came back in just a couple of minutes and took off his clothes and got back into bed with me."

"But it wasn't Fred."

"No. I was half-asleep by then. The room was dark and I expected Fred. I didn't realize it was someone else until he climbed on top of me. No greeting, no asking that I remember, just pushed himself on me."

"Murcheson, the guy who lived in the apartment."

She tilted her head. "I didn't know who it was. I started to say something and he put his finger on my lips and I kept quiet." She looked at Jim and then looked away. "I can't explain why I didn't push him away or fight him. Why I let him. Why I let all of you. But once I'd let the second guy do what he wanted, I sort of gave up thinking and just let it happen."

"Yeah, well, we were young and stupid. We took advantage of you, of the situation."

She looked at him for a long moment. "I was young and foolish too. Like I said, I knew what Fred wanted from me."

"He was not someone any of the rest of us trusted. I don't know why we…"

She had put her hand on his and he stopped talking. "Trust wasn't something I thought about either. Maybe we don't when we're that young." She gave a low laugh and he wondered what seemed funny. "But it doesn't really matter. I met you and that was wonderful. Our time together is one of my best memories."

"Mine too," he said and in that moment, he knew he meant it.

He must have sounded sentimental for she looked at him then in a different way and shook her head. "Please don't say you still love me. This isn't some movie where the star-crossed lovers are reunited in their golden years."

"We aren't in our golden years."

"You know what I mean."

"Is your husband good to you?"

"Paul? Yes, we make a good team. We understand each other. We come from the same world." She smiled at him. It wasn't shy anymore. "What about you? Do you have someone who's good for you?"

"I did but I let her go."

"Can you get her back?"

"No, she's married and happy."

"Then let her be and look for someone else."

"Is there anything I can do for you?" Jim said. "I want to do something."

She didn't say anything and he went on. "I would have come back if you'd told me about the baby."

"If I'd known it was yours, if I could have been sure, I might have told you. But I couldn't be sure, and I couldn't ask you to take on another man's child." She paused. "Have you met him? What's he like?"

He dodged the question. He didn't want to say he hadn't spent any time with the boy. "How is it you haven't met him?

"I…" She looked over his shoulder for a long moment, then looked him in the eye. "I've been afraid to. I know that sounds crazy. What mother wouldn't want to meet her child? But I had to box up all the feelings I had for him and put them far, far away in my heart. I had to pretend it didn't happen or I think I would have lost my mind. Maybe someday I won't feel this way but right now, I just can't."

He wanted to say he'd been afraid to meet Jason as well, but he didn't. "What can I do now?" he said instead.

She thought for a moment. "Take care of my boy. I don't know what kind of father he had growing up, but you could watch out for him. Be sure he has someone who cares what happens. And if you're his father, then you know what to do."

He nodded but she said, "Promise me."

"I promise."

She smiled and he smiled back and he knew she was getting ready to leave him again and he couldn't bear it. "Isn't there something I can do for you?"

She picked up her bag and stood up. He stood up too. She came over to him and put her arms around him and he held her for a moment and for that moment all the years were gone. Then she tipped her head up and said, "Send me a picture of you with my son." She pulled away and he watched her walk out the door. She waited for the traffic and then hurried across the street to her life.

70

Wednesday was Karina's short day at work and Derek knew she'd be home when he got back from campus. He knew his best bet was to play the answering machine recording for her just as he had for the dean and to get her on his side. Maybe that could overshadow the paternity problem. She certainly didn't want him to lose his job over Mary Alice's indiscretion. They had a good life and they were both invested in keeping it. Being proactive was clearly the way to go here too.

She was sitting at the dining table reading the paper when he got there. "What happened to the answering machine?" She didn't look up at him, and her voice carried some antagonism from the night before.

"I have it with me."

"Whatever for?"

"I got a disturbing message from a student and I took it over and played it for the dean."

She looked up at him then. "Suicide threat?"

"No, fortunately not that. Just malice. Do you want to hear it?"

"Of course."

He got the machine out of his briefcase, set it up in its usual place, and pushed the button. He watched Karina's face as she listened to the message, saw her jaw tighten.

"Okay if I erase it now?"

She nodded. "Who is this girl? Do you know her?

"Yes." He sat down across the table from her and told her about Mary Alice's spring visits to his office, about her showing up in the summer school class. "What I don't understand," he said, "is why she would do this. She got an A so it isn't payback of any kind."

"She never flirted with you?"

"They all flirt with me, but that's all it is."

"Well, not this one."

"No, you're right."

"What did the dean say?"

"That she'll have a talk with the girl and tell her to leave me alone. She isn't a major in my department so there's no reason for her to take any more classes from me. I think that should take care of it."

She nodded and looked at him. "It seems odd that both of these things should happen this week."

"Doesn't it though?" He hoped he sounded equally baffled. "It's an odd coincidence but I don't think they're related. I can't imagine she knows the kid in Oregon."

She kept looking at him.

He took the lead again. "Do you want to talk some more about what I told you last night?"

She looked away and then back at him. "It all seems so unlike you. You have such respect for women. I just can't see you doing this."

"We were young and stupid. I didn't think. I was pretty drunk and the guys egged me on and I caved. Peer pressure can be pretty strong."

"I know. I see it all the time at school. Teenagers." She thought a moment. "Are there going to be legal consequences?"

"About the message? No, I think the dean can handle it."

"I meant about that night in the apartment."

"No, the statute of limitations has run out."

"Is that a good thing? I mean what you guys did was pretty awful."

"I know, but the girl involved didn't press charges and she isn't pressing any kind of charges now. In fact, none of us have heard from her. Only from this kid. And he's interested in the paternity issue."

"So I don't understand why you haven't given him your DNA. You either are his father or you're not. Hiding behind whatever Bruce Houghton had to say doesn't seem very—I don't know—ethical."

"You're right and I've reconsidered. In fact, I called the kid and asked him how I can best get him my sample."

"What did he say?"

"I didn't reach him. Just left a message."

"And you've had the answering machine unplugged all this time."

"I never thought of that."

"Well, let's hope he calls back."

"I'm sure he will." He got up and went into the kitchen and brought back two beers. She shook her head and he returned one to the fridge. He put his beer on the table and came around to her side and pulled her up to meet him. He put all the passion he could into the kiss. "Forgive me?"

Her smile wasn't quite what he'd hoped for, but the next kiss was better.

71

As Jason neared the little house where Landon had gone in, he began to lose his determination so he didn't slow down as he neared the house. Instead he continued on to the tavern. The place was empty except for the bartender setting up and a very old man at the far end of the bar with a mostly empty beer glass in front of him. The bartender looked him up and down when he came in. The old man kept his eyes on his beer.

Jason ordered a beer he didn't want and put the cash down on the polished wood of the bar. He took a sip, then said, "You got a pay phone?"

The bartender motioned with his head to the left. "Back by the john."

Jason pulled out his wallet, his calling card, and the list with Derek Walsh's number on it.

72

Derek and Karina were halfway up the stairs to the bedroom when the phone rang. "Go get it," she said.

"It can wait."

"No, I don't want the phone ringing again and again."

He kissed her and went down the stairs. He was hoping it wasn't going to be Mary Alice on a rampage.

"Derek Walsh?" The voice was young, familiar, but he couldn't place it.

"Yes?"

"This is Jason Kirchner. Is your wife there?"

"Why?"

Karina had come down the stairs and stood across the table from him.

"I left you a message about an hour ago. I want to speak to you both about getting me the sample."

"I don't think we need to involve her. You can just tell me what you want me to do."

"No. It's not going to work that way. Unless you want me to call your dean and give her more details."

Derek said nothing.

"Walsh?"

"I'm here."

"Do you have a speaker phone?"

"Yes."

"Then put it on."

Derek pushed the button on the phone and sat down at the table and looked at his wife. "He's on the phone, Karina, and he wants to talk to you too."

She frowned but sat down near the phone.

"Mrs. Walsh? Are you there?"

"Yes, I am."

"Do you know what this is all about?"

"Yes, my husband told me."

"Did he tell you he has repeatedly refused to give me a sample?"

"He told me he called you today and offered to do it."

There was a pause. "Yes, I got that message."

Derek spoke up. "All right, now that that's clear, what do you want me to do?"

"I put a swab kit in the mail to you yesterday overnight mail. Please use it when you get it and mail it back today. Send it to Nancy Chandling. You have her address, right?"

"What's Nancy got to do with this?" Karina asked.

"She's offered to get the tests run."

"I'm not happy having her know my results," said Derek.

"I don't care," Jason said. "Will you do it?"

"Yes," Derek said. "Are we good if I do this?"

"If you're my father, I will want medical history from your family."

"I can do that."

"Mrs. Walsh, will you call me when the swab has been mailed?"

"Yes, I will. I promise."

"Okay." He recited his number. "You can leave a message if I'm not there. Thanks, Mrs. Walsh." There was a click and a dial tone.

They continued sitting at the table. Karina looked at him and he shook his head and looked away.

"What will you do if he's your kid?"

"What is there to do? He's 27. He's not a child."

"That wasn't the answer I was hoping for, Derek."

"What? You want a stepson who's five years younger than you are?"

"It's not about wanting. It's about what's true, what's real. If he's your son, he's your son."

"Well, I don't think he is. But if he is, we'll cross that bridge later." He smiled at her but she didn't smile back.

73

Jim went on sitting in the coffee shop. He watched the café across the street but it was too far away for him to see Rhonda. He'd thought he was keeping his expectations low but he was saddened and disappointed by their conversation. He'd wanted her to feel some spark of those old feelings they'd had for each other, the kind of spark he had been feeling all night and all morning before she came to him. And maybe she had and didn't want to say so. After all, she was married.

He was also surprised at how she had described that night. He hadn't thought of her as participating, as agreeing or not agreeing. In fact, he hadn't ever thought about that night again in any detail. It was just how he met her. Once they started dating, started falling for each other, none of that mattered. He never cared if a girl he slept with was a virgin. He knew guys collected that like scalps but he preferred a girl with experience. The sex was better and the emotional attachment wasn't so overwhelming.

He'd never assumed Rhonda was a victim of that night. She had never brought it up in those weeks they were together, never complained about it. He'd known plenty of women victims over the years, real and self-diagnosed, and she hadn't been like that. Not then and not now.

He wasn't sure what to do now. He wasn't going to pursue Rhonda. That was out of the question. And he wasn't in love with her. He could see that now. But he admired her. She wasn't angry, she wasn't bitter, she didn't feel sorry for herself. She had taken responsibility for her part in that night in the apartment. That was something he didn't see very often, except maybe with Pete and the guys Pete knew in AA. He wondered if Rhonda was in a 12-step program, if that was why she was so calm about it all.

So now what? Wait until the results came back? He wanted to know now. And then it occurred to him. What if the results didn't matter? What if he could just step in and be the dad to Rhonda's son regardless of the DNA finding? Walsh had made it clear he wasn't interested. Landon would make a terrible father and hadn't Pete said that Murcheson had kids? He thought some more. He was probably the only one with any emotional stake in this. He had enough money to help the kid. He didn't have the complication of a wife who'd have to accept anything. Why couldn't this work?

He went out to his car and found his phone. Hit Nancy's work number on speed dial. One of the other nurses answered. "She's with a patient. Can I take a message?"

He gave his name. Said he was coming over to see her. It was urgent.

74

After Jason hung up the phone, he went back to the bar. His beer had disappeared so he ordered another. As he put his money down, he said, "What goes on in the little house next door?"

The bartender said nothing, just stared at him. Jason stared right back. Finally, the guy said, "Why do you want to know?"

"I saw my cousin come in here and then go in there. I didn't want to interrupt if it was something…you know."

"Who's your cousin?"

"Fred Landon."

"You're pretty young to be Fred's cousin."

"Well, actually, my dad is his cousin."

"Why were you following him?"

Jason hesitated, then said, "He owes me money."

The bartender stared at him again, then said, "That sounds like Landon." He turned around to the phone on the wall, dialed a number, and asked for Fred. "There's a guy here says he's your cousin and needs to talk to you." He listened and then hung up. "He says okay. Go on over."

"Thanks."

"Don't thank me. Those guys don't like being interrupted."

Jason got off the bar stool and headed for the door.

"Hey, kid," the bartender said. "You'll do better if you buy them a round." He held up a six-pack of long necks. Jason looked at him and then went back to the bar and paid for the beer. Then he made his way to the front porch of the little house.

He raised his hand to knock but the door opened and a cloud of cigarette smoke escaped. Landon was standing with his back to the door, laughing. "Come on in, Tom," he said as he turned. Then, he said, "Who the hell are you?"

"Jason Kirchner."

"Who? Oh, right." He smiled but his eyes were cold. "The prodigal son with no father."

6 GUYS, 1 GIRL, 1 NIGHT | 239

75

Nancy got a second call from Jim about 12:30. He was in the lobby. She had just taken the vitals of six of her charges on the ward when the call came through. She had four more to do and so she made him wait. She wasn't quite sure what *urgent* meant but if he was in the lobby, it wasn't that urgent.

When she came out of the elevator, she saw on him on a couch off by himself. He looked tired, worn out, and she felt a strong stab of love and sympathy. She sat down next to him. "What's so urgent, Jim? Work is really busy today."

"I know. I'm sorry. I just had to talk to you. It won't take long. How is Kirchner getting the DNA tested?"

"Well, he gets the samples to me and I have them run here at the lab through my friend Jane. Why?"

He frowned. "Do you have any results yet?"

"No, I just gave her your sample and Murcheson's this morning. I don't know about Derek's or that other guy."

"Two other guys."

"No, Lonnie Tillstrom's out of the picture. Pete found him and he apparently never went into the bedroom. Turns out he's gay."

"Huh. That leaves Landon then."

"Haven't heard anything about his swab although Murcheson told Pete he would find him. Why? What's up?"

Jim looked at her and hesitated. She smiled at him but he didn't smile back. "You talked to Rhonda, didn't you?" she asked.

"Yes."

"And?"

"And I want to be the father."

"You what?"

"I want to be the father. Look, I loved her once and I want to do something for her. She got such a raw deal from us and we never knew it. So this seems the least I can do. I can be a father to her kid."

She could see he was serious. "Oh Jim, honey, that's not how it works." She reached over and took his hand. "You are the father or you aren't. DNA will show that. Wait and find out."

His eyes turned dark. "But what if I'm not? What if it's Walsh? That would be a disaster. He's way too self-centered. Or what if it's Landon, who's a royal fuck-up? No, Murcheson and I are the only real possibilities and Murcheson already has kids, I think. It should be me. I'm the one who loved her."

Nancy felt a big sigh well up in her throat. "Don't you think Jason deserves the truth?"

"The truth could be disastrous."

"Okay, I'll grant you that's possible." She put up a hand to slow him down. "But what if he finds out later that you lied to him and that you aren't his father? Any trust he'd have in you would disappear and he'd be worse off than ever. And that certainly wouldn't honor Rhonda, which is what I think you want to do."

"But I've got money to help him with. I've got connections in lots of different places. I could send him to college, help him get a good job."

She wanted to smile at his desperation. He sounded young and eager again, something she hadn't heard from him in a long time. It was actually very sweet. And she hated now to be the voice of reason. "But maybe he doesn't need or want any of that. He's an adult, Jim. A self-sufficient adult."

"Then how else am I going to make this right?"

"I don't know, but I'm sure you'll find a way." Her beeper went off and she pulled it from her pocket and typed in a couple of numbers. She stood up. "I've got to go back to work. How about you stick around and come and have dinner with us tonight? Maybe we can brainstorm some ideas of how to help."

She saw the hesitation in his eyes and she said, "Come on. Stick around until this is settled. It won't be too long now. You know where the key is, right?"

He nodded, and she leaned down and kissed his cheek and headed back over to the elevators.

76

"Who is it, Landon?"

Jason could hear a deep, raspy voice, probably one of the smokers.

"Nothing but trouble," Fred said over his shoulder, laughing again. He turned to Jason and Jason held up the beer. "Well then, come on in. We never turn down free drinks."

Jason nodded and stepped inside. He didn't close the door behind him and Fred didn't seem to notice. The room was not all that large. It was clearly a living room. There was an old plaid couch and a couple of easy chairs shoved back against the wall. In the center of the worn and faded rug was a card table with five folding chairs filled with four men. The men were big and burly, all except the guy with the full ashtray next to him. He was wiry and much older. Cards and money were on the table. Beer bottles too.

Jason handed the six-pack to Fred, who said, "We're in the middle of a hand. I hope you can wait." He took his seat at the far side of the table, facing the door. He put the beers down on the rug beside him, then opened his cards, which had been in his hand all along.

"Sure," said Jason. What else was there to say? He moved over to the mantel of an old fireplace across from the couch and leaned against it.

The men went back to their game with the seriousness of surgery. No one asked Fred or Jason about what was going on. There was no chitchat at all, just bids and requests for cards from the dealer. While Jason didn't care what happened in the game, he wanted Fred to win the hand so that he would feel more amenable to giving him the sample. And that's what happened. Fred swept the small pot of bills towards himself. By the groans and "not again" comments, Fred was a constant winner. *Why shouldn't he be?* Jason thought. *I'll bet he's a pro.*

Fred tidied the bills, folded them, and put them in the pocket of his jeans. "How about we take a break, guys, so I can see what this young man wants." He handed each of them a beer from the six-pack. Took the last two out of the carrier and handed one to Jason. "Let's step outside," he said and led the way through a kitchen that was astonishing in its tidiness. There was a door out to a tiny back porch.

Fred settled down on the porch railing and opened his beer. "How did you find me?"

"Followed Murcheson to the casino. Followed you here."

"Do you think you're my kid?"

"I don't know. That's what I want to find out."

"I already gave the sample to Tom."

"Then you don't deny being there."

"Of course not. The whole thing was my idea."

The casual pride in his face pissed Jason off. "How could you do that to her?"

"I didn't do anything to her. I had sex with her. She had sex with me. People do that all the time. In fact, millions of people are doing it as we speak."

"You know what I mean. Set her up to service your buddies."

"That was a stroke of genius. Some of those guys had so much trouble getting laid. I knew they'd appreciate the favor."

Jason wanted to punch Landon's smug face. "Did you tell her what you had arranged?"

"I don't remember. She was happy to be there with me. I remember that. Pretty eager."

Jason took a deep breath, held himself back. He knew that Landon was taunting him, picking a fight with him. It was his choice to react—or not. "You're scum, you know that?" he said finally.

Landon tilted his head and smiled. "That's not a word I'd use. I prefer 'expedient' or…" he thought a moment, "'spontaneous.' I like that word." He waited for Jason's response. When there wasn't one, he said, "Look, I've got to get back to the game. You got anything else to say?"

Jason put his hand in his jacket pocket. Landon reached over and grabbed the wrist. "I don't have a gun," Jason said. "Though you're worth shooting, that's for sure." He slowly pulled out the sample kit.

Landon let go of his wrist. "I told you I already did that and gave it to Tom."

"I'd like one of my own."

Landon looked at him, then shrugged. He put out his hand, took the kit, used it, and handed it back. He got up then from the railing and moved to the back door. As he opened it, he turned. "Kid, if it turns out it's me, don't come back. Just let it go. You don't want to get to know me." Then he went through the door and closed it behind him.

77

The special delivery package arrived about an hour after the phone call with Kirchner. Derek heard the doorbell ring, heard Karina thank the guy, heard her come up the rest of the stairs. They hadn't gone up to the bedroom after the call, hard as he'd tried to get the mood back or create a new one. It wasn't the sex he wanted but her tenderness, her forgiveness, to feel that they were on the same side in this. But while she wasn't unkind, she held herself apart. Now she stood by the dining table holding the thick envelope.

"Go ahead and open it," he said.

There were only two things inside, the swab kit and a small piece of paper with instructions for its use. Karina handed the kit to Derek. "Do you need me to read this?"

"No." He used the kit and handed it back to her. "Is there a return envelope?"

"No. I'll take it over to the post office. I'll need Pete's address."

He pulled out his address book, wrote down the information, and handed it to her.

"Thanks, babe." He looked her in the eye, wanting to see what he was looking for. It wasn't there yet, but the anger was gone and that would have to do for now.

78

Jim sat in his SUV in the hospital parking lot and placed a few calls to Seattle. He made some business decisions, put off some others. He reassured two high-strung clients, both male. He coaxed another tentative prospect into meeting him for breakfast a week from Saturday morning with her parents so that they could see what kind of an agent he'd be. As a prospective father, he could see how he might do some of this work differently, especially with young musicians. Maybe this whole thing could renew his interest in his work.

It was just past 2 when he got off the phone. He headed towards Pete's, keeping his eye out for a tavern where he could get some lunch and play some pool. He found one a few blocks from the house, ordered a sandwich and a draft. The place was empty and after one game of solo pool, he bought a couple of six packs to go and went on over to the house. The key was still in the same place in the backyard and he let himself in through a side door. He turned on a basketball game, poured himself a beer, and settled in. In about 15 minutes, he'd dozed off.

The doorbell brought him back to the surface. He figured it was a solicitor but when it rang again, he opened the door. A really big man stood there, well-dressed, professional. Vaguely familiar. They looked at each other and slowly the big man grinned. "Jim Leeder, I presume." He stuck out his hand. "I'm Tom Murcheson."

Jim shook his hand, opened the door wider, and moved back into the house. Murcheson followed him into the living room. "Chandling or his wife here?"

"No, Pete will be back about 6 though. Is there something I can do?"

"I have Fred's DNA sample. I wanted to get it to Chandling."

"Well, you can hang out till they get back if you want or I can give it to Nancy. Or you could take it over to her at the hospital where she works or I could do that. The tests are being run there by a friend of hers."

Murcheson came further into the room. Jim took his seat again on the sofa, muted the TV, and motioned to him to sit down. "Beer?"

"Sure, why not? I can get them." Murcheson headed into the kitchen and returned with two bottles. He handed one to Jim and then sat down across from him. The two men looked at each other and then looked away.

"Hell of a mess, huh?" Murcheson said, taking a long pull from the bottle.

"You can say that again. You think you might be the father?"

"Have you met the kid?"

Jim nodded.

"He certainly doesn't look much like Walsh. Too dark, too tall, different body type. He doesn't seem to look much like me or Fred but that doesn't really mean too much. You can father a kid that looks like your wife's Great-Aunt Matilda." He drank from the bottle again. "Think he's yours?"

"I don't know. But I wouldn't mind." He could see the surprise on Murcheson's face.

"Well, I've already got two girls who are costing me a fortune." Murcheson smiled, "so if he's mine, you're welcome to him."

"You mean that?"

"What do you mean?"

"Are you willing to let me tell him I'm his dad even if your DNA is the match?"

"Why in the world would you want to do that?" The frown that creased Murcheson's forehead was deep and lasted a long time.

"I've got my reasons."

"I don't know. That seems crazy." Murcheson worked on his beer. "I don't suppose you want to share those reasons."

"Not really, no."

The two men were quiet for a long moment. Finally, Murcheson spoke up. "You don't think Kirchner should know the truth? You know there are some serious medical reasons for the truth." He chewed on his lower lip. "And your willingness to take on the responsibility doesn't absolve any of the rest of us from what we did."

"Do you regret what we did?"

"Of course I do. It was stupid and thoughtless. Two lives were seriously affected and not for the better." He looked at Jim. "Most of my friends think I became a lawyer for the money and in a way they're right. But I also believe in justice and doing some good in the world, and what we did wasn't good. It wasn't good for that girl and it certainly wasn't good for the kid."

Jim nodded. "I want to do something to make it up to her—to him."

"Well, we have that in common. What about Walsh? Has he changed his tune?"

Jim hadn't given Walsh's reaction much thought, he'd been so caught up in his own. "You mean not admitting anything? I don't know. I sort of doubt it. He can be pretty adamant and self-protective. What about Fred?"

Murcheson shook his head. "My cousin is a piece of work." He told Jim a little of what he had learned though he didn't mention the rape cases. Instead he just painted Fred as a bad apple. "We all need to hope that Kirchner is not Fred's kid." He looked at his watch and stood up. "I've got to head back to Salem before the traffic gets impossible." He reached in his pocket and pulled out the swab in its plastic bag. "Give this to Pete's wife for me."

Jim stood too. "You haven't answered my question. About letting me be Kirchner's dad."

Murcheson studied him and then smiled. "I think it's best that the truth come out. Once that happens, maybe we can help each other to help him out."

Leeder felt another surge of disappointment. No one was agreeing with what he thought was the best option all around.

79

Pete Chandling left work later than he'd hoped. It was nearly 6:10 when he got to his car. The worst of the traffic would be over but it would still take a while. He'd had a call from Nancy. Leeder was at the house and staying for dinner and wanted to talk about the whole thing. Pete was glad Jim had come to his senses about all of it. He just wished Walsh were in town so that this meeting could be all three of them making decisions together. Walsh's absence was going to have a big impact. He wished they'd been able to settle this before Derek went back to Virginia.

He could hear the shower running when he came in the door. A glance into the guest bedroom showed Jim's bag open on the bed. Pete went on into the kitchen and began to pull stuff out to see what kind of a dinner he could put together. Nancy had promised to be home no later than 7:30. They could always do takeout but something more substantial seemed important to provide. There were sausages from Sheridan's that he could grill, some potatoes, enough salad stuff. He sliced the potatoes, added butter and salt, and made a foil packet for the grill. Then he made a pot of decaf and was just sitting down to go through the mail when Jim came in. Jim got a beer from the fridge and sat down across from him.

Pete put down the mail and looked up. "What's going on, Jim?"

Jim seemed to hesitate for the slightest moment and then the story tumbled out. Meeting Rhonda again a few days after the night in the apartment, their weeks together, the Dear John letter. Seeing her again that morning. The telling took a while. There were some long pauses. Pete knew to wait. Jim mostly kept his feelings out of it but that didn't surprise Pete. That wasn't Jim's way. But he knew his friend well enough to know that a highly romantic heart was in there somewhere, buried under the cynicism of the music business, and that this was all painful for him.

After the last silence had gone on long enough, Pete said, "Do you think you are the father?"

"It would make sense, wouldn't it? Seeing as how I slept her with a bunch of times."

"I'd think so. It certainly improves the odds."

"Do you think Nancy will have results tonight?"

"I don't know. We'll find out when she gets here." Pete looked at the kitchen clock and got up from the table. "I need to put the food on." He took the tray of meat and potatoes out to the back patio and started up the gas grill. Despite the trees and shrubs that lined the yard, the air was hot and still. Deep August. He turned the sprinkler on in hopes it would cool things down enough for them to eat outside.

When he went back into the kitchen, Nancy was just coming in. He hugged her, always so glad to feel her body next to his. She hugged him back, went over and put her arm around Jim, kissed Jim's cheek, and said, "Do I have time for a shower before we eat?"

"Yes," Pete said, "but don't dawdle. Food in twenty."

Jim went in and turned on the news. Pete set about making a salad. He thought about Jim, about what he'd just heard. He felt sad for his friend, who had lost so much. Rhonda, the child that might be his, then Nancy. He felt lucky to have what he had.

Nancy came out in a loose cotton dress, her hair hanging wet and curly. Pete felt a surge of pride and of love. She took the salad out and plates and silverware on a tray. Pete stepped into the living room and called Jim to dinner.

"I told Pete about Rhonda and me," Jim said as soon as they sat down.

"I'm glad you did," she said.

Jim nodded. "Do you have any results yet?"

"No, Jane wants to do them all at once."

"Well," Jim said, "I've got Fred Landon's sample."

Pete looked at him. "How did you get it?"

"Murcheson came by this afternoon with it. I told him I'd pass it along to Nancy." He took a bite of potato. "You know, we have three of the four now. Couldn't your friend just run these? If one of them is positive, we don't need Walsh's sample. If they're all negative, then Walsh is it and his sample will confirm it. Either way we'll know." He paused. "I need to know, you guys."

Nancy looked at Jim and then at Pete. "I don't know why not," she said. "We can take Fred's swab to Jane after dinner. Maybe she can run them tonight. I'll call her after we eat."

They ate in silence for a few minutes. Then Nancy said, "Did you tell Pete about wanting to be Jason's father?"

Jim didn't say anything so Pete spoke. "I can see why, Jim. You feel a special responsibility to Rhonda. I'm so glad you're willing to take that on if it works out that way."

Jim kept his eyes on his plate but said, "Actually I want to be his father however the tests come out."

Pete looked at Nancy, who gave him a look he recognized—skepticism. "Wow," Pete said.

"Yeah," said Jim. "I feel it's the right thing to do. But Murcheson won't go along with it."

"You asked him?" Nancy said.

"Yeah, he said Kirchner should have the truth. Medical stuff and all that."

"He's got a very good point," Nancy said.

"But you don't agree?" Pete said.

"It's not that," Jim said. "I want the kid to have a dad who has a stake in it. Not just a random sex act."

"Because you loved his mother," said Nancy.

"Yeah. It's a lot better reason than just sperm."

"But what about what Jason wants?" said Pete. "We're talking about him as if he's a child. He's an adult, a man, and he wants the truth."

"Pete's right, Jim," said Nancy. "You guys already made decisions that have determined much of the course of his life. You can't do that again."

"But what if it's Landon? Murcheson says he's bad news."

"But we're not saying you can't have a relationship with Jason," Pete said. "We just don't think you should lie to him."

"That isn't going to happen anyway," Nancy said. "I promised Jason I would bring him the results in a sealed envelope and that's what I'm asking Jane to do. No one should know the results before Jason does."

Jim scowled and looked away. "So you guys aren't going to help me do the right thing?"

Pete could hear the disappointment in Jim's voice but he couldn't fix that. "The truth is the right thing," he said although he wasn't sure he believed it. But he knew Nancy did and that was what was important. He went on. "Look at it this way. If Derek is the father or Fred Landon, God forbid, Jason will need your support more than ever."

Nancy looked over at him. "Our support, I mean," Pete said.

"You don't think Walsh would make a good father either?" Jim turned his gaze back into the conversation.

Nancy shook her head. Pete felt a need to defend Derek, at least a little bit. "He's a great guy and a good friend, but his priorities aren't exactly family-oriented." There was a moment of silence and then Jim began to chuckle and laughter spread around the table, breaking the heaviness that had been stuck between them.

Pete got up and cleared the dishes. Jim went into the kitchen for another beer. He brought out two in case Nancy wanted one, but she shook her head when he held it out to her.

When Pete came back out and sat down, Jim said, "That idea of *our* helping the kid. Murcheson said that too, that we could help each other to help him."

"Did he have any specific ideas?" Nancy was folding and refolding her napkin, a habit Pete found endearing.

"No. He said it just as he left. But I guess we could put some money together to help him buy a house or go to school." He looked at Nancy. "If that's what he wants."

She smiled at him and Pete saw Jim relax, saw again how much Nancy's opinion mattered to Jim, just as it did to him.

"Do you think we could also do something for Rhonda?" Jim said. "To make things up to her." He told them about the shabby little house, the two old cars, her job as a waitress.

No one said a word for a bit. The heaviness was back. Then Nancy spoke. "Those are such great intentions, but you're going to have to tread lightly in all of this. People have their pride and their dignity. Rhonda has a husband who is probably providing as best he can. He may not take kindly to an old boyfriend wanting to help. Or worse yet, the pack of boys who had sex with her when she was a teenager. I can see a lot of problems in anything like that." She paused and put her hand on Jim's arm. "I think you just have to let her go again."

After a moment, she went on. "I also think you guys have to be prepared for Jason to be resistant and maybe even offended by your offers. He's very independent. He's had a hard life and he's a survivor. He may take your money, but I don't think you can earmark it for anything specific like college or a house."

"That's a good point, Nance," Pete said. "You know, I'll bet Murcheson could help us set up a trust for him, one that Jason could access when he's 30 or 35. We could all contribute to it between now and then. What do you think?"

"I like that idea," said Nancy. "Jim, if you're Jason's father, would you object to that?"

"Well, I guess not. I mean that could be separate from anything else I did for him. Yeah, I could talk to Murcheson about that."

"Sounds like we have a plan," said Pete. "Now what?"

"Now I'm going to call Jane and see if she can run the three tests tonight and if she can, I'll call Jason and arrange to hand him the results in the morning." Nancy stood up and went inside.

"Okay if I drive her to the hospital?" Jim said.

"Fine by me but ask her." Pete grinned at his friend.

"Right," Jim said, grinning back.

80

Nancy got to the coffee shop a few minutes early. She got a hot tea and a glass of water and commandeered one of the outdoor tables. The air was cooler at 7:30 than it had been in days past. Maybe the summer was starting to ease its grip. She'd been up early, dressed for work in case the time ran short, and then she'd headed to the hospital at 6:30 so she'd get there before Jane went off the night shift. She hadn't slept well and neither had either of the men. She'd heard Jim get up several times and Pete had tossed and turned.

Jane had asked her if she wanted to know the results but Nancy said no, the tests weren't for her. They were for the boy. So she'd taken the envelope and driven here. She turned her pager off. She didn't want Jim or Pete to pressure her. Now she put the envelope on the table and sat back to wait. Part of her hoped it would be Jim. Being Jason's father might change him for the good. Yet again, it might not change him at all. People change very, very slowly. She knew that. And she also knew that most changes came from inside, not an external event.

She closed her eyes, listened to the traffic, the birds, the sound of the espresso machine inside the shop. Then she heard a chair scrape on the sidewalk and she looked up at Jason, who sat down and then shifted his chair so he too could watch the street. "Do you want anything?" she said.

"No, I already had coffee." He too looked tired, older than the last time she had seen him and it had been only a few days.

They didn't say anything for a while, and the silence was okay between them, almost companionable. She wanted to watch him, figure out what he was thinking, but she knew that wasn't fair, that what he was thinking was none of her business. He looked over at her and then glanced down at the envelope.

"Like I said on the phone, we have three test results: Jim's, Fred's, and Murcheson's. If they're all negative…"

"Then it's Walsh, by default."

She nodded. "Do you have a preference?"

He didn't look at her and she felt awkward. "Forget I asked that," she said. "That wasn't the right question again."

He looked at her then and nodded.

"Would you like me to just go so you can open this in private?"

He hesitated, then said, "No, stay." He reached over and picked up the envelope, broke the seal, and took out the three pages. He looked at each one, then folded them back up, and put them back in the envelope. He put the envelope on the table and looked out at the street.

"Is it okay?" she said.

"Yes, it's okay."

They sat like that for a few minutes. Then he looked over at her and nodded at the envelope.

She reached over and took it, pulled out the sheets, and read through them. Then she put them back in the envelope and smiled at him and at the way things work out.

EPILOGUE

Rhonda was still tired when she got up. She hadn't even heard Paul leave. They'd been short-staffed at lunch the day before and she'd had to stay on and work the first part of the dinner shift as well. No real breaks to speak of so way too many hours on her feet. Paul wanted her to quit, kept saying they'd manage somehow without her salary and tips but she knew that wouldn't be easy and she didn't really want to stay home all day. Well, today she wanted to stay home.

There was coffee made and the breakfast all laid out for her. Paul was good about things like that. She ate, got dressed, pulled some hamburger out of the freezer for dinner. She could bring some salads and fries from the café to go with it. She poured a little bit more coffee and stood out on the back porch and watched the fall morning come on. The doorbell startled her and she looked at her watch. 8:15. Jehovah's Witnesses probably. She shook her head and went to be polite.

But it was Jim Leeder and when he turned to smile at her, she saw the young man beside him.

She knew it was her boy. She just knew. The boy looked shy and as scared as she suddenly felt.

Jim spoke and broke the tension. "You made me promise to get you a picture of me with our son," and he handed her a little camera. "Jason and I want you to take that picture."

Jill Kelly is a writer, painter, editor, and coach. Her first memoir, *Sober Truths: The Making of an Honest Woman*, was a finalist for the prestigious Oregon Book Award. She is the author of a second memoir, *Candy Girl: How I Gave up Sugar and Created a Sweeter Life between Meals*; two thrillers, *Fog of Dead Souls* and *Broken Boys*; and two relationship novels, *When Your Mother Doesn't* and *The Color of Longing*. Jill lives in Portland, Oregon, with four cats, many books, and two easels.

She loves to hear from readers at **jill@jillkellyauthor.com.**

27397828R00162

Made in the USA
Columbia, SC
26 September 2018